MAYHEM AT THE
ORIENT EXPRESS

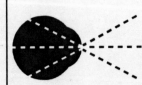

This Large Print Book carries the
Seal of Approval of N.A.V.H.

MAYHEM AT THE ORIENT EXPRESS

KYLIE LOGAN

WHEELER PUBLISHING
A part of Gale, Cengage Learning

GALE
CENGAGE Learning

Detroit • New York • San Francisco • New Haven, Conn • Waterville, Maine • London

GALE
CENGAGE Learning·

LIBRARY OF CONGRESS CATALOGING-IN-PUBLICATION DATA

Logan, Kylie.
    Mayhem at the Orient Express / By Kylie Logan. — Large Print edition.
        pages cm. — (A League of Literary Ladies Mystery) (Wheeler Publishing Large Print Cozy Mystery)
        ISBN 978-1-4104-6239-8 (hardcover) — ISBN 1-4104-6239-0 (hardcover) 1. Large type books. I. Title.
PS3612.A944237M39 2014
813'.6—dc23   2013035581

Published in 2014 by arrangement with The Berkley Publishing Group, a member of Penguin Group (USA) LLC, a Penguin Random House Company

Printed in the United States of America
2 3 4 5 6   18 17 16 15 14

For Koula, George, and the entire staff of Something Different Gallery in Cleveland, Ohio.

Thank you for your continued support, your discerning eye when it comes to art, and most important, your friendship.

ACKNOWLEDGMENTS

I have a very clear memory of the day I got my first library card. My dad had taken me to the closest library branch, and when we were done, I was so excited, I ran into the house, waving the pink cardboard card in the air so my mother could see it. And the first book I ever took out with that card? I remember that, too — *Horton Hatches the Egg,* that great Dr. Seuss classic.

Books still give me that kind of a buzz and I know you, as a reader, understand. For us, books are the magic carpets that take us on all sorts of adventures.

That's what I was thinking about when I came up with the idea for the League of Literary Ladies Mysteries, my love of classic books, and yours, too. This new series gives me the opportunity to explore the wonderful classics I've enjoyed through the years, and I've started with one of my favorites, *Murder on the Orient Express.*

7

Nobody does twists and turns better than Agatha Christie, and having the chance to reread her masterpiece was a treat in itself. So was the opportunity to take her story and riff off it with a Lake Erie island setting, a cast of eccentric supporting characters, and the League of Literary Ladies itself, four very different women who become a book discussion group thanks to a neighborhood squabble — and a court order!

As with every book, I owe special thanks to a whole host of people for their help with *Mayhem at the Orient Express,* including Tom Colgan, my editor at Berkley Prime Crime; his assistant, Amanda Ng; and my great and fabulous agent, Gail Fortune. My thanks, too, to Shelley Costa, who over cups of coffee, spent many an hour going over plot points and making suggestions. Like me (and you!) these are people who know and love books, the stories they tell, and the places they transport our imaginations.

1

If it weren't for Jerry Garcia peeing on my pansies, I never would have joined the League of Literary Ladies.

No, not that Jerry Garcia! Jerry Garcia, Chandra Morrisey's cat. In fact, it was that peeing incident, and the one before it, and the one before that . . .

Well, suffice it to say that if it weren't for Jerry's less-than-stellar bathroom habits, there never would have been a League at all.

Jerry, see, was the reason I was in Mayor's Court that Thursday morning.

Again.

"That damned cat . . ." I bit my lower lip to hold in my temper and the long list of Jerry's sins I was tempted to recite. After all, Alvin Littlejohn, the court magistrate, had heard it all before.

Then again, so had Chandra Morrisey, and her cat was still peeing on my pansies.

Chandra was standing to my right, and I swung her way. "He needs to be kept in the house. That's all I'm asking."

It was all I'd asked the week previously, too, and just like that time (and the time before and the time before that), Chandra rolled eyes the color of the gray clouds that blanketed the sky outside the town hall building. "Cats are free spirits," she said, her voice as soft as the rolls of flesh that rippled beneath a tie-dyed T-shirt that fit her like a second, Easter-egg-swirl-of-color skin. "They are the embodiment of nature spirits. If we don't allow them to roam free, we impede their mission in this world. They can commune with the Other Side, you know." Like it would help the information sink into this nonbeliever's skull, Chandra looked at me hard.

If I were still back in New York City, I would have given her a one-finger salute and been done with it. But we were, in fact, on an island twelve miles from the southern shore of Lake Erie, and as I'd come to learn in the six weeks I'd lived on South Bass, people here were a different breed. They moved slower than folks back in the Big Apple. They were friendlier. Considerate. More civilized.

Well, except for Jerry.

10

And, obviously, his owner.

"This is ridiculous!" I threw my hands in the air. Not as dramatic a gesture as I would have liked, but hey, like I said, people here were considerate, and my goal in coming to the island in the first place was to blend in. "You're wasting my time, Chandra. And the court's time, too. All you need to do is —"

"All Chandra needs to do?"

Honestly, I was so fixated on Jerry's loony owner, I'd forgotten Kate Wilder was even in the room. She stood on my left, tapping one sensible pump against the black-and-white linoleum. "It's not like I have time for this, Alvin, and you know it," she grumbled, her arms crossed over the jacket of a neat navy suit that looked particularly puritanical against flaming orange hair that was as long as my coal black tresses, but not nearly as curly. "We could settle this whole thing quickly, if you'd tell her . . ." Kate was a pretty, petite woman who looked to be about thirty-five, the same age as me. Her emerald green eyes snapped to mine. "Tell Ms. Cartwright here to cut down on the traffic at that B and B of hers and there won't be anything left for us to discuss."

"Oh, we'll still have plenty to talk about," I shot back. "Especially if your constant nagging about traffic means my renovations don't get done by the time I'm scheduled to open. Come on, it's not like it's any big deal. It's just a few trucks coming down the street now and then."

"A few?" Kate ticked the list off on her fingers (which is actually a pretty pithy way of putting it, since while she was at it, she was ticking me off, too). "There was the truck that brought the new windows, and one that took care of the heating and air-conditioning, and one from the painters, and one from —"

"I thought you said you were busy and had better things to do?" Ah yes, me at my sarcastic best! Not one to be intimidated (see the above comment about New York), I, too, crossed my arms over my black turtleneck and adjusted the dark-rimmed glasses on the bridge of my nose, the better to give Kate the kind of glare anybody with that much time on her hands — not to mention nerve — deserved. "Apparently, you don't have anything better to do than spend your time looking across the street at my place. Once the renovations are complete —"

"At least those trucks won't be spewing fossil-fuel exhaust fumes near my herb garden." Chandra tugged at her left earlobe and the three golden hoops in it. "Once *she* gets rid of those —"

"And *she* cuts down on the traffic jams —"

"And *she* takes care of that damned cat —"

"All right! That's it. Quiet down!" In the weeks I'd been appearing before Alvin in the basement courtroom, I had never seen him so red in the face. He fished a white cotton handkerchief from his pocket and mopped his forehead. "This has gotten . . ." There was a plastic bottle of water on his desk and he opened it and took a gulp. "This situation has gotten out of control. You're out of control."

I would have been willing to second this last comment if he'd kept his gaze on Chandra. When it moved to Kate . . . well, that was understandable, too. But when it slid my way and stayed there, I couldn't help myself. My chin came up and my shoulders went back.

Alvin scraped a hand through what was left of his mousy-colored hair and pointed a finger at Kate. "You're mad at . . ." He arced his finger in my direction. "Her because of the traffic. And you're . . ." His slightly trembling finger remained aimed at me. "Mad at her . . ." The accusatory

13

gesture moved to Chandra. "Because her cat —"

"Pees on my flowers. All the time. What's going to happen in the summer when I have guests and they want to sit out on the front porch and —"

"I get the picture." A muscle jumped at the base of Alvin's jaw, but he kept his gaze on Chandra. "And you, Chandra, you're mad at Kate. Do I have that right? Because . . ." He flipped open a manila file on his desk and consulted the topmost piece of paper in it. "Because Kate plays opera too loud on Sunday mornings."

Chandra nodded, and her bleached blond, blunt-cut hair bobbed to the beat. "I do my meditating in the morning." She said this in a way that made it sound like public knowledge. For all I knew, it was. From what I'd heard, Chandra Morrisey had lived in Put-in-Bay (the little town that was the center of life on South Bass) nearly all of her nearly fifty years. "She's messing with the vibrations in the neighborhood and that affects my aura."

"Oh for pity's sake!" Kate's screech fell flat against the pocked tiles of the drop ceiling. "She hates opera? Well, I hate that creepy sitar music that's always coming from her place. And I don't have time for

14

this. Any of it. I need to get to the winery."

"Oh, the Wilder Winery!" If we hadn't been enmeshed in our own little version of a smackdown, I might have laughed at Chandra's attempt at a la-di-da accent. "Play your screechy opera at the winery, then, why don't you," she suggested to Kate. "And leave the rest of us in peace."

"Which actually might be possible," Kate snapped back, "if it weren't for you, Chandra, and those stupid full moon bonfires you're always building." She fanned her face with one perfectly manicured hand. "The smoke alone is bound to kill somebody one of these days. Add your singing to it —"

"It isn't singing." Chandra was so sure of this, she stomped one Ugg-shod foot. "It's chanting."

"It's annoying," Kate countered.

"And it's getting us nowhere." Me, the voice of reason. "It all comes down to the stupid cat. If you'd just make Jerry Garcia —"

"In the animal kingdom, cats are among the highest beings, intelligence-wise." Need I say that this was Chandra talking? The heat kicked on and blew my way and it was the first I realized she was wearing perfume that smelled like the herbal tea they sold in the head shops around Washington Square

15

Park back in New York.

I wrinkled my nose.

And ruffled Chandra's feathers.

Her eyes narrowed and her voice hardened. "In fact," she said, "the ancient Egyptians —"

"Are dead, mummified, and poofed to dust. Every single one of them," I reminded her. Then I added, just for the sake of a little drama, "They died from the germs because they let their cats pee anywhere they wanted. Like on their neighbor's flowers."

"Oh, yeah?"

It was the ultimate in bad comebacks, and yes, I knew better. I swear, I did. I just couldn't help myself. I answered Chandra with a, "Yeah," of my own.

It should be noted that, at this point, Alvin dropped his head on his desk.

I'm convinced he would have kept it right there in the hopes that when he finally looked up, we'd all be gone, but at that moment, the door to the courtroom opened.

"Oh. I'm sorry. I didn't know you were busy." The woman who poked her head in, then stepped back, looked familiar. Short. Round. Dark hair dusted with silver. I'd been introduced to Marianne Littlejohn, the town librarian and Alvin's better half, at a recent potluck.

Only the evening of the gathering, her eyes weren't puffy and her nose wasn't red. Not like they were now.

"Marianne! What's wrong?" Yes, this would have been a perfect thing for Alvin to say, but it wasn't the magistrate who raced to the door and grabbed Marianne's hands. It was Chandra. She drew Marianne into the room. "Your aura is all messed up."

"It's . . . it's . . ." Now that it was time to explain, Marianne hiccuped over the words. "I've had such terrible news." Kate checked the time on her phone. "And that's a shame, really, but we need to finish up here. I've got to get over to the winery —"

"And I've got someone coming to repair the stained glass window in my front stairway," I piped in, refusing to be outdone by Miss I'm-So-Important. "So if I could just pay a fine or something, I'll be heading home. And by the way . . ." I hoped Kate could see the wide-eyed, innocent look I shot her from behind my glasses. "I hear the stained glass artist is going to be driving a really big truck."

A head toss from Kate.

A click of the tongue from Chandra.

A whimper from Marianne.

And Alvin was on his feet.

His teeth clenched and his palms flat

against his desk, he turned to his wife. "Marianne, honestly, this isn't a good time. We're kind of in the middle of something and —"

"I know. I said I was sorry." She sniffled. "It's just —"

"That we need to finish up," Kate said.

"And get out of here and back to the B and B," I put in.

"Nobody's going anywhere. Not until you women learn to get along!"

In all the weeks I'd been appearing in court thanks to my neighbors' not-so-neighborly complaints, I'd never heard Alvin raise his voice. Now, it ricocheted against the walls like buckshot on a barn door.

We pulled in a collective gasp and as one, took a step back and away from his desk.

Alvin, apparently, was as surprised by his outburst as the rest of us.

"Look what you've reduced me to!" he said, suddenly ashen and shaking like a hoochie-koochie dancer. "I've been doing this job for nearly thirty years, and in thirty years of weekend drunks and fighting fishermen and vandals tearing up the mini-golf course . . . in thirty years I've never lost my temper. Now you three . . ."

Since Marianne was standing next to me

and sobbing, I can't say for certain, but I think Alvin growled to emphasize his point.

That was right before he pulled in a long breath and let it out slowly. "Maybe what we all need," he said, "is a time-out."

"Great." Kate reached for her Coach bag and slung it over one slim shoulder. "I'm out of here."

"No. That's not what I meant. You're not going anywhere, Kate. Not yet. None of you are." Alvin sat back down and folded his trembling hands together on the desk in front of him, his suddenly flint-hard gaze hopping over each of us before it came to rest on his wife. "You have the floor, honey. Tell us what's going on. That will give us all a chance to take a few deep breaths and get our collective heads back where they belong before we figure out what we're going to do about the problems in Ms. Cartwright, Ms. Wilder, and Ms. Morrisey's neighborhood."

"Okay. Sure." In a perfect mirror image of her husband, Marianne clutched her hands together at her waist. "It's the library. Our funding. We're . . ." A single tear slipped down her cheek. "Oh, Alvin. What are we going to do? We're going to lose Lucy Atwater's grant!"

It goes without saying that this meant something (and apparently something important, from the looks on the faces around me) to everyone but me. Newcomer, remember, and I leaned forward, to remind Marianne that I was there. And I was lost.

"Lucy Atwater," she said, her voice clogged with tears. "She died . . . oh, it must be twenty years ago now. Don't you think, Chandra? Wasn't it the winter Bill Smith over at the hatchery fell into the fish tank and drowned? It must have been right after that, because I remember Lucy telling me how much she missed Bill. They used to date, you know. Well, I'm not exactly sure it could be called dating. But they'd step out together and —"

Alvin cleared his throat.

Marianne gulped and collected herself and the quickly untangling threads of her story. "When Lucy died, she left the library a chunk of money. It funds most of our programs, but there's a catch. We can only get our yearly payment if we have an ongoing book discussion group. And . . ." Marianne's shoulders rose and fell in a slow-motion shrug. "These days no one's signing up."

"People are too busy," Kate said.

"Yes, of course, that's part of the problem." Marianne dug a tissue out of her purse and touched it to her nose. "There are so many other distractions these days, books aren't high on enough peoples' lists. The other part of our problem is that there are so many summer visitors here to the island. They don't sign up for programs because they know they're not going to be around long enough to participate more than once or twice. I don't know what to do. I'd hate for kids to come to the island in the summer and stop at the library and . . ." A fresh cascade of tears started and Alvin handed Marianne his handkerchief. She blew her nose. "Wouldn't it just be awful for some poor, sweet child to show up at the library and find it closed?" she wailed.

"It's really too bad," Kate agreed. "Now can we leave?"

In the hope that she was actually right about something, I grabbed my purse.

Chandra didn't move a muscle. That is, until she slipped an arm around Marianne's shoulders. "Of course you're upset. Who wouldn't be?" With her other hand, she grabbed for the denim hobo bag she'd plunked on a nearby chair when she entered the courtroom. She opened it, dug around inside, and came up holding a small glass bottle.

"It's neroli oil," Chandra said, pressing the bottle into Marianne's hand. "Rub it on your solar plexus. You know, right here." She pressed a hand to a spot just under her own stomach. "That's your Manipura chakra, and remember what we talked about when you came for your last crystal healing? That's the chakra that corresponds to feelings of fear and anxiety, and that's what we need to contend with first before we look for an answer to your problem. No worries," she added, when Marianne gave the bottle a questioning look. "Neroli smells really nice, zesty and spicy with a little flowery note. Go on, Marianne, just pull up your sweater and —"

"Not in my courtroom!" Alvin was on his feet again, and one look from him and Marianne blanched and handed the bottle back to Chandra.

With a sigh of epic proportions, Kate dropped into the nearest chair and checked her text messages. "This is a perfect example of everything I've been telling you, Alvin," she said, her fingers flying over the keyboard. "I told you, the woman plays sitar music. Loud. Day in and day out. Chandra's nuts. Do you get what I'm talking about now that you see her in action? Someone needs to do something about the music and the bonfires and the chanting."

"Actually . . ." I stepped back, my weight

against one foot, lest Alvin get lost in the moment and forget the real reason we were there. "What someone needs to do something about is Jerry Garcia. That stupid cat —"

"Is nicer than a lot of people I know," Chandra grumbled.

Since she really didn't know me, I didn't take this personally.

Kate dropped her phone back in her purse. "Can we leave now? It's obvious nothing's going to get done. And I don't have time for this nonsense. Just tell Bea here" — she cast an icy green glance in my direction — "to cool it with Grand Central Station, and the Good Witch of the North over there . . ." She looked toward Chandra. "To put a sock in it, and —"

"And the cat!" I butted in before Kate could get even more carried away. "Don't forget the freakin' cat!"

Honestly, I hadn't even noticed that there was a thick legal book on Alvin's desk until he picked it up and slammed it back down.

That got our attention. So did his voice. He spoke in what was nearly a whisper, each word so clipped and so precise, there was no doubt that he meant what he said.

"I've had enough. We're going to solve this problem once and for all. And we're going to do it right now."

"Make Bea close her B and B?" Kate asked.

"Make Chandra keep her cat inside?" I countered.

"Make Kate turn off that horrible music?" Chandra retorted.

Alvin banged a fist down on top of the book. "No. None of those things. What you women need to do . . ." His gaze moved from one to the other of us. "What all of you need to do is learn to get along. You're neighbors. Start acting like it. You have to stop talking *at* each other and start talking *to* each other. And I'll tell you what, I'm going to go down in South Bass history, because I'm the one who's going to make sure you do it."

Yeah, I sounded as skeptical as I was feeling when I asked, "You're going to sentence us to talk to each other?"

Alvin's smile was sleek. "I'm going to do you one better than that," he said. "I'm going to make each of you report to the library at seven o'clock, this Monday, and every Monday for the next year. I'm sentencing you three to be a book discussion group."

Marianne's miserable expression morphed into a smile.

Chandra's mouth dropped open.

Kate (do I even need to say it?) rolled her eyes.

Good thing one of us didn't lose her head. "You can't do that," I said. "It's not legal."

"Well, it's not illegal," he told me. "And believe me, it beats all the other things I could do to you. You don't want to find out what those things are."

I had to agree with Alvin there.

But just for the record, that didn't mean I had to like it.

From the looks on their faces, I'm pretty sure Kate and Chandra didn't either, and I left the town hall with a cynical smile on my face, thinking it was the first thing we'd ever agreed on.

No, at that point, we didn't think of ourselves as the League of Literary Ladies. Not yet, anyway. I'm pretty sure we didn't think of ourselves as anything but royally pissed, not to mention inconvenienced.

But then, that was before the murder. And the murder?

Well, that changed everything.

2

A library was the last place I wanted to be.

Not that I hate books or anything, it's just that . . . Well, it's a pretty long story, and it doesn't matter at this point, anyway. Let's just say that I spent the weekend stewing about Alvin Littlejohn's creative sentencing, and by the time Monday evening came around, that stew was at a rolling boil.

At the risk of sounding too much like my across-the-street neighbor, Ms. Kate "Oh-I'm-So-Uppity" Wilder, I didn't have time for reading books, much less talking about them. Add to that the fact that I didn't have the patience to sit around when there was so much to do back at the place I called Bea & Bees (no, there were no hives in the garden yet, but someday I hoped there would be), and that I didn't have the inclination to spend another minute in the company of my two unneighborly neighbors, and I confess, I almost opted for the

Rambo approach. I pictured myself barricaded in at the B and B, eating tinned meat, chopping up the furniture for fuel, and fighting to the death if anybody actually noticed I hadn't shown up at the library and came to collect me.

Not to worry, after a few moments of dramatic daydreaming, my cooler-headed self prevailed. She usually does.

After all, I reminded myself, I didn't want to *not* comply with Alvin's ruling and end up on the radar screen of the Put-in-Bay Police Department.

With that in mind, I arrived at the room in the library basement next to the boiler room, the one someone with more of an imagination than a decorating budget had dubbed the Executive Boardroom.

I slipped off my lightweight spring jacket and flopped into a metal chair with a gray plastic seat, paying little attention to the shelves that lined three of the room's institutional green walls. They were stacked with books, mass-market paperbacks mostly, and rather than worry which of them would be our first official homework assignment, I took off my glasses long enough to clean them on one of those lint-free cloths and ran my fingers through my unruly hair. As ready as I'd ever be, I propped my elbows on the table, braced my chin in my hands, and waited.

Kate was the next to arrive.

"Oh." Obviously, she'd expected to be the first one there, and she pulled to a stop just inside the door and glanced around the room as if deciding which of the chairs at the round table would afford her the power position within the group. Since there were only five chairs, it wasn't like she had a lot of choice.

She slapped a leather portfolio on the table and took off her tan Burberry raincoat. "You got here early."

"I just finished hanging some pictures in one of the bedroom suites at home. It seemed like a good place to stop for the day."

"I hope the room doesn't face Chandra's house." Kate took a compact out of her purse, checked her makeup and freshened her lipstick. "She might have heard the pounding on the walls and figured the spirits were trying to communicate from the Other Side."

Hey, the woman was a royal pain, but I had to give credit where credit was due. I laughed.

Kate had chosen the chair directly opposite mine, and she studied me for a moment, apparently trying to decide if my amusement was genuine. I guess I passed the test, because after she glanced over her shoulder toward the door, she leaned a little nearer. "You know it's not her real name, don't you?"

My questioning look said *huh?* way better than words could have.

It was Kate's turn to laugh. She had straight, even teeth, and they were blindingly white. "Chandra. Our woo-woo friend. Her real name is Sandra. A couple years ago, she insisted we all start calling her Chandra because she thought it sounded more mystical, but a lot of the old-timers still call her Sandy."

I felt my smile get bigger. "Sandy. Yeah. I can see that. She looks like a Sandy."

"And smells like a Chandra." Kate wrinkled her nose. "All those herbs and potions and oils. I swear, if the woman put half as much effort into fixing up her house as she does into concocting all that weird stuff she's always giving people to use, all our home values would skyrocket."

I had seen Chandra's house, of course; I knew exactly what Kate meant. Though it wasn't a dump by any means, Chandra's place was . . . eclectic, a spare, single-story house, each outside wall painted in a different color: turquoise, orange, pink, purple. She saved the sunshiny yellow for the garage door. The house was surrounded by a veritable forest of wind chimes and fountains, gnomes and sparkly twirling suncatchers. I shuddered to think what might pop up in her overgrown garden once the weather was warm and Chandra really got into the spirit of outdoor living.

"You're thinking about summer." Chalk one up for Kate; she was an annoying little twit, but she was perceptive. "When your windows are open, that's when you'll start hearing the music."

"And the cat will visit more often, I imagine." Just thinking about it, my head started to pound. "I'm considering tiny electric fences. One for each of my flower boxes."

For about half a second, she thought I might actually be serious. Then her smile bloomed. "I'm thinking about something a little more irritating than opera. Hip hop?"

I joined in the good-natured fun. "Knowing Chandra, she'd be out in the street, dancing to the beat."

"Broadway show tunes?"

"I have a confession. I like Broadway show tunes. I even know most of the words. If you start playing them, I'll start to sing. And

I'm pretty sure you don't want to hear me sing."

"Then zydeco."

"Klezmer."

"Polkas."

"Yanni."

"No." Kate groaned. "Chandra actually likes Yanni! You'll hear a lot of him this summer, too."

By this time, we were both laughing, and I decided that maybe I'd misjudged Kate. Maybe, like me, she was annoyed at being dragged into Alvin's courtroom — again — when she had more important things to do. And irritated about being forced to read and discuss a book she'd likely have no interest in. Maybe that explained the way she'd acted when we were in court together a few days before. Maybe Kate was simply rushed. And overworked. Maybe she really was as busy and as important as she made herself out to be.

"The workers are nearly done at my place," I said, proving once again that I can act like an adult when the situation calls for it. "There will be less traffic soon."

"Well, that's a relief." Kate sat back. She must have just come from the family winery, because she was wearing a tweedy brown suit with flecks of orange in it that matched her hair. I was wearing jeans, sneakers, and a navy blue sweatshirt, and I felt like we'd reversed roles and that I was the country bumpkin and she was the power broker from the big city.

"I've got my first guest checking in on Sunday," I said, and maybe I wasn't just making conversation; maybe I was reminding myself that running Bea & Bees wasn't just my new career. It was my chance at starting over, and I planned to be as darned good at it as I was at everything else I'd ever tried in my life. "Kind of a red-letter day for me."

"First guest. Let's hope it's not the last."

"No reason it should be. Once the summer tourist season starts —"

"The island will be hopping. Yeah, that's true. Around here, from Memorial Day to Labor Day, the place explodes with visitors. Fishermen, boaters, families, partiers."

"Which only reinforces the fact that I won't lack for guests. I've already taken a few reservations for the summer season. Once I start advertising, things are bound to pick up even more."

"Right."

It wasn't what Kate said, it was the way she said it. And the fact that she *tap, tap, tapped* one finger against her leather portfolio when she did.

I hadn't realized I sat up a little straighter until it was a done deal. "What?" I asked her.

Her smile, so leisurely just a short time before, was suddenly tight. "That place of yours, I can't help but wonder if there might have been a better use for land that close to the lake. It may have made more sense to tear down that monstrosity of a house than renovate it. That way, the land could have been repurposed, let's say for —"

"Growing grapes?" No grape was ever as sour as the sudden tone of my voice. But then, I'd just realized why those words *repurposed* and *better use for land that close to the lake* and *monstrosity of a house* sounded so familiar.

"You're the one." I pointed an accusatory finger directly at the cute little freckles on the cute little bridge of her cute little nose. "You're the one who submitted the objection to the township board of trustees when I first tried to buy the property. I always wondered who the troublemaker was. You!" Another jab in her direction, just for good measure. "You're the one who wanted to stop me from opening the B and B."

"Busted." She didn't sound at all guilty about it. Kate sat back, as nonchalant as if we'd been talking about the weather instead of the place I hoped was going to be my home and my refuge for who knew how long. "I've got nothing against you personally," she said, and she didn't give me time to throw in a sarcastic *thank you very much* before she went right on. "But let's face it, you show up here out of nowhere and chances are you don't know anything about running a B and B on an island in the middle of Lake Erie."

"And that's your business, why?"

Her phone vibrated, and she checked the message on the screen before she said, "It's not. And honestly, I don't care if you succeed or go belly up. I do care that when you fail and you go running back to the mainland with your tail tucked between your legs, that hulking Victorian house of yours is going to stay empty because these days, nobody's going to be able to afford to buy it, especially after all you've sunk into the renovations. It's going to fall into shambles and that's going to hurt everyone's property values."

I didn't even realize I was clinging to the tabletop until I looked down and saw that my knuckles were white. "That's only if I fail," I said, snapping my gaze to Kate's again. "And I have no intention of failing."

I prayed she was about to give me some smart-alec comeback, because I was ready for her. Yeah, I had pledged to be as polite and considerate as my island neighbors, but enough was enough.

And I'd had enough of Kate Wilder.

Before I could make that stunningly clear, the door popped open and Chandra walked in.

"Oh my, isn't the feng shui off in this room!" She shivered, reached into her purse, and took out a small spritz bottle.

"I swear, Chandra." I slapped a hand on the table. "If you spray that, I'm going to hurt you."

She pouted. "It's only lavender water. Lavender helps promote serenity. Seems to me this room could use a big ol' dose of that." She lifted the hand holding the bottle.

I popped out of my chair.

Marianne breezed into the room. "I'm glad to see things are going so well." She was either oblivious, or she had nerves of steel; she stepped between me and Chandra and took a seat. "You're all here, and right on time. This is going to be the most fun book discussion group ever. We're going to have such a good time."

I would have liked to point out that I could already be having a good time if she'd given me half a moment and I had the chance to snatch that bottle out of Chandra's hand, toss it on the floor, and stomp on it.

But I didn't have a chance because another woman walked into the room. She was short and wiry, with a head of silvery hair that framed a face as wrinkled as an old blanket.

"Hope I'm not late." The woman was wearing tan Carhartt bib overalls and when she got nearer she brought with her the musty scent of the lake in spring. She glanced around the table, nodded to the other three women, and stuck out a hand to me. "Luella Zak." Her grip was firm, her handshake rock-steady. "We haven't met, but we have a connection. My daughter Meg is the one who's going to be doing your baking for you over at Bea and Bees."

I'd sampled a half-dozen bakers' wares since I'd been on the island, and Meg's muffins and breads were by far the best, and I told her mother so.

"Hiring bakers. Hiring cleaners. Renovating the house." Chandra had gone around to the other side of the table and — thank goodness — she tucked that bottle of lavender water back where it came from. "There's been plenty of talk on the island since you bought that place, Bea. People are wondering how you can afford to do everything you're doing."

In a polite world, I would have given her an answer. Then again, in a polite world, she wouldn't have brought up the subject in the first place.

I was well within my rights to ignore her.

"So . . ." Maybe she was immune to the bad mojo in the room, or maybe Luella really didn't give a damn. She dropped into the chair next to mine. "I hear there's a book discussion group starting."

"And you want to join?" Like anyone could blame me for sounding so cynical?

Apparently, Luella didn't. Her blue eyes gleamed. "Boy, there's nothing I love more than reading," she said and added for my benefit, "I run Zak's Charter Fishing. Used to be my business and Joe's, my husband, but he's been dead nearly ten years. So now I'm the one who takes tourists out on the lake for perch and walleye. They fish, I read. I've always got a book with me." As if to prove it, she pulled a tattered copy of a historical romance out of the pocket of her overalls. "Just finished this one today while I was waiting for the guys over at the marina to do some work on my boat. I'm all set for a new book." She looked toward

Marianne. "How is this going to work? And what are we reading?"

"Well . . ." Marianne glanced around the table. "I suppose it's up to all of us. This is a democracy, after all."

"Not exactly," Kate grumbled. "Or we wouldn't be here in the first place."

Rather than deal, Marianne got up and walked over to the bookshelf along the back wall of the room. "I suppose the first thing we'll need to do is choose a book to read. And we'll need something we have five copies of. So . . ." She riffled her fingers along the shelf at eye-level, plucked a book from the stack and spun around. "There's this one. *Darkness on the Edge of Death* by FX O'Grady. Everybody loves FX O'Grady."

"No!" My objection came out a little too loud, and way too fast, and I didn't even realize it until I saw that the other women were staring at me. I tried for a smile that even I knew didn't look genuine. "I hear those books are scary. I don't like to read scary books."

"That's because you don't have a clear concept of life after death," Chandra pointed out right before she made a face. "Although, if I remember the movie right, it didn't exactly portray those who have crossed over as a very friendly bunch. There were zombies, and shapeshifters, and some pretty nasty things happening in a cemetery."

"Scared the bejesus out of me." Luella, apparently, wasn't one to beat around the bush. "The book and the movie. Couldn't sleep for a week after and even then, had to keep the lights on."

I hoped another weak smile would convince them. "See? If the book is that scary . . ." I jiggled my shoulders to get rid of the cold chill that had settled there. "I'd rather not read it."

Marianne weighed the book in one hand. "They say O'Grady has retired, you know. He's not writing anymore. So since there won't be any more new books from him, this really would be a perfect opportunity."

She slid a look my way and apparently took pity on the abject terror in my eyes. She slipped *Darkness on the Edge of Death* back on the shelf, and I breathed a sigh of relief. "Well, here's a different sort of classic," she said. "And there are one, two . . ." She counted below her breath. "We've got enough copies for everyone. How about it, ladies?" She held up the book so we could see the cover. "What do you think of a real mystery classic, *Murder on the Orient Express?*"

"I adore Christie and wouldn't mind reading it again." Luella reached for a copy of the book.

Kate took a copy, plunked it on top of her portfolio, and stood. "Now that that's settled," she said, "we can get out of here."

"Well . . ." Chandra turned the book over in her hands. "There was a movie, wasn't there?" she asked no one in particular. "I'd rather watch the movie than read the book."

Because no one objected to Kate's attempt at a quick getaway, I sidestepped toward the door.

"You mean we're not going to start talking tonight?" Luella looked from one of us to the other. "I thought we might have a lot to say about the influence of classical mysteries and . . ."

Her words trailed away. But then, like I said, I got the feeling Luella wasn't the type who wasted her time. And since Kate was already on her way out the door, I was hot on her heels, and Chandra was checking out the nearest stack of DVDs, I think she pretty much got the message.

3

"One guest checked in this morning, and I've already had someone call and ask about rooms for the last weekend in June. You've got to admit, Jason, this was a good move. I told you I could do it."

"I don't have to admit anything." Since my attorney, Jason Arbuckle, was back in New York and at the other end of the phone, I couldn't see his face. But, hey, I'd known Jason a long time; I pictured him with his bald head gleaming and that omnipresent toothpick twitching in the left corner of his mouth, the way it always did when he tried to stand up to me and realized from the start there was no way he could. "It just doesn't make sense, Bea. You. On an island. Running a B and B."

"It makes plenty of sense, and you know it," I told him. "I wanted out of New York, and I got out. I was looking for a place that was laid back and quiet, and I found it." I was doing a last-minute check on the downstairs parlor, just in case my guest wanted to sit in front of the fire later in the evening. Thanks to the crackerjack cleaning crew I'd hired as soon as the painters and decorators were done with the house, the room was pristine, from the tin ceiling to the antique Oriental carpet in shades of indigo, madder, and tobacco that looked perfect with the leather furniture I'd brought with me from New York.

Speaking of which . . .

"You got an offer on the condo?" I asked Jason. It wasn't the only reason he would call on a Sunday, but it was the best one.

"You don't have to sell," he said.

"But you got an offer."

"If you keep the condo, you can always decide to come back."

"If I don't keep the condo, I can always decide to come back and buy another condo."

He grumbled, but he gave in, just like I knew he would, and when he told me how much the offer was for, I agreed to it on the spot.

Ater all, I had a guest settled in upstairs in Suite #1, it was lunchtime, and I was starving. I was not inclined to dicker.

Finished with Jason, I raced up the stairs

to tell my guest, Amanda Gallagher, that I was going out to pick up some lunch, asked her if she wanted anything (she didn't), and headed out of the house.

For about fifteen seconds.

It was downright chilly out, considerably colder than it had been earlier in the week, and I whirled back inside and grabbed my heavy jacket. If what the weather forecasters said was true, we had snow heading our way, and the nip in the air told me they just might be right. Yes, it was officially spring, but according to the people I'd talked to at the grocery store the day before, snow in April isn't all that unusual in Ohio. It would pass in a day or two, they assured me, and added that the daffodils just peeking out of the beds around the house were as hardy as the rest of the island's residents; they wouldn't mind a bit.

I fished in my left pocket for my gloves, and in my right pocket for my knitted hat, and thus attired and as cozy as I was likely to be with a brisk wind racing south over the lake from Canada, I stayed with my original plan, which was to walk into town. South Bass is only a little more than four miles long and about a mile and a half wide, and smack dab at its narrow center from north coast to south is the town of Put-in-

Bay. I'd been smart enough to buy property not far from downtown. The location was convenient for me, and for all those guests I hoped to host over the summer, and the chance to get out and walk in the brisk air without seven million other people milling around me was more of a treat than I can say.

Content and with the kind of spring in my step that I had only dreamed about back when I was still in New York and desperate to get out, I paused in front of Chandra's, listening to the not-so-melodic clang of her windchimes while I took a good long look back at Bea & Bees.

As much as I hated to admit it, Kate was right when she said the house was a monstrosity. Turret, wraparound porch, six suites for guests that each included its own bathroom, and the common rooms: parlor, dining room, kitchen. There was also a full basement, an attic I hoped I would someday need to convert into more guest rooms, and my own private first-floor suite, which included my bedroom, a bath, a sitting room, and a back porch I had yet to have the leisure to enjoy.

The place had been for sale for a couple years before I discovered it, and from what I'd heard, plenty of people had looked at it before me. It intimidated the hell out of every single one of them. Honestly, I could see why. My little piece of real estate was directly across the road from a postage-stamp-sized area of green space that included a picnic table, a park bench, and a few battered trees that leaned away from the wind. There was a three-foot drop to the lake just beyond the little park, and most days, Lake Erie slapped gently against the narrow, rocky strip of shore. Today, the waves were more of the crashing variety. Even twenty feet away, I felt the cold sting of spray.

As all the architectural magazines say, homes near water are plenty desirable, and romantic, too. But what most people don't realize is that they also require more maintenance than most normal human beings are willing to commit to. Add to that the fact that island real estate is scarce, and thus expensive, and it was easy to see how folks had been scared away. Sticker shock plus endless upkeep and the cost of the renovations the place sorely needed when I stumbled on it? Yeah, even the bravest speculators and the smartest investors had run off screaming into the night.

Fortunately for me, I'd never been accused of being especially brave or exceptionally smart.

I looked past the newly installed Bea & Bees sign tastefully highlighted with gold gilt and painted in shades to match the house's fresh coating of teal paint and accents of rose, terra cotta, and purple. Automatically, my gaze went to the distinctive chimney with its ornamental brickwork that hugged the outside of the house all the way from the first floor to the slate roof, and my heart squeezed. She was the pride of the neighborhood.

Well, at least I thought so.

As for what my neighbors thought . . .

I spared exactly one second looking at Chandra's rainbow house and at Kate's across the street from it, a modern, one-story number right on the water that had a sloping roof and natural-colored shake siding.

What the rest of the world thought of Bea & Bees, I really didn't care. I had found my home sweet home, and discovered my bliss, to boot, and nothing and no one — not Jason who was worried I'd be lost forever in middle America, or Jerry Garcia the unsanitary cat — was going to scare me away.

Buoyed by the thought, I made my way downtown in record time. (The cold temperatures might have had something to do with how quickly I walked, too.) Once summer arrived, the island would teem with tourists, but on a cold (and getting colder) Sunday afternoon in April, things were pretty deserted. A couple of restaurants stayed open year-round to accommodate the couple hundred hearty souls who stayed on the island through the winter months, but I passed them by without a second thought.

I knew where I was headed, and I knew what I'd order when I got there, and since I visited the establishment at least three times a week, my feet knew the way as surely as if I had a yellow brick road to follow.

Before I knew it, I stood in front of the island's newest eating establishment, the Orient Express.

Yes, I thought about the book I was supposed to be reading for our discussion group. Well, for about a nanosecond, anyway.

No, I had yet to start the assignment.

And yes (again), I was fully aware that the next day was Monday and I'd better get off the stick, but really, I'd been busy all week with the last of my unpacking, and I'd made a couple trips to the mainland on the ferry to check out landscaping plants at a garden center and do some other necessary shopping.

Even if I were so inclined (and I wasn't), I wouldn't have felt guilty.

For now, all I cared about was the tingle of anticipation that coursed through my bloodstream like some kind of crazy-making drug. How could I think about books or anything else when just a few short feet away, on the other side of the door in front of me, lay Nirvana?

Peter Chan's as-good-as-anything-I'd-ever-eaten-anywhere-in-the-world orange/peanut chicken.

I pulled in a breath of icy air and the glorious aromas of soy sauce and stir fry that wafted out of the building. The Orient Express had opened only a few weeks earlier in a nondescript strip that included a souvenir store and a knitting/quilt shop, and already, Peter and his stellar takeaway cuisine had a reputation on the island for fresh ingredients, terrific service, and reasonable prices. Once summer started, I anticipated long lines at the counter, and truth be told, I am not a fan of long lines. Not to worry, I already had a plan: I'd get my fill of the fabulous, fabulous orange/peanut chicken before that. Then I could afford to be generous and let the tourists enjoy Peter's culinary talents. Either that (and I was thinking this was actually the better plan), or I'd pay the small upcharge and have dinner delivered right to my doorstep.

Unfortunately, in spite of the weather, it looked as if I'd have to start sharing Peter a little sooner than I anticipated. Through the front window, I saw that there was already a customer at the front counter. His back was to me, so I couldn't see his face, but I did see that he was a tall, broad man wearing a tan trenchcoat and a brown fedora.

Disappointed? Yes, a little. Until I reminded myself that Peter was quick and efficient so it shouldn't take him long to take care of this man. And besides, the orange/peanut chicken was worth waiting for.

I was all set to stroll right in and take my place in line when I heard the baritone grumble of the customer's voice and saw him poke Peter square in the chest with one finger.

Hey, even in New York, where shrinking violets get walked all over, this was not the way we put in our takeaway orders.

Curious, I ducked to my right and out of both men's line of vision, the better to watch what was going on.

As if he were moving in slow motion, I

saw Peter flatten his hands against the front counter and lean forward. He was shorter than the other man, slimmer, and wearing a white apron tied around his waist, and he had one of those paper surgical masks looped around his neck and hanging down on his chest.

Not exactly the picture of a tough guy, but whatever the customer had said, Peter gave back as good as he got. His voice was quieter, and higher-pitched; I couldn't understand a word. But I couldn't fail to miss the fact that Peter's eyes spit fire.

His teeth clench over his words, Peter reached under the front counter and came up holding a single sheet of white paper. He waved it in front of the customer's face.

The man stepped back and shook his head, and I caught a couple words. "Not me. Don't know what . . . You're crazy . . . It's not what we're talking about, anyway."

Peter slammed the paper down on the counter, and the customer whirled toward the door. The stranger's voice rumbled its way out to the sidewalk. "It was a bait and tackle shop once. It can be a bait and tackle shop again."

Before I could move to get out of the way, the man slammed out of the door and plowed right into me.

My knees buckled and I would have hit the sidewalk if he hadn't grabbed my arm to keep me upright. This close, I saw that the man's brown eyes were small and set close together and his cheeks were doughy. The hand that held my sleeve was meaty, the fingers short and as fat as sausage links. The man's mouth opened and closed, and though I'm definitely not the rose-colored-glasses type, I found myself hoping he was fighting to form the words of an apology. When he came up empty, dropped his hand, and stalked away, I couldn't help but be annoyed.

"Well, then." My spine stiff with indignation, I tugged my jacket back in place, nudged my glasses up to the bridge of my nose, and took a deep breath. Undeterred and as hungry as ever, I walked into the Orient Express.

What to say to a proprietor who's just had a knock-down-drag-out with a customer?

No worries. Like I said, I'm from New York. Though it wasn't a daily occurrence, I'd seen my share of confrontations back in the big city and, truth be told, I'd been involved in a couple myself. I knew the drill. When in doubt about what's politically correct or morally right, pretend nothing happened at all.

At least if you're smart.

But like I may have mentioned before . . . me and smart (at least that kind of smart) . . . not two concepts that are usually included in the same sentence.

The moment I was inside the door, I asked Peter, "Are you all right?"

I actually thought he might throw the same question back at me. After all, I was the one who'd nearly been flattened by the man in the trenchcoat, and Peter is usually nothing if not chatty and concerned that his customers have just the right experience at the Orient Express.

Except this time, I guess he was so upset by the incident I'd witnessed inside the restaurant, he didn't even notice my close encounter with the sidewalk.

He was standing right where I'd last seen him, his face screwed into an expression I refused to call inscrutable, his hands balled into fists, and his mind clearly a million miles away. In fact, I walked all the way to the front counter before he even noticed I was there.

Peter had a narrow face with even, pleasant features. At least when it wasn't flushed and his teeth weren't gritted. He shook himself back to reality. "Bea! What can I get you?"

No small talk? There usually was.

No asking what was happening back at the B and B? He always had before.

I excused the lapse in customer service because I figured he was upset, and placed my order for orange/peanut chicken.

No laugh along with the line that if I wasn't careful, I was going to get addicted?

Nope. Though Peter had always teased me before about my inability to try anything new now that I'd found the dinner dish of my dreams, this time he merely scratched my request onto an order pad.

"Sorry to be so disorganized today," he said when he was finished getting out a bag and tossing a few of those plastic pouches of soy sauce in it along with a complimentary fortune cookie. He touched a hand to the surgical mask around his neck. "Been doing some remodeling up in the apartment," he said, and he glanced up at the ceiling of the restaurant. I knew that Peter had just moved from the mainland and that he lived above the Orient Express, so it made sense. "It'll be just a couple minutes," he said.

End of small talk.

He disappeared into the back of the restaurant and shut the kitchen door behind him so quickly, a stream of air shot up front and made the piece of paper I'd seen him wave toward his disgruntled customer float to the floor.

It would have been rude of me not to stoop to retrieve the paper.

As for reading it . . . come on, it's not like anybody could blame me.

It was plain computer paper. No big deal there. But the words on it were plenty funky. Each letter was cut from a magazine or newspaper, a hodgepodge of both upper- and lowercase, some bold and dark against the white paper, others outlined in black, like a ransom note in a mystery novel.

You won't get away with this, it said. *I won't ever forget. I swear, I'll make you pay.*

Strange. And shocking.

I was staring at the note, wondering what it meant and if it had anything to do with the fight Peter had with the man in the raincoat, when the door to the restaurant opened and shut behind me.

Startled, I jumped — and smacked the paper back on the counter where it came from.

When I turned to greet whoever had walked into the Orient Express, I looked (I hoped) as casual as if nothing unusual had happened.

That was made just a little easier when I

saw that the next customer in line was Luella Zak.

"Hey, nice to see you." She moved quickly and efficiently, as only a person can who is completely at ease with her own body and satisfied with her place in the world. Luella stuck out one calloused hand and I shook it. "Finish the book?" she asked.

There were a couple other things I'd learned in New York. One was that when reluctant to admit the truth, it is perfectly acceptable to sidestep it.

"Not quite," I replied. "I've been kind of busy."

Luella grabbed a to-go menu and quickly read it over. "Meg tells me your place is really shaping up. Can't wait to see it."

"You'll have to stop by sometime." It was the polite response, and besides, I didn't have anything against Luella. Unlike the other members of my book discussion group, she seemed like a reasonable and reasonably nice lady. "I've already got one guest," I added, tooting my own horn.

"Bully for you!" Luella emphasized her point by poking a fist in the air. "Innkeeping's not an easy business, but I can tell, you've got what it takes. You care about the kind of experience your guests are going to have. You must, otherwise you wouldn't have hired the best baker on the island! Speaking of customer service . . ." She looked across the counter at the closed kitchen door. "Where's our friend Peter today?"

"Getting my orange/peanut chicken."

Luella laughed. "You, too? I swear, that stuff's got some magic drug in it. I walk in here and tell myself I'm going to have something else and when the time comes to order, the words just sort of spill out of my mouth. Orange/peanut chicken."

"Got it right here!" Peter came out of the kitchen holding the to-go container with my lunch in it, stopped and gave Luella a look. "You, too?"

"Me, too!" She stepped up to the counter. "As a matter of fact, Peter, give me two. It's supposed to snow, you know, and that way if it does, I'll have an extra in the fridge for dinner one night this week."

Peter wrote up Luella's order while I counted out the money for mine.

"Don't forget to finish your reading," Luella called to me as I was leaving.

I told her I wouldn't forget — which didn't mean I'd get around to it — and headed outside only to find that it was even colder than when I walked in a few minutes earlier. But maybe that was a good thing, after all. Otherwise I might have stood outside watching Peter, wondering what his beef had been with the man in the trench-coat, and what it had to do with the creepy, threatening note I found.

A blast of cold wind brought me to my senses, and I hauled the food bag up in my arms and started toward home. Peter might have tried his best to act as if nothing was wrong, but I knew better, and knowing it, a chill that had nothing to do with the falling temperatures crept up my back. Something was up, and it was not something good.

Good thing the street was deserted. That way, nobody gave me a weird look when I barked out a laugh. But then, I'd just found myself thinking I could have used some of Chandra's mystical powers. Where's a good crystal ball reader when you need one?

4

If I had any fantasies about a leisurely stroll into town for the next day's book discussion group meeting, they dissolved in a flash when I looked out the window.

Monday morning, there were snowflakes dancing in the air. By afternoon, that dance had turned into a choreographed routine, and by the time I needed to leave for the library, it was a full-fledged Busby Berkeley production number.

I hoped the folks I'd talked to at the grocery store were right about how the snow wouldn't hurt spring flowers, because by dinnertime, the poor daffodils in the front beds were smothered. That was about the same time I discovered that my new roof had a leak. In an ironic twist of fate that did not leave me laughing, just as I was putting pails on the floor of the bathroom in Suite #6 to catch the drips, my sole guest, Amanda Gallagher, announced that there was no way she could go out in the elements.

"I expect," she said with a tilt to her chin that showed more chutzpah than I'd expected from a woman who'd been as quiet as the proverbial mouse since she checked in, "that you will be providing dinner."

Side note here: I'm not morally opposed to cooking. In fact, I'd been known to do it myself a time or two, mostly when I'm trying to impress some guy and figure he'll be blown away by my mother's bolognese. But there is a reason they call it a bed-and-*breakfast,* after all, and remember, I'd hired Luella's daughter Meg to take care of the breakfast part.

Always the good sport (well, always when I'm so inclined), I opened a couple cans of chicken soup and left it simmering on the stove, showed Amanda where to find crackers, bread, and the blueberry muffins left over from breakfast, pretended I didn't hear her mumbled comment about how canned soup wasn't exactly what she had in mind when she mentioned dinner, and left the B and B.

Stepping through the three inches of slush that had accumulated in the driveway to get to the garage and the four-wheel drive SUV I'd bought specifically so I could easily pick up guests at the airport and the ferry, I did my best to distract myself from all the above-mentioned aggravations by humming the music from one of those wintry car commercials that feature sparkling snow and shiny, doughty vehicles that make it over the river and through the woods without a hitch.

Yeah, the same commercials that never bother to mention how when the streets are coated with a layer of ice, no vehicle — SUV or not — is going anywhere fast.

Halfway to the library, I felt the tires lose their grip. I slid to the right, overcompensated (hey, I never even owned a car back in New York so I can't be expected to drive like a pro), and ended up on the side of the road in what looked like a week's worth of carnival snow cones.

Grumbling, I slipped the car into reverse, then back into drive a couple times, gently rocking it until the tires caught hold and I jerked forward. When I got stuck again in the drive leading to the library parking lot and tried the same maneuver and it didn't work, I gave up with a groan, shoved the car into park, and left it right where it was. Kate's black BMW was the only car in the lot and, let's face it, no library patron was dumb enough to come out on a night like this. I wasn't worried about Luella. Though I barely knew the woman, I knew she was capable of taking on the elements — and winning every time. As for Chandra . . . for all I knew, she'd just use some hocus-pocus and poof into our midst.

Who would have guessed that a little white-knuckle driving would be the highlight of my evening!

Well, honestly, I should have. I mean, right after I stepped into a puddle of mush that lapped up over the tops of my ankle boots and soaked my feet.

I squished into the basement meeting room right on the heels of Kate's well-shod heels and watched her brush snow from her shoulders before she peeled off her wool coat and hung it on a nearby chair. "Worst I've seen it in April," she said.

"You're not kidding." Chandra slipped into the room right behind me. "And some idiot parked right in the middle of the driveway."

She knew what kind of car I drove and she was looking right at me when she said this. Which was exactly why I didn't dignify the comment with a reply.

"And just in case you haven't heard . . ." Since she didn't get a rise out of me, Chandra plunked into the closest chair, unbuttoned her coat, and removed her knitted hat and mittens. "The ferry isn't running. I got that news straight from Jayce Martin." Briefly, her gaze flickered to Kate, but when she didn't get whatever reaction she hoped for, she looked back my way. "Jayce is the ferryboat captain. Stopped at the grocery store on my way over here and saw him there. Not that he needed to tell me about the ferry. One look at the way the wind is whipping up waves on the lake, and I knew. The airport's shut down, too. Whoever's on the island is staying on the island. At least for tonight. And whoever's over on the mainland sure isn't coming home."

"Then we're all one big, happy family." Kate's smile was tight and her voice was acid. How she managed both while she was texting away, I couldn't say. Nor did I need to. That was because Luella arrived.

"Wow." She unzipped her hooded jacket and stomped her feet. "Bad and getting worse. I hear we could have a foot of snow by morning. Good thing we're in here and not out there."

I was so not in the mood to think about it, and would have debated the issue if Kate hadn't beat me to the punch. "Better when it's time to leave," she grumbled.

"So . . ." Chafing her weatherbeaten hands

together, Luella took the chair next to where I sat down. "Saw Marianne upstairs and she says she'll be a few minutes. She's closing things down before Alvin picks her up so all we'll have to do is turn out the lights and lock the back door behind us. She asked me to get things going. Who wants to begin? You did all read the book, didn't you?"

Kate studied her nail polish.

Chandra blushed a shade darker than the raspberry-colored sweater she was wearing along with a filmy turquoise scarf and orange jeans.

I cleared my throat. "I did. I read the book."

Eye roll from Kate. "Doesn't it figure? Teacher's pet. I should have known."

"Really?" My spine stiff, I turned her way. "We're going to be that juvenile about the whole thing? Won't that be fun for the next year!" I plopped back, my arms crossed over the front of my black cardigan. "I just so happened to have a little downtime yesterday evening," I explained, though why in the world I thought I had to, I wasn't sure. "I started reading, and you know what? I couldn't stop. It's a good story. Even though I knew how it ended, I kept reading. Seems to me that's the highest compliment you can give any author."

Luella's blue eyes gleamed. "This is exactly the kind of conversation I was hoping we'd have in this group. How about you, Chandra?" She looked that way. "What did you think of the book?"

Chandra dug into her denim bag and brought out the book along with a DVD. "I watched the movie. That counts, doesn't it?"

"At least I've got an excuse." Kate's phone vibrated, and she checked a message, then deigned to turn her attention back to the rest of us. "We've been doing inventory at the winery all week. Come on, Chandra, what kept you from reading? Wrong phase of the moon?"

"Hard to concentrate," Chandra said, "what with so many bad vibes rolling across the street from your house. Speaking of which, you're messing up the atmosphere in here, Kate, what with all that texting. Electronic signals interfere with —"

"Please!" Kate turned the word into two syllables. "All this mumbo jumbo of yours is what got us sent here in the first place. If you hadn't proved to Alvin just how off-kilter you are —"

"Me?" Chandra reached into her purse, brought out a little bottle, and spritzed the air all around where she was sitting. "I'm not the one poisoning the atmosphere in here."

"You think?" The scent of lavender wafted through the room, and Kate wrinkled her nose. "If it wasn't for you, Chandra —"

"If it wasn't for you, Kate —"

"If it wasn't for all of us. So why don't we just get down to business, because I'll tell you what, there's sure no way in hell I'm going to spend the next year coming here every Monday just so I can listen to this sort of bullshit."

Honestly, I didn't mean to hop to my feet at the end of my little speech, it just sort of happened. No worries. Since I was already standing, I was able to push my glasses down to the tip of my nose and glare at Kate over the frames. My cold, damp socks added a chill to my voice.

"Let's drop the attitude," I told her. "And you, Chandra . . ." I swung that way and repeated the glare. "We get the message, all right? We know you're" — I added air quotes here for emphasis — " 'one with the Universe.' So stop knocking us over the head with your Earth Mother routine. It's getting us nowhere, and it's only making a bad situation worse. And, yes, ladies, in case you need the reminder, this is a bad situation.

"We have to be here. You don't like it. I don't like it. Nobody likes it but Luella, but then, Luella . . ." With my blood boiling and my temper so near snapping I waited to hear the *thwang,* I somehow managed a lopsided look that someone who didn't know me well might have mistaken for a smile. Those who did know me? They knew that when I brought out the sarcasm guns, it was time to back off. At least if they were smart.

"Luella, you weren't condemned to the seventh circle of book discussion hell like the rest of us. Okay, all right. I get that we're all annoyed and we'd rather be home doing something else. Heck, I'd like to be in front of a roaring fire with a glass of really good pinot noir. But we're not. We can't be. And it isn't just because of Kate and her opera or because of Chandra and that damned cat, and it sure as hell isn't just because of whatever you think it is I've been doing to make the ol' neighborhood go to hell in a handbasket. It's because we've all . . ." Another look at Luella to be sure she understood she wasn't included in my scathing assessment.

"We've all been acting like horses' patooties," I reminded them, "and it needs to stop. At least while we're here every Monday

66

evening. Let's suck it up, ladies, and make the best of it. And if we have to make the best of it, we might as well make it quick. So let's stop wasting time." I dug in the pocket of my coat where I'd tucked my copy of *Murder on the Orient Express* to keep it dry on my way from the car to the library and slapped the paperback on the table. "Let's just talk about the damn book."

Ignoring their slack-jawed stares, I plunked back down in my chair just in time to hear Luella croon, "Way to go, New York, it's about time you started acting like a big girl."

Not everyone shared her sentiments.

Kate's head was so high, her arms so tight to her sides, I was pretty sure she was going to keel right over.

Chandra sniffled and grabbed for a lace-edged hanky.

"So . . ." I might have spoken my piece, but I was in no way done. Still hopping mad — at them for being the reason I was here and at myself for giving in to the anger that pounded through me like the waves against the island that night — I shot a laser look back and forth between them. "Who's going first? Nobody? Then I will."

In an attempt to curb my runaway temper that didn't work, I clutched my hands together on the table in front of me and flipped like mad through my mental Rolodex, reminding myself of all the things that had occurred to me as I read through *Murder on the Orient Express* the evening before. Heck, it wasn't like anyone was listening to me, and it sure wasn't like anybody cared. The way I figured it, I might as well say what was on my mind.

"One of the things that struck me as interesting," I said, "was the pacing of the story. The book was written when, in 1934? It seems a little . . . I don't want to say dry. It's a classic, and it deserves to be. But obviously, the world was a slower place then, and the pacing of the story reflects that, don't you think? As I was reading, I couldn't help but wonder, what if the book was written today? And what if Agatha Christie was just some wannabe writer who no one ever heard of? The pacing is deadly, the characters are stereotypes, and often insulting stereotypes, and the dialogue doesn't exactly sparkle. These days, would the book ever make it out of the slush pile of unsolicited manuscripts on an editor's desk and get published?"

I guess it was expecting a lot to think someone might actually answer me, since their mouths were still hanging open.

The silence only made me more determined. Not to mention annoyed. "What? I've made some perfectly valid points, and they're worth discussing. So, come on, people!" I slapped the table. "Discuss!"

Chandra was the first one to shake herself out of her stupor. She leaned closer, her eyes wide. "Are you an English teacher or something?" she asked.

It was the first I realized that the day's annoyances had piled up and pushed me over the edge. Slush pile? Had I actually said the words *slush pile*? I cringed and reminded myself not to make the same sort of mistake again. "I was an English major in college," I said. The truth if not the whole truth. Then again, the whole truth was the reason I was on the island in the first place, and not something I was willing to share. "I guess some of that stuff about pacing and dialogue and such, I guess it just sort of stays with you."

"Well, it sure stuck with you!" Luella clapped a hand to my shoulder. "You make some valid points."

Kate's phone vibrated. She read the message and popped out of her seat. "Pacing, characters, yadda yadda yadda. That's terrific. Really. And we can discuss it all next week," she said, grabbing her coat and heading for the door.

When no one stopped her, I figured she was onto something. I needed time to regroup and regain my composure before I said something else incredibly stupid, so I slipped *Murder on the Orient Express* back in my pocket and put on my coat, too. "Next week. That sounds good."

"But . . ." When I got to the door, I could feel Luella's gaze on my back. Just like I could hear the disappointment in her voice.

Even the guilt couldn't stop me.

In record time, I was in the car. I didn't so much back out of the drive as I slid down it and out onto the street.

After the tension of the meeting and the slip of the tongue that I prayed I'd handled with my English major explanation, I knew there was only one thing that was going to make me feel better.

With any luck, the Orient Express hadn't closed because of the snow.

So I never said my timing was impeccable, did I?

I guess I proved it when I saw the lights still on inside Peter Chan's place, shouted a hallelujah, parked the car, and raced through the snow to the front door.

That's when I realized Kate was already

standing in front of the Orient Express and Luella and Chandra were parking in front of the restaurant, too.

"Well, look at this!" In spite of the swirling snow, Luella's smile was a mile wide when she got out of her truck. "Looks like there is something we can all agree on after all."

"I was just . . ." I began.

"I just thought . . ." Chandra said.

"It really doesn't mean . . ." Kate grumbled.

"Oh, come on, you three." Luella hauled open the door and stepped back to let us walk into the restaurant ahead of her. "Think about Peter's cooking. If that's not enough to make you act like civilized adults, nothing is."

One sniff of the delicious aromas making their way out of the kitchen and into the frosty night air and I knew she was right.

I stepped inside and the other women followed.

"Peter!" He wasn't behind the front counter so I figured he was in the kitchen and I raised my voice so he was sure to hear me. "You've got customers."

No answer.

Apparently, like me, Chandra was a regular and knew Peter's routine. "He's probably working upstairs in the apartment," she said, and she opened the door that led to the stairway and called up.

No answer.

"Well, he must be close," Luella decided, drawing in a deep breath. "It smells great in here, like he's been cooking."

"And he's had at least one customer." Kate bent down and picked up a pink knitted glove with a frilly cuff in shades of blue and purple. "Let's just hope she didn't order all the orange/peanut chicken."

It wasn't my imagination. There was a collective intake of breath, and I'm pretty sure it had nothing to do with us being worried that Peter might actually run out of orange/peanut chicken — and everything to do with being struck with horror when we realized that we were all crazy about the same dish.

"Whoever lost it, she'll come back and look for it." I shook myself out of the thought, plucked the glove out of Kate's hand on my way by to drop it on the front counter. "It's so cold out, how could you possibly not want one of your —"

All set to set the glove on the counter, I froze and stared at the strip of floor behind the front counter.

The strip of floor that wasn't empty.

"Gloves." Leave it to Kate to refuse to accept anything but perfection. Even when it came to a sentence I hadn't finished. I could practically hear the disapproval dripping from her voice when she came up behind me and said, "That's what you meant to —"

Kate stared at the strip of floor behind the front counter.

The strip of floor that wasn't empty.

"Bea? Kate? What's with you two?" I'm pretty sure the next person who spoke was Luella, but it was kind of hard to tell seeing as how the voice sounded as if it came from a very deep cave. I'll bet she was the one who grabbed my arm, too, but then, Luella's the type who would notice right away that I was swaying on my feet.

The hold on my arm tightened when Luella looked behind the front counter.

"What in the world is wrong with all of you?" Chandra's laugh dissolved when she joined us and saw what we saw.

The four of us stood side by side, leaned forward, and took another gander at what I'd seen the moment I walked up to the front counter of the Orient Express.

Peter Chan on the floor.

His eyes bulging.

His mouth open in a silent scream.

A knife through his heart.

5

What's left to say after you've found a body with three of your not-best friends?

I didn't have the answer, and apparently, Luella, Kate, and Chandra didn't, either, because nobody was talking. After we called the police, gave our statements, and left the Orient Express, we somehow all ended up back at Bea & Bees, and we were in the parlor sitting in front of that roaring fire I'd envisioned earlier. Like me, the other women stared into the flames. Like me, I knew they were grossed out, upset, and feeling terribly sad, not only at the senseless loss of life, but at a disturbing and frightening act that was surely going to send out shockwaves that would ripple through island life for who knew how long.

"I never thought . . ." We'd sat in silence for so long, each lost in her own thoughts, that Chandra's comment made us jump. She sniffled and adjusted the knitted afghan she'd grabbed from a nearby chair and thrown over her shoulders when we came into the room. "I mean, I've never seen anything like . . ."

"Me, either." Kate was on the other end of the couch from Chandra and the couch was directly across from the fireplace. Though the logs hissed and popped, the warmth of the fire didn't seem to make its way over to her. She wrapped her arms around herself, leaned forward, and shivered. "Did you see the expression on Peter's face? It was —"

"What a horrible shame." Luella had taken the wing chair to the left of the couch, across from the chair where I was sitting, and on the other side of the mahogany coffee table. In spite of the orange glow of the fire, her face was pale. "Terrible thing, murder. To think anyone could have done such a thing . . ."

"Not something you'd expect here on the island." I didn't realize I'd spoken out loud until I heard my own voice. It was so small, it was nearly lost beneath the sounds of the crackling flames and the howling wind outside. "In the big city, maybe. But here . . ."

"Horrible shame," Luella muttered. "Horrible shame."

Chandra scrubbed her hands over her face. "I wonder if Peter had family."

"He never talked about them if he did," I said. Then before any of them could point out that I was the new kid on this block, and thus probably didn't know nearly as much as they did about the island and the people who lived there, I added, "Not that I knew him all that well, but we chatted when I went in to pick up food. He never said anything about a wife or kids."

Kate was as still as stone. "He was always so charming and friendly."

"Not true!" Once again, I spoke without thinking, and I flinched and braced myself for the firestorm of criticism I knew was sure to come. Being picky, petty, and picayune was what Kate and Chandra were all about.

When no one jumped in to bite off my head — not yet, anyway — I went on to explain, "Yesterday when I stopped in at the Orient Express, Peter was . . ." I thought back to the scene. "He was distracted," I said. "There was this man in the restaurant when I got there, and from outside, I heard them arguing."

Chandra's hands flew to her neck. "The killer?"

"We don't know that. We can't know it," I

76

pointed out. "But after the man left, I went in and placed my order, and Peter wasn't his usual talkative self. Then again, I can't blame him. It was a pretty ugly incident."

"Somebody we know?" Luella was asking about the man Peter argued with, of course, and the only response I could give her was a shrug.

"I've never seen him before," I admitted. "The rest of you . . . maybe you'd know him. He was tall and broad. He had small, brown eyes and a sort of doughy face. Not exactly fat, but padded, if you know what I mean. He was wearing a tan trenchcoat and a brown fedora. Kind of an Indiana Jones look without the Harrison Ford face or body to go along with it."

Chandra's smile was watery. "There you go, talking like an English major again. Your description's so good, I can picture him, and he sure doesn't sound like anybody I know. Maybe . . ." Her eyes widened. "Maybe you walked in and interrupted something. You did say they were arguing, right?"

"Yeah, but —"

She warmed to the theory and didn't give me a chance to finish, or to mention the creepy note I'd found when Peter went into the kitchen. "Maybe he was going to kill

Peter yesterday, and then you showed up and he couldn't. And so he left, and he went back today and . . . and . . ." The tears on Chandra's cheeks glistened in the light of the fire.

And I realized that a good innkeeper has duties that have to come before talking about murder. I had extra boxes of tissues upstairs in the linen closet and I headed out to fetch them.

At the bottom of the stairway that led to the second-floor guest rooms, I bumped right into Amanda Gallagher.

"Sorry," she gasped, flinched, and stepped back at the same time she cinched the belt on her robe. I'm nobody's idea of tall, but I had a few inches on Amanda, and she looked tinier than ever swathed in turquoise chenille. She had porcelain skin and hair the color of corn silk, and in the glow of the chandelier in the stairwell that I'd dimmed for the night, she seemed ethereal, like a wisp that had blown in on the tail of the winter wind. "I thought I'd just . . ." She sidestepped around me and in the direction of the back of the house. "I was going to make some tea."

"Of course." I stepped back so she could get by, and when she did, I realized something was off. Automatically, I reached for the decorative basket I kept on a table just inside the front door. "I've got slipper socks," I said, offering Amanda a pair at the same time I looked at the sturdy fur-trimmed boots she wore. "I know you weren't planning on staying here long and you may not have come prepared with everything you need."

She grabbed a pair of socks and tucked them in the pocket of her robe. "Speaking of that . . ." A gust of wind rattled the front door and Amanda shivered. "I don't know if the ferry is running —"

"It's not," Chandra called from the parlor, and I couldn't exactly fault her for eaves-dropping. After all, there wasn't exactly a talk fest going on in there.

Amanda's slim shoulders drooped. "If I need to stay another night —"

"Of course you can," I assured her. "They say no one's leaving the island, and for sure, no one will be coming. I've got plenty of room."

"Except . . ." Amanda's cheeks flushed the same color as the cabbage roses on the wallpaper in the hallway. She plucked at her robe. "I wasn't planning to stay more than a couple nights. That is, I hadn't exactly made arrangements, if you know what I mean, and . . ."

I had never been accused of being slow, but let's face it, I was new to this innkeeper thing. In fact, I was new to the service industry. It took me a couple moments to catch on to what she was getting at.

"The cost of the room. Of course!" I made up my mind in an instant and hoped my smile softened the edges of talking business. "The weather isn't your fault. How about if I charge half the rate I quoted you for however long you stay, including last night."

Relief swept over her expression and she disappeared down the hallway and into the kitchen.

"Well, that was a lousy business decision."

When I turned around, I found Kate leaning against the wall outside the parlor, her arms crossed over her chest and her top lip curled in disapproval. "Your business shouldn't suffer just because she can't afford to stay here."

"And what should I do? Tell her she should go sleep in her car?" Honestly, I wondered how people like Kate could look at themselves in the mirror. Then again, when you don't have a conscience in the first place, maybe things like kindness and common sense don't figure into your way of thinking. Shaking my head, I turned back around to head out on my original mission and Kate walked over to the door. She'd slipped off her boots when she came into the house and she reached for a pair of slipper socks. Before she grabbed a pair, though, she stepped back and made a face.

"Wet spot," she said, looking down at the floor and shuddering. "Now my socks are wet and —"

"Take two." I tossed her another pair of slipper socks. "That way you can take off your socks and —"

My words were interrupted by a knock on my front door.

"Go. Get the tissues." Kate leaned backward and took a quick look into the parlor. "Chandra needs them bad, and she's going to start wiping her nose in that pretty afghan of yours if you don't get them fast. I'll answer the door."

She did, and I raced upstairs. I had my head inside the closet outside the main bathroom when I heard the rumble of a man's voice.

"Bea!" Kate called up to me. "There's a man here who's looking for a room for the night."

"I was staying in a cottage over on Mitchell," the man called out, following Kate's example and raising his voice loud enough for me to hear. "But the heat went off.

Someone in town told me you had a generator, so I figured I'd take my chances and see if you have a room."

I loaded my arms with boxes of tissues decorated with flowers and butterflies and hurried back to the stairs. "Of course," I said, starting down. "I've got six rooms and only one guest and —"

Three stairs up from the front entryway, I froze and looked down at the man who was looking up at me.

The same man who'd plowed into me outside the Orient Express the day before.

The man who I'd seen arguing with Peter.

"Excellent!" Apparently, I don't have as memorable a face as I always thought. Without a flicker of recognition, the man lifted the duffel bag that he'd set on the floor next to him and stomped his feet against the hallway rug. He took off his fedora and a sprinkling of snowflakes landed on the floor. "I'm frozen to the bone. I can't wait to get settled," he said.

"Is it him?" Behind the man, Kate took one look at my expression (I am clearly not subtle when I'm gobsmacked), and mouthed the question.

I nodded in response and scrambled, wondering if there was a way I could announce that I'd remembered there were guests in every single one of my rooms. Before I could, the kitchen door at the end of the hallway swung open, Amanda stepped out, saw our little clutch at the bottom of the stairs, and swung around and back into the kitchen.

"Ted Brooks." Apparently, this newest guest thought my hesitation was due to the fact that we hadn't been properly introduced. He held out a hand and with no choice, I shook it. "I run Island Properties. You may have heard the name." He looked back and forth between me and Kate, and she knew what he was talking about; she nodded. "I own a number of cottages here on the island and rent them out to tourists. That's why I came to South Bass yesterday. To check on my properties, make sure everything made it through the winter okay."

"Competition, huh?" I hoped my smile looked as casual as I intended. It was better than letting him in on the flood of ideas racing through my mind:

Peter.

This man.

Murder.

Ted's laugh rattled me out of my thoughts. "This experience tonight, it's really got me thinking, that's for sure. I mean, about getting generators for the cottages. You know, in case any summer storms knock out the power. But heck, that would cost a small fortune."

There wasn't much I could say, about the generators or to discourage him from staying, so I led the way up to Suite #2 and allowed him to step inside the room ahead of me.

I have never been a fan of froufrou but, let's face it, a rambling house needs its share of ambiance and guests expect a certain amount of kitsch in a Victorian B and B. For the room Amanda was staying in, I'd gone all out: wallpaper studded with violets, lacy curtains, antique photographs in gilded frames. In Suite #2, I'd toned things down a bit. The walls of this room were painted a tasteful, deep green, and the four-poster bed was hung with maroon damask bed curtains. The shelves near the window were filled with leather-bound books.

Ted was apparently not a bric-a-brac kind of guy. He looked around and nodded his approval. "Hey, maybe we could come up with some kind of arrangement," he suggested. "You know, if it ever happens that my guests can't stay in one of my cottages for any reason, like there's no electricity, I could have them come here to your place."

I said I'd think about it, told him breakfast

would be on the table at nine, and high-tailed it out of there, my mind still racing. Same tune, different words. The racket went something like this:

Ted Brooks fought with Peter.

Peter was dead.

Ted was in my house.

Good thing that sturdy oak door to his suite was shut before I started back downstairs. Otherwise, he might have heard me gulp.

I deposited the tissues where Chandra could grab a box, then kept walking. My original intention was to follow Amanda's lead and go into the kitchen and make a pot of tea, but heck, as genteel as that sounds, I knew there were better ways to soothe the battered spirits of four women.

When I walked back into the parlor, I was carrying a tray with four fluted crystal glasses on it, and a bottle of Dom Perignon.

Kate took a gander at the label and her eyebrows rose. "1986. You must have been saving that for a special occasion."

"It was a gift." It was true, and as far as I was concerned, of no consequence. I poured and when she walked past the room, I offered to get another glass for Amanda. She declined and headed up the stairs, and I passed the glasses around.

"We're not . . ." When the bubbles in her glass tickled Chandra's nose, she held the Waterford a little farther away. "I feel guilty. Like we're celebrating something. And we shouldn't be."

"Don't think of it as a celebration." My mind still reeling, I didn't bother to sip. I took a nice big gulp and tipped my head back, enjoying the tickle of the bubbles in my throat. "Think of it as a way to help thaw the ice inside all of us."

"I'll drink to that." Luella took a long drink and smacked her lips. "Good stuff," she said.

"It should be." Kate sipped and nodded her approval. "That vintage . . ." She thought about it. "I'd say that bottle cost more than five hundred."

"Dollars?" Chandra nearly choked on her first sip. She swallowed, burped, and pounded her chest. "Well, if that's the case, I'd say the least we can do is toast." She raised her glass. "To Peter."

It was a somber reminder of why we were all there in the first place. We clinked our glasses together and settled back.

After another couple sips, Chandra sighed. "I suppose it's pretty fitting that we're sitting here drinking champagne tonight," she said with a wistful look at the fire. "Today is my anniversary."

I would have offered my congratulations if Kate's top lip hadn't curled. "Was that your first wedding, Chandra?" she asked. "Or your second? Or maybe it was your third?"

Chandra did not seem to hold these questions against her. She took another sip of champagne and answered matter-of-factly. "Second. You know, when I married Hank."

"Hank!" Luella threw back her head and laughed. "There was a match made in hell if ever there was one. You and Hank Florentine are like oil on water."

"You got that right." Chandra grinned and downed the rest of her champagne. "That man is pigheaded and stonehearted. I should have seen it from the start. Even when you know a guy is bad for you, sometimes you just can't help yourself. It's the whole moth-to-the-flame thing. You ladies know how it is."

Kate shook her head. "I don't know that. Not at all. The smart way to approach any relationship is to evaluate things from the start. If there are that many obvious problems, why start dating in the first place?"

"I'm afraid I can't really relate, either." Luella's glass was empty and she set it on the table near her elbow. "Joe, he was the love of my life, the only man I ever needed."

It wasn't until I finished my own champagne that I realized they were all looking my way, waiting for me to say something. Anything. About my love life.

Collecting my thoughts and steeling my nerves, I refilled the glasses, and when I was done, I sat back down. Not to worry, I had anticipated that someday I might face this sort of questioning, and I was ready for it. The trick was making my story sound convincing.

I wrapped my fingers around the stem of my glass. "My husband, Martin, died last year," I said, and since I guess I was expected to add some romantic insight into the comment, I added, "And I do think he was the right man for me. Even though he was twenty years older."

Something about this statement appealed to Chandra; her eyes sparkled. Or maybe that was because of the champagne. "Oh, a trophy wife!"

Back when I concocted the story, I told myself that folks would think this. I didn't actually expect anyone to come right out and say it. I hadn't prepared a response, so I covered with a laugh. "Nothing that interesting, I'm afraid. Martin owned an antiques store in Chelsea and I used to shop there. That's how we got to know each other. When he died . . . well, I sold the shop and moved here."

"Which explains the great furniture." Kate stroked one hand lovingly along the arm of the butter-soft leather couch.

"And it explains how you were able to afford this place and all the renovations." Who else but Chandra would have the chutzpah to put this into words? "We've been wondering, you know. All of us."

"I haven't." Kate distanced herself from this tacky little foray into my private life, and for this, I was grateful. It gave me a chance to finish the last of my champagne. When I was done, I set down my glass. "I'm afraid that was my last bottle of champagne," I told them.

"Not to worry!" Chandra popped out of her seat and scampered into the hallway to tug on her boots. "I'll go home and be back in a jiffy. I've got a couple bottles of stuff."

"Oh, no." Luella moved pretty darned fast for a senior citizen. She was out of her chair and had a hand on Chandra's arm to stop her before Kate and I caught up. "No way you're going to bring some nasty, herby stuff over here and tell us it's good for us. We'd all drink it, just to be polite, and I'll tell you what, I don't feel much like being polite. Not tonight."

■ ■ ■ ■

Lucky for us, Chandra returned with a six pack of beer, but it wasn't the only thing she brought from home. No sooner had she stepped into her rainbow house than she realized her electricity was off, too, and so was her heat. She returned with a sleeping bag and a promise to stay out of the way if only I'd let her sleep there for the night, and I told her not to worry about it and promptly showed her up to Suite #3.

That taken care of, I rummaged through the freezer and found margarita mix. And as long as we were in the kitchen crushing ice and blending, I pulled out a jar of salsa, a bag of tortilla chips, and some brie and crackers and set them on the granite counter to the right of the stove so we could pull up tall stools and make ourselves at home.

Believe it or not, I was halfway through my first margarita before a weird thought hit. "Hey, Orient Express."

Kate dredged a chip through the bowl of salsa. "Not open. Because of the murder. We can't order Chinese food."

"Not what I meant." There was a string of gooey brie on my finger, and I wiped it away with one of the purple cocktail napkins I'd set out. "Peter's restaurant was the Orient Express, and we're reading . . ." I used the royal *we* just to be polite and as a way of including Kate and Chandra even though they hadn't read the book. "We're reading *Murder on the Orient Express,* and there was a murder at —"

"The Orient Express."

We all finished the thought together. Had it been any other night, we might have laughed. Instead, our hands stilled over snack dishes and libations and our expressions sobered.

A shiver snaked over my shoulders. "It's weird when you think about it. I mean, the similarities."

Shaken from her momentary paralysis, Kate sipped her margarita. "There's the name of the restaurant, of course. That's a no brainer."

"And the note!" It was the first I had a chance to mention the note I'd read when it blew off Peter's front counter, and I told them all about it.

" 'You won't get away with this. I won't ever forget. I swear, I'll make you pay.' " Luella repeated the words I'd told her I'd seen cut out and pasted to the page. "What do you suppose it means?"

"I didn't know then and I don't know

now," I admitted. "But think about how weird it is. There was a threatening note in the book, too. It was sent to the victim before he was killed."

"Creepy." Kate wrapped her arms around herself.

"Strange." Chandra put down the chip she was about to take a bite out of.

"And we've got a snowstorm, too," Luella said. "That's just like in the book, too. The victim and the detective and the suspects, that's why they're all together. The train they're traveling in hits a snowbank and is stuck. They're trapped."

"We're kind of trapped, too." Though my kitchen was newly renovated and brightly lit, Chandra's gaze darted from corner to corner. "It's like the movie. All the suspects gathered together with no place to go. No one can leave. No one can arrive."

Well, not exactly, because for the second time that night, someone knocked on my front door.

6

Considering the kind of night it had been, I wasn't taking any chances. In an effort to look as decent as possible when the situation was anything but (both weather- and murder-wise), I made sure I wiped the salsa off my mouth before I went to the door. As it turned out, I was glad I did. First impressions are important, after all, though come to think of it, I don't think I'd ever made the sort of first impression the woman on my front porch did.

I was wearing my sweatshirt, jeans, and, since they were the closest footwear to the door when I slipped off my boots, my pink fuzzy bunny slippers.

She was cocooned in a sable coat that brushed the tops of her knee-high leather boots. Alligator — I'd recognize it anywhere, even in the midst of a blinding snowstorm — and the three-inch-high heels made her tower over six feet.

I'd scooped my hair back into a ponytail, the better to man the blender, but it's pretty rambunctious hair to begin with, and great curling wisps of it had already escaped my ponytail holder and were whipped around by the wind.

In spite of that stiff wind blowing off the lake, every strand of her brown chin-length hair was perfect. Just like her manicure, her makeup, and the hoop earrings crusted with diamonds that winked at me in the light of the porch lamp.

The perfume she'd ladled on? Not so perfect, at least to my nose. But plenty expensive. I caught a hint of jasmine and vanilla and wondered if she wasn't sniffing the air around me and picking up on the unmistakable aroma of lime and tequila.

"Ms. Cartwright?" The woman's voice was sultry and just a tad condescending. But then, there was the whole tequila/messy hair thing. "I was told you might have a room available for the night."

When I said, "Of course," my words were blown away by the wind, so I motioned her to come in and I shut out the storm.

"The electricity is off on most of the island," she said, sighing with satisfaction as the warmth enveloped her. "I heard you had a generator and were open for business. The roads are terrible. I was sure I was going to get stuck out there somewhere." She jiggled shoulders that were wide for a woman, but in perfect proportion with the rest of her body.

"You're not the only one who's been stranded," I told her. "But your timing is just right. I've got a couple extra guests, but there are still three rooms left."

I told her the rate, and this time, I didn't offer a special weather-related discount. Like I said, sable coat, alligator boots.

"I'm so glad I got here when I did. The weather's getting worse and worse." She offered a hand encased in a leather glove and I shook it. "Mariah Gilroy," she said by way of introduction. "I threw some essentials into my tote bag . . ." She had the leather tote slung over one shoulder, and she touched a hand to it. "That way, I could leave my suitcase in the car."

"If you'd like me to get it . . ." I'd already stepped toward the door when she stopped me, one hand on my arm. Which, come to think of it, was a good thing. Bunny slippers, remember.

"I wouldn't ask anyone to go out in that weather. Not for anything. Like I said, I've got everything I need for tonight. I'll worry about the rest of it in the morning. For now, if you could just show me to a room, I would be forever grateful. I need a long, hot bubble bath to thaw out."

I waved her toward the stairs and let her climb up ahead of me, and it wasn't until I turned to follow her that I realized we had an audience.

From the doorway of the kitchen, Chandra grinned and gestured up and down, one hand flat, her fingers splayed, as if to say *ooh-la-la!*

Kate nodded. I suppose that was her way of congratulating me for not offering Mariah a reduced rate.

Luella grinned and gave me the thumbs-up.

I hurried and caught up to Mariah at the top of the steps. I was right when I said her timing was good; now that the three suites at the front of the house were filled, Suite #4, the first door to the left of the stairway, was the most logical one to show her to, and something told me she was just the woman for the room.

I opened the door, turned on the faux Tiffany lamp on the cherry dresser, and showed her around. This was the most spacious and the most audacious suite at Bea & Bees, from the canopied bed to the shelves of bric-a-brac. It also happened to be the only suite that had a fireplace in the bathroom.

One look at it and Mariah cooed with glee. "You don't mind if I burn it?"

"I can start the fire for you if you like," I told her, and since there was already kindling and logs piled next to the fireplace, I did just that while she got herself settled.

Once the fire was crackling, I told her about breakfast, wished her a good night, and left Mariah slipping out of her boots.

I was all the way back to the kitchen before I realized Mariah wasn't the only new arrival. There was a middle-aged man standing near my back door. Buzz-cut hair, square jaw, arms crossed over his chest. If the dark blue uniform wasn't a giveaway, the gun he had strapped to his hip would have been.

Put-in-Bay's finest.

And he didn't look happy.

His eyes snapped to mine. "So you're one of the ones causing all this trouble."

I hoped he was kidding and decided in an instant that he didn't know the meaning of the word.

Dumbstruck, I pulled to a stop just inside the kitchen door. Kate wasn't complaining about traffic, was she? On a night like this? Or maybe it was Chandra, upset at all the cars that were now lined up in my driveway, too close to her precious herb garden.

I took a couple steps farther into the room, one bunny-shod foot in front of the other, and my smile as tight as my voice. "Me? Trouble?"

I swear, if Kate was behind this, I was going to . . .

Since Kate was seated at the countertop eating the last of a pint of Ben & Jerry's Chunky Monkey that I was sure had been in my freezer when I left to answer the front door, my suspicions were assuaged.

And Chandra? She was sitting next to Kate, her back impossibly straight, her head improbably high. She took a swig of beer and thumped her bottle back on the black granite countertop. "No trouble here at all, Officer," she said, each word as clipped as if she were biting it in two. "We can't imagine what you're talking about."

"Bunch of noisy women, partying." He shook his head in disgust. "I should have known you'd be behind something like this, Chandra."

She hopped off her stool. "You think? Then you should know something else. We're not sitting here just drinking and eating." Her gaze landed on the blender, half-filled with limey green margarita, and on the plates and bowls of snacks scattered all around, and she swallowed some of her outrage. "Okay, so yeah, we are sitting here drinking and eating. But that's not all we're doing. As a matter of fact, we were talking about Peter's murder. You know, about all the clues and such."

"Really?" The way he pursed his lips, I could tell he wasn't as impressed as he was simply amazed. "Is that so, Ms. Cartwright? Because I'll tell you what, I stopped over here just to talk to you for a minute, but if I'm interrupting your own private investigation . . ."

There's no buzzkill like a visit from the police in the middle of the night. I bunny-stepped over to the counter and put on a pot of coffee. "Don't be silly." Yeah, bad choice of words. From the tilt of the cop's bullet-shaped head to the chip I swore I could see on his shoulder, this guy was anything but. "We're just talking. That's all. And yes, the subject of the murder came up. Of course it did. What happened tonight has upset all of us."

He glanced around the kitchen. "You don't look upset. None of you."

"Pish tush!" Luella brushed him off with the flick of one hand. "That's for us to judge. Just like it's for us to decide how we can best handle how upset we are. Being with friends . . ." She glanced around at us. "Well, if you ask me, that's the best way any of us can handle the kind of trauma we've been through tonight."

Were we friends?

This didn't seem the moment to debate it.

Done with the coffee, I got out mugs and offered one to the cop, who declined with the tip of his head.

"Speaking of the murder, there are a couple interesting things we noticed," I began.

"Yeah, like how it's just like the one in *Murder on the Orient Express*." Her cheeks flushed, Chandra cut me off. "That's what we're reading, for your information. You know, for our book discussion group at the library."

Was that a smile I saw on the cop's pug-ugly face?

I must have been imagining it, because the next second, his mouth thinned.

"Don't give me that bull, Chandra," he said. "You haven't read a book in thirty years. Not unless it was some book about tarot cards or how to make that stinky incense you cook up in the basement."

"You're wrong," she shot back and not

one of us disputed this. For one thing, this was not the time to quibble about the differences between reading a book and watching a movie based on that book. For another, I wasn't sure I liked this cop's attitude.

"We found a clue," Chandra said and yes, she was stretching the truth. Well, just a little bit, anyway. Again, I didn't bother to interrupt. See above about attitude. "When we walked into the Orient Express tonight, before we realized what had happened to Peter, we saw a woman's glove on the floor."

The cop simply stared.

Chandra stepped closer, leaned in, and tapped her forehead with one finger. "Hello! Don't you get it? A woman's glove on the floor? That's got to mean something. Like that Peter was murdered by a woman."

All this time, the cop had stayed near the door that led out onto the little porch and from there, to the backyard. Now, he took a couple steps farther into the kitchen. He scrubbed one finger under his nose. "Or it could mean that the Orient Express is a public establishment. You know . . ." He leaned toward her and tapped his forehead with one finger. "Like lots of people come and go in the place. A woman's glove!" He chuckled. "That doesn't mean any more than the pack of chewing tobacco we found behind the counter."

"Well, Peter wasn't a chewer." Me. I had no intention of getting in the middle of whatever was going on between Chandra and the cop, but it was a legitimate comment, and we were in my kitchen, after all. "At least I'd never smelled tobacco on him. So that could mean —"

"That the murderer was a man!" The cop's eyes flew open in mock surprise. "Or that the murderer was a woman who likes a good chew now and then. Or that the Orient Express is a public establishment." He pronounced these last two words slow and loud, like we hadn't heard him the first time he'd pointed this out. "You four, you're playing games, and murder isn't about games. Leave the investigating to the professionals."

"We're not investigating." Chandra crossed her arms over her chest. "We're observing. And what we're observing is that the whole thing, it's a lot like *Murder on the Orient Express.* I mean, come on." She glanced around to where we were lined up on the opposite side of the kitchen from the cop. "Did you take a look at the chick who just came to the front door? It's like she just stepped out of the book. Like that Princess . . . Princess . . ." Her memory came up empty, and Chandra screeched her frustration. "You know who I mean."

"Princess Dragomiroff."

When I supplied the name, Chandra nodded. She stood tall and pulled back her shoulders, trying for a British accent that fell way short, but was as funny as hell. "Oh, so proper. And so regal."

"And so well dressed," I added, because the other women hadn't gotten a really up close look at Mariah.

"And then there's the note." Kate licked her spoon before she put it in the kitchen sink. "The one Bea saw on Peter's front counter yesterday."

"And the fight Peter had with . . ." Luella pointed to the ceiling, indicating Suite #2 and Ted Brooks.

There was exactly zero humor in the cop's laugh. "Don't tell me, let me guess. All that is just like in the book, too."

"Well, yeah." As strange as it sounded, it was the truth, so I wasn't embarrassed to admit it.

"And you're the one . . ." He looked my way. "You're the one who had both these experiences? You saw the fight? And read the note?"

Why did he make it sound like a bad thing?

I nodded.

"And that was after you read the book, right?"

"No, it was before, but —"

The cop's grin was sharp enough to cut me off. "Somebody" — since he was looking at me when he said this, I had a pretty good idea who that somebody was — "has an overactive imagination."

It was not the first time in my life I'd had that said about me, but this time, it sounded less like a compliment, and more like an accusation.

My shoulders shot back. "I'm not making any of this up. Why would I?"

The cop pursed his lips. "Sometimes when people get a little taste of the spotlight . . ."

"That's what you think's going on here?" My pink bunnies preceding me by a couple inches, I marched across the kitchen to face him. "You think because we were unfortunate enough to stumble across a body that all of a sudden, we're trying to get our names in the papers? Or our faces on the news?"

"As a matter of fact, that's exactly what I came over here to talk to you about. Glad I found you all together. Saves me from making a stop at each of your places." He glanced around from Luella (looking like she really didn't give a rat's ass), to Kate (who'd lost patience with the whole thing and had out gotten another pint of ice cream and was digging into it), to Chandra, who, I swear, looked like her head was going to pop off at any moment, to me.

"We'd appreciate it," the cop said, "if you ladies didn't talk to the press. No interviews."

"Like anybody could get to the island tonight to interview us anyway," Kate reminded him.

"Well, no phone calls, either. We'd like to keep the details of the murder under wraps until we're a little further along in our investigation."

"No one's called. Not any of us." The other ladies' nods confirmed my statement.

"That doesn't mean they won't." The cop had been holding his hat in one hand, and he plopped it on his head and back-stepped toward the door. "As near as we can figure, Peter died somewhere between seven and eight this evening. That means folks have had a couple hours to call their friends and neighbors over on the mainland and tell them what's going on. Sooner or later, the press is going to get wind of the whole thing. You know when my guys arrived on scene to talk to you, folks were watching from that new bar across the street. I'm sure they knew who you four were. They're talking about you. And when they call those friends on the mainland, they're sure mention your names."

This was something I hadn't even considered when I made the original call to the police. Not that thinking about it would have stopped me from fulfilling my civic duty. I consoled myself with the fact that because I was a newcomer, those folks over at the bar might not know who I was, and that made me feel better.

At least until my phone rang.

I checked caller ID. "WNWO."

"That's the NBC affiliate TV station in Toledo," Kate said.

My hands in the air, I backed away from the phone. "See?" I looked at the officer. "Not answering it. I have nothing to say."

"Me, either," Luella chimed in.

"Or me," Kate added.

"Or me," Chandra said.

When the cop walked out the door, he was laughing. Only not like it was funny. "That," he said, "would be a first."

It wasn't until the door banged shut behind him that I felt some of the tension inside me ease. I'd already poured myself a cup of coffee, but there was still an inch of margarita left in my glass and I reached for it and wrapped my fingers tight around the green cactus that served as the stem. "What's that guy's problem?" I asked no one in particular.

Chandra's laugh sounded like air escaping from a balloon. "Sorry." She laughed some more and washed it down with a slug of beer before she was able to talk. "We forgot to introduce you. That was Hank."

My mouth fell open. "Hank —"

"Yep." Chandra grinned. "My ex number two. Cranky son-of-a-bitch, isn't he? Hank, he has this funny way of losing his cool whenever he has to deal with a situation that involves me. And me? I just love it when I can get under his skin like that. Makes life worthwhile."

Luella spooned sugar into her coffee and stirred, her expression thoughtful. "I'd say we all handled him just fine."

"Yeah, except for him not believing what Bea said. About the note, and the fight."

I appreciated Kate coming to my defense, but honestly, I didn't need it. I sloughed off the whole thing with a lift of my shoulders and divided what was left of the margarita mix in the blender between my glass and

Kate's. "No worries. He'll spend some time thinking about it, and then he'll come around. I predict Hank will be back here tomorrow asking about the note. And the fight."

"You've had experience with cops." Luella didn't say it as a question, so I didn't feel obliged to answer.

In fact, I leaned against the counter, my head tipped to one side. "What Hank said . . . about the time of Peter's murder . . ."

"He said between seven and eight," Kate reminded me.

"Which was after the ferry stopped running."

It took a couple seconds, but they all got the message. I knew this for a fact because suddenly, each of their complexions was the same color as the margarita in my glass. Something told me mine was, too.

"You mean . . ." Chandra latched on to my arm with both hands. "Are you saying . . ."

"I'm just saying what old Hank didn't want to say," I told them. "Nobody can get here. And the ferry's not running to the mainland. That means the killer's still on the island."

7

The next morning, I woke to the sight of snow swirling outside my window, and the sounds of howling wind and pounding waves.

Or maybe that pounding was all in my head.

"Margaritas." Standing in the kitchen watching wave after snowy wave hit the windows, I grumbled and scrubbed my hands over my face, reminding myself that I had a houseful of guests and I needed to get a grip. There was a time when I used to party hearty until the wee hours of the morning. These days? It looked like the laid-back island life was already getting to me. A couple margaritas, and I was ready to head back to the sack. Of course, there had been that champagne, too . . .

"Good morning." The good news was that when she dragged into the kitchen, Luella didn't look much more chipper than I felt.

She'd stayed behind to help me clean up the night before and by the time she was ready to leave, the storm was worse than ever. I'd talked her into sleeping on the pull-out couch in my private suite. Now, she scraped her hands through her hair, shook her head to clear it, and reached for a coffee mug. "Need help with breakfast?"

She was the answer to my prayers, and I told her so. Together, Luella and I warmed a cinnamon and sour cream coffee cake and cut up fruit for a compote. In an attempt to thumb my nose at the weather, I set the cherry table in the dining room with a lace cloth and the yellow and white china I'd bought in London a couple years earlier. The dishes and chunky mugs were decorated with cute cartoon characters who offered advice like, "Start each day with a smile and get it over with."

Take that, snowstorm!

By nine o'clock, we were ready, and at nine fifteen, I heard the first footsteps against the oak floors upstairs.

When he walked into the dining room, Ted Brooks scowled. "I can't believe it's still snowing." As if he needed to reinforce what he'd no doubt already seen from the windows in his suite, he knelt on the dining room window seat and peered outside. If he was trying to make himself feel better about the weather, he'd picked the worst possible moment; the snow fell fast and hard, the wind blasted, and it looked like we were smack in the center of a snowglobe that had been given a good, hard shake.

"Terrible." His brows veed over his small, dark eyes, Ted stopped at the buffet to pour coffee and grab some of the scrambled eggs Luella had insisted on making. "A good hot breakfast," she'd said. "That will cheer folks up."

If the frown on Ted's face meant anything, her plan wasn't exactly working.

Mariah showed up just a minute later. That morning, she was dressed in black pants, a teal turtleneck, and a black silk jacket lavished with teal and cream embroidery. I directed her to the buffet, but before I could attempt small talk, I heard a small voice call out from the top of the stairs.

"Miss Cartwright?"

Amanda Gallagher peered over the railing, the collar of her chenille robe pulled up around her ears and a scarf wrapped around her neck.

"I'm afraid . . ." She shifted from foot to foot and I saw that she was wearing a pair of those slipper socks I'd offered her the night before. "I'm not feeling well," she said.

"I think . . ." She sniffled loud enough for me to hear it at the bottom of the steps. "I think I've picked up a bug of some sort. I was wondering . . . If you wouldn't mind . . . That is, I hoped you could bring some breakfast up to my room."

Of course I said yes.

Of course I was grumbling about it when I went back into the kitchen.

"I didn't exactly promise room service," I told Luella, who was busy making another batch of toast, and looking more awake than she had just a few minutes earlier.

"No worries." She put a friendly hand on my shoulder. "I'll take it up to her. You butter the toast and get it out to the dining room."

"But you shouldn't have to —"

She was already walking into the dining room to grab a plate for Amanda. "Like I said, not a problem. It's the least I can do to repay you for your hospitality." A gust of wind rattled the windows, and Luella shivered. "Chances are if I'd started for home last night, I would have gotten stuck on the road somewhere. Believe me, I'm grateful to have your roof over my head. Nobody's going anywhere. Not today."

"Is it true?" When the door between the kitchen and the dining room swung open, I heard Mariah's breathless question. "Mr. Brooks here tells me the ferry isn't running."

"I'm afraid he's right." While Luella filled a plate and took it up to Amanda, I refilled coffee cups. I weighed the wisdom of mentioning Peter's murder to my guests and decided against it. Once the storm passed and Ted and Mariah were on their way back to the mainland, no doubt they'd hear plenty about the murder. For now . . . well, for now, there was no use giving the island a black eye. Or worrying anyone. Maybe the good thing about being snowed in was that no one could spread the word that there was a murderer loose somewhere on the island.

Unless the murderer happened to be staying in Suite #2 and already knew that.

I couldn't help myself. As much as I tried, I couldn't forget that argument I'd heard between Peter and Ted. No more than I could forget the way Peter looked when we found him there behind the front counter of the Orient Express.

"So . . ." Yes, that was me, doing my best to sound chipper while I offered my guests a sunny smile that didn't match the sour feeling in my stomach. Hoping to drown it with some really good French roast, I

113

grabbed a cup of coffee and sat down at the head of the table. "What's everyone going to do today?"

Ted talked around a mouthful of eggs. "Wish I could go check on my properties." He washed down the eggs with a big gulp of coffee. "But that doesn't look like it's going to happen. With the power off, I've got to think about broken pipes and flooded cottages, and with the way the snow's still coming down and how heavy it is, I'm worried about roof problems, too." He finished a piece of coffee cake in two bites. "Since I can't get out and drive around, I suppose I'll stay in my room and go through some contracts," he said. "When it comes to being a landlord, there's always paperwork to take care of."

"And you?" I asked Mariah.

"Do?" Her laugh was throaty and her smile was as bright as my English breakfast china. "My nails, I think." She popped out of her chair and took her coffee upstairs with her.

Ted's gaze followed Mariah until she was out of the dining room door. "Must be nice to be so carefree," he said. "I've got cottages to worry about. I don't know, maybe I should take a chance and drive around for a bit."

A confession here: my imagination has a tendency to run away with me. At times in my past, this was a definite asset. Not so when that imagination was running in the direction of wondering if Ted was running away from the law.

I shook away the thought. It was that, or risk tipping my hand. If Ted was as innocent as all that driven snow outside, it would be the worst innkeeping faux pas imaginable. If he was guilty . . .

"I'm not sure that's a good idea," I said, and good thing the comment covered both what I was thinking and what Ted had been talking about, because I wasn't sure which I was addressing. I shook away the thought and gulped down some coffee. "From what I've heard, everything on the island is at a standstill."

Okay, so not everything. And apparently not everyone, either.

My doorbell rang.

I hurried out to the front entryway and opened the door to find Kate, who was struggling to keep on her feet because of the wind. She had a computer case in one hand and an overnight bag in the other, and she was coated, head to toe, with snow.

She shouted over the noise of the storm. "I hate to ask."

Before she could, I motioned her inside and closed the door.

It wasn't very far from Kate's house to mine, but Kate had been fighting the storm all the way; she was breathing hard. Her boots were caked with snow, and she slipped them off and put them on the area rug I'd set out near the door. "I don't mean to be a bother," she began.

"But your electricity is off, and so is your heat."

Her come-and-go smile told me she was glad I'd said it so she didn't have to. "I'd go to the winery. There's a generator there. But . . ." There were tall, thin windows on either side of the front door and she looked that way and at the snow that slammed into the front of the house. "No way the roads are passable, and I could never walk all the way over there. It was hard enough getting here."

I felt as awkward offering help as she did asking for it. After all, there was that letter she'd written to the township board about how she was sure the B and B would be nothing but a nuisance in the neighborhood. Nuisance, huh? Looked like this was one nuisance that had literally turned into a warm port in a very bad storm.

And now was not the time to mention it.

I took the overnight bag out of Kate's hand and set it down on the steps. "Suite #5 is open," I told her. "And breakfast is in the dining room."

Kate shook her head. "I had yogurt at home. But I'll gladly grab a cup of coffee, and I saw a computer in your kitchen last night. If your Wi-Fi is working . . ." Computer bag in hand, she was already padding into the kitchen to settle herself on one of the high stools at the countertop.

While I watched Kate, Luella started down the steps. "She's got a cold, poor thing," she said with a look over her shoulder at Amanda's room. "I told her I'd bring up tea with plenty of honey and lemon. You do have honey and lemon, right?"

I thought I did. Maybe. I went into the kitchen to look, and Luella followed me.

"By the way . . ."

Luella sounded pained, and though I didn't know her well, I was pretty sure she wasn't the type of woman who was easily intimidated. By anything. My head already in the pantry, I stood up and turned around.

Luella looked at the ceiling. She glanced at the floor, fingering the cell phone she carried in one hand. "Meg called while I was upstairs with Amanda."

Was that all that was bothering Luella? I

brushed off her uneasiness. "If Meg is worried about getting fresh breakfast pastries over here for tomorrow's breakfast, tell her to forget it! No way I want her to come out in this storm. We'll get by. Even if it means we'll be serving Cheerios."

Luella nodded. "That's nice of you, really, but that's not why she called. Seems her heat is out and . . . I hope you don't mind, Bea. I know it wasn't my place and it's not my business and . . . but . . . well, I told her to bring the girls and come over here."

While I was still processing this, Luella jumped back in. "I'm sorry. I should have asked you first, it's just that I was thinking of poor Meg there alone . . . you know her husband, John, he's with the National Guard and stationed overseas, and she's got little Isabelle and Mila, and I was thinking of them there at home in the dark and the cold and they've got a big old Hummer and they're right down the street, so I'm pretty sure they can make it this far safely, but —"

"Luella." I stopped her before she could get any further. "I already know Meg is the best baker on the island. Tell me, is she any good at any other kind of cooking?"

Luella didn't see where this was headed so all she did was give me a tentative nod.

"These folks are going to want lunch," I

told her. "And I'm pretty sure my cooking isn't going to earn any five-star ratings. Of course Meg and the girls are welcome to stay here. I don't mind at all, and we can use the extra help. They can have Suite #6 and you can stay up there with them if you'd like."

Relief swept over her expression at the same time Luella caught sight of a jar of honey and reached around me to retrieve it. "I saw some ground beef in your freezer last night when Kate was rooting around in there for the ice cream," she said, and while she was at it, she grabbed a couple cans of diced tomatoes out of the pantry. "With the meat and these tomatoes, I can make sloppy joes for lunch. I'll get right on it as soon as I make tea for Amanda." Her arms loaded, she deposited the items on the table, but not before she gave me a wink. "I make pretty mean sloppy joes, and it's the least I can do to thank you. We can serve the sandwiches along with pickles, and if you've got potatoes, I can make —"

"Hiya! Hiya! Hiya!"

The strange sound was halfway between a song and a chant. When it floated into the kitchen, Luella swallowed her words and we exchanged glances.

"Hiya! Hiya! Hiya!"

"Kate . . ." She was sitting at the counter-top, her laptop open in front of her, furiously typing, and I looked that way. "That wasn't you, was it? Are you watching a movie on the Internet or something?"

Kate glanced up from her work. "I didn't hear —"

"Hiya! Hiya! Hiya!"

This time, she did hear, and she jumped off the stool and moved to the back door. "It sounds like it's coming from outside," Kate said. "But that's impossible. Nobody in their right mind would be out there on a morning like this."

Exactly what I was thinking, which, truth be told, was why I wasn't surprised when I looked out the back window and saw Chandra on the porch. She was wearing a long purple coat, tall, sturdy boots that were covered with snow, and a knitted hat pulled down around her ears. That in and of itself wasn't weird considering the weather. What was a little weird was the fact that she was pacing the length of the porch and that she had a bundle of some kind of greenery in her left hand. Whatever it was, it was smoldering, and the musty perfume of the burning weeds snaked inside and tickled my nose.

"Hiya! Hiya! Hiya!" Chandra shook the

bundle of greens and the smoke billowed and was blown away on the next gust of wind. "Hiya! Hiya! Hiya!"

"Isn't that just what I was saying to Alvin in court the other day?" Kate's mouth pulled into an I-told-you-so smirk. "The woman needs to be committed."

"She does if she's planning on spending the morning out in this storm," I agreed. "I wondered why Chandra didn't come down to breakfast. I figured she was a late sleeper."

"What you should have figured is that the woman is as nutty as a fruitcake." Kate must have known what I was going to do, because she backed away from the door. That gave me a chance to go out into the little mud-room just off the porch and pull open the back door.

"Chandra!" The name whistled away on the wind. I tried again. "Chandra, what on earth are you doing?"

She waved the bundle and a puff of smoke stung my eyes.

"I'm working to repair the island's aura, of course," she called out.

We weren't going to do that by screaming at each other.

I waved her inside.

Chandra must have been cold. She obliged.

121

She stepped into the mudroom, and maybe she was doing me a favor and getting rid of any snow before she walked into the kitchen, or maybe she was trying to get her circulation going again. Either way, she stomped her feet and handed me the smoldering bunch of greens so she could pull off her hat.

"I'm sure the murder has seriously damaged it," she said.

Luella and Kate were standing just inside the door, and Luella leaned forward. "Damaged what? Your thinking? Because I'll tell you what, honey, you're nuts to be out there in this weather."

"But we've got to do something, don't you see?" Another couple stomps, and Chandra stepped into the kitchen. When it comes to cleaning, I'm not obsessive/compulsive, but I know a disaster waiting to happen when I see one. I got a couple kitchen towels out of a drawer and dropped them on the floor so Chandra could stand on them and drip.

"Anytime something like a murder happens, well . . ." Chandra shivered, either from the cold or from thinking about Peter. Maybe both. "We've got to do something to get the island's aura back in line. Right now, it's pretty darned dark, and that isn't good for anybody. The way I see it, we needed to start with a cleansing. That's what . . ." She reached over and plucked the smoking bundle out of my hands so that she could wave it around. "That's what I figured I needed to do first."

"First." I'm not sure any of the others picked up on this, but trust me, I didn't miss it. The fact that Chandra apparently had a plan was something of a surprise. I only hoped that whatever she was planning wasn't so out there as to add any more odd smells or smoke — I waved one hand in front of my face — to the house.

When I opened the back door, a burst of cold air had come into the kitchen, and since it still lingered like the hand of some unseen specter (see, I was telling the truth about having an imagination!), Kate and Luella went to sit at the counter, farther from the door. Chandra peeled out of her coat and kicked off her boots. There was still coffee in the pot, so I filled four mugs and passed them around.

"What are you planning, Chandra?" I asked her.

"You mean after I finish this?" She grabbed a piece of coffee cake and wolfed it down, and I realized I was being a lousy hostess. I pulled out dishes and flatware so everyone could grab a piece.

123

"The way I figure it . . ." Smiling her approval, Chandra pointed to the coffee cake with her fork. She swallowed. "The way I figure it, we've got to find out what happened to Peter, or the island's karma is going to be completely destroyed."

"Oh, for heaven's sake!" Kate rolled her eyes.

"No, wait." Luella put a hand on Kate's arm. "Let her finish. Chandra might be onto something."

"Thank you." Chandra sat up and pulled back her shoulders. "What I was thinking is that there are so many people here on the island who depend on the tourist season for their livelihoods. I do tarot card readings for plenty of tourists, and chakra realignments and crystal healings. And you depend on tourists, too, Luella. Bea, so do you. And Kate, whether you want to admit it or not, I know you can't possibly survive on the sales of the wine you ship to the mainland. You need the tourists who come and tour Wilder Winery and buy wine to take home."

"Yes, of course." Kate had a bite of coffee cake on her fork and she stopped with it halfway to her mouth. "But what does that have to do with —"

"If people are afraid to come here for vacations, none of us is going to survive,"

Chandra said. "That's why we have to figure out who murdered Peter before the ferry starts running again and the killer gets off the island."

Kate's laugh was sharp. "Isn't that what the police are for?"

Chandra had put plenty of sugar in her coffee; she shouldn't have looked quite so sour. "You heard Hank last night. We offered him some darned good theories, about the woman's glove and the fight Peter had with . . ." She leaned back on the stool and peered at the dining room door, though since it was closed, she couldn't see Ted and he couldn't see us. "The fight with Ted, and the threatening note, and the Princess."

Blank stares all around.

Chandra gave us a hard look. "The Princess. The one who came to the door last night. You know, like the princess in the book."

"Mariah!" I laughed. She did remind me of Princess Dragomiroff in the Christie classic: haughty, well-dressed, aristocratic.

"Hank's not listening to any of it," Chandra continued. "And believe me, if there's one thing I know about Hank, it's that he can be as stubborn as a rusty old lock. We've got to show him. We've got to be detectives. You know, like that Parrot guy in the book."

I don't know why I bothered, but I corrected her. "Poirot."

"Yeah, him." Chandra warmed to her idea. "I read the book last night," she said, beaming with pride. "Cover to cover. And I'm telling you, if the weird little guy in the book can do it, so can we. Besides, we've got to do something or everybody's feng shui is going to be out of whack."

"Hmm . . ." Luella drummed her fingers against the granite countertop. "It would be an interesting exercise. And I'd bet it would make Alvin plenty happy to know you three are working together."

"Yes, but —"

My protest was interrupted by Kate. "I liked Peter. He was a nice man, and he knew a thing or two about wine. He didn't live on the island that long, but he'd already ordered a few bottles from me."

"I liked Peter, too," I admitted. "But . . ."

They were staring at me. Every single one of them.

And all I could think about was the way we'd found Peter the night before. That, and how as a newcomer in the close-knit community, I understood something about how he must have felt when he came here to start a new business.

"Where do we begin?" I asked.

Leave it to Chandra to have the answer. She popped off the stool and threw an arm into the air. "We'll use our little gray cells," she announced in an accent that could only have come straight out of the movie she'd watched before she read the book. "Just like that Hercules guy!"

8

Was I worried about Chandra and her crazy idea that we could be detectives?

You bet'cha!

Which is precisely why I made sure to keep her busy and as far away from my guests as possible. No easy thing considering we were getting to the point of being wedged in like kippers in a tin.

Thank goodness it is a big house.

When I saw Ted go into the parlor to turn on the TV, I made sure to send Chandra up to Suite #6 to help Meg and the kids get settled, and when she did that a little too quickly and barreled down the stairs with a sort of gleam in her eye that I remembered Albert Finney having when he played Poirot in the movie version of *Orient Express,* I intercepted her and assigned her to Luella's sloppy joe team.

Luella was also in charge of the french fries, and in no way was I worried about her. Luella (poor delusional thing) thought the idea of us working together to figure out what happened to Peter was a good one. That meant she wouldn't go rushing headlong into anything silly. Or solo. And Kate? As much as I hated to admit it, it was admirable that Kate wanted to see justice done in Peter's name. Surprise, surprise, the woman had a heart. But I knew she also had a brain. She'd never try to corner my guests to interrogate them. Not in an obvious way, at least. And never in a phony Belgian accent.

By lunchtime when we set the table, we had those sloppy joes ready along with a nice variety of pickles that Kate had arranged artistically on one of my Depression-era glass platters, Luella's kick-ass french fries (she was a wizard with seasoned salt), and a batch of chocolate and oatmeal no-bake cookies Meg had pulled out of her freezer and brought along as a way of thanking me for my hospitality.

It was the perfect lunch for a snowy day.

Now if only Chandra didn't open her mouth and say something she shouldn't to someone she shouldn't say it to.

The thought burned in my brain as I directed Ted and Mariah to the buffet. Amanda, it should be noted, was still feeling too punky to come down, so while Luella made up a plate for her, I informed my guests that the other ladies and I would leave them in peace and take our lunches into the kitchen.

"Don't be ridiculous." Of course this was Mariah, ever gracious and acting like the lady of the manor even in my house. The dining room table seats twelve, and she waved at all the empty chairs, expertly showing off the nails that had been mauve at breakfast and were now candy apple red. "It makes no sense at all for you to be crammed in the kitchen when we've got so much room here. Besides, I'm just dying to hear more about each of you, and about the island."

It was exactly what I had been dreading, and exactly what Chandra had been waiting for. I hoped the look I shot her reminded her to be careful and to take it easy. When her eyes flashed like the island lighthouse, I knew I was in trouble. Too bad I'd just taken a bite of sloppy joe, otherwise I might have been able to say something before she scraped her chair closer to the table and pinned first Ted then Mariah with what I think was supposed to be a clever, detective-like look that came off more like the desperate, eager expectation of a dog waiting for a scrap to fall from the table. That was, of course, right before she blurted out, "Have you two heard about the murder?"

I was seated directly across from Ted, so I couldn't fail to notice that he blanched. It was Mariah, though, who spoke first. She was the type — no big surprise — who eats a sloppy joe with knife and fork, and she paused, the flatware poised over the sandwich on her plate.

"Not a murder here on South Bass, surely." She dismissed the very thought with a twitch of her very red lips. "You're talking about something you saw on the news this morning that happened somewhere else. Or perhaps something that happened here ages ago?"

"Yeah, if last night counts as ages ago." Chandra again, her eyebrows rising and falling with the excitement of sharing the lurid secret.

This time, I was ready for her.

Sort of.

Before she could add anything to what she thought was the piercing look she darted between Ted to her right and Mariah on her left, I cleared my throat to deflect their attention.

"I'm afraid it's true, and I figured you hadn't heard since we've all been stuck inside since last night. It's a terrible thing."

"And not something that usually happens here, that's for sure," Luella added, defending the honor of the island.

"But a murder? Really?" Mariah set down her silverware, her hands fluttering above her plate like anxious butterflies before she pressed them to her ample bosom. "How awful!"

"It was. It is." I saw Chandra open her mouth and knew if I didn't speak fast, she was going to say something about the game being afoot. "Ted . . ." I did my best to make this sound like nothing more than a simple statement of fact, no guilt intended. "I believe you knew the victim. It was Peter Chan."

Talk of murder or not, Ted had just taken a chomp out of his sandwich, and he held up a finger to signal that he couldn't answer me while he chewed, his jaw working up and down like pistons in an engine. He swallowed, washed down the mouthful with a glug of coffee, and pounded his chest.

"Name doesn't sound familiar. I don't think I knew him at all."

Far be it from me to pretend I was a detective, but the way Chandra was squirming in her seat, I envisioned her losing control at any moment, pointing a finger, and screaming out *j'accuse* with all the French outrage she could muster.

I couldn't let that happen, and the reasons should be fairly clear:

1. I couldn't offend Ted if he wasn't our murderer. Hospitality and all that, and besides, he was a paying guest.
2. If Ted had killed Peter, we couldn't afford to tip our hand. He might be desperate, dangerous — and I was responsible for the welfare of the people under my roof.

In an effort to throw him off his guard, I stammered. Just for the record, I am a lousy stammerer. "I'm so sorry. I could have sworn it was you." I pretended to think it over. "It's funny, isn't it, how our memories can play tricks on us? When I stopped at the Orient Express on Sunday —"

"Oh, the restaurant?" Ted grabbed a napkin and wiped a dribble of tomato sauce from the corner of his mouth. "Why didn't you say so in the first place? Really? The Orient Express? That building is one of the properties I own here on the island!"

"So you must have known Peter Chan. He was one of your tenants."

Ted glanced toward Kate, who'd made this pronouncement. "Chan! Is that what you said?" He looked back at me. "Peter Chan? I thought you said Jan. Peter Jan."

Yeah. And I just fell off a turnip truck.

"Not only was he your tenant, but you were there." Me again. Hoping I came off as merely interested, not burning with curiosity. "Sunday afternoon. You were walking out of the Orient Express as I was walking in."

Ted's face crumpled with the effort of remembering, then cleared when he snapped his fingers. "Yeah. Of course. You bumped into me as I was leaving."

My smile was angelic. After all, I was the hostess. "You bumped into me," I reminded him ever so gently, though *plowed into me* was a more accurate way to describe it. "But then, I can see how you might not remember. You and Peter were having something of a knock-down-drag-out argument when I arrived."

"Were we?" Ted was to acting what I was to stammering. He refused to meet my eyes. "I wouldn't exactly call it that. I was —"

"Angry."

"Upset," he insisted.

"It looked a little more personal than that."

"Well . . ." There was a bowl of sloppy joe meat and more sandwich buns on the buffet, and he got up for seconds. Don't think I didn't notice how much time he took to arrange the food just so on his plate, then again when he sat back down and squirted a ketchup design on his fries.

"You were having a business disagreement," I suggested.

He dredged a fry through ketchup and chomped it down. "No, no, nothing like that."

"But from what Bea says . . ." Kate sat back, regarding Ted with a look so perceptive, it made me certain that Wilder Winery was in capable hands. "Bea says it was a pretty heated discussion. Come on, Ted, you're a man of business. You and I both know there's nothing that can press your buttons like some dispute over rent, or utilities, or upkeep on a property. Believe me, been there, done that. I know my temper's gotten out of control a time or two when it comes to that sort of thing. That's why I understand."

Slick. Oh yes, I had to give Kate credit for that. She was as poised under the pressure of this impromptu interrogation as Chandra was dramatic and transparent.

Cool as a cucumber and as icy as the wind

from Canada that battered the house.

I told myself not to forget it, just in case Kate ever decided to write another letter about me to the township board.

Ted was about to bite into another fry and he changed his mind and set it back on the plate. "In light of the fact that Peter Chan is dead, I can understand that you're curious. And I know it's only human to jump to conclusions. I mean, about a landlord and a tenant and a dispute. But honestly, that's not what happened at all. You see, I called ahead to the Orient Express before I stopped in. To order lunch." His head was bent, and he raised his small round eyes and looked across the table at me. "It's going to sound silly."

"We won't know until you tell us," I replied.

He played with a fry on his plate, trailing it back and forth through the sea of ketchup. "Well," he said with a sigh, "it was all because when I called, I told the man who answered the phone — Peter, I know that now and didn't then — that I was hungry and willing to try just about anything. He decided to make up a dish of something he called orange chicken."

It wasn't my imagination; a sigh went 'round the table.

"When I placed my order, I said I didn't care what I ate, but I had one stipulation. I said I was allergic to peanuts. Peter said not to worry. And when I got there, well, good thing I checked before I walked out, because if I'd taken even one bite, it wouldn't have been pretty. There were definitely peanuts in that orange chicken."

Another sigh, and yes, I was just as guilty as the other ladies. I thought about the perfect blend of ingredients, the sweetness of the orange juice, the crunchy peanuts, and my mouth watered.

Right before I told myself to get a grip.

"So you and Peter were arguing about peanuts?"

Ted's brow folded into a dozen creases. "I'm sorry to hear the poor guy's dead, and I wish I could tell you more, but really, things just kind of got out of control, what with me telling him the peanuts could have killed me and him telling me that I'd never told him I was allergic. I did tell him. Of course I did. But honestly, there wasn't anything else for us to fight about. I never saw the guy before that afternoon."

"You rented him space and never saw him before?" A plain and simple question from Luella, and she folded her hands on the table in front of her, waiting for Ted to answer.

"All done via email. And the contracts were sent through regular mail." His explanation was short and sweet. Then again, his sloppy joe was getting cold. He dug into it, and I wondered if he was telling the truth. If Peter and Ted didn't know each other, why had Peter waved that note under Ted's nose?

In an effort to look casual, I picked up a pickle spear. "Then what," I said, and bit into the pickle to emphasize my point, "about the threatening note?"

Ted's doughy face blanched. "How do you know anything about a threatening note?" he asked.

Which wasn't at all the same as answering my question.

Before I could point that out, Mariah's fork clattered against her plate. "The whole thing is perfectly dreadful," she said, touching her napkin to the corners of her mouth. "I thought . . . That is, I was hoping island life would be less . . . eventful. You see, I was hoping to settle down here."

This was news, and eager to turn the conversation away from threatening notes, frightening arguments, and murder, I glommed right on to it. Maybe a little time-out would put Ted at ease. And make him more likely to tell the truth.

"As a newcomer to the island, I might be able to answer any questions about relocating here," I said.

"And we can certainly help out when it comes to where to live and things like that," Kate offered.

Yeah, I thought, as long as where you decide to live doesn't bring too much traffic past Kate's house.

I wiped the notion from my mind along with the bitter little smile that threatened to give away my thoughts, and gave Mariah my full attention.

"What are your plans?" I asked her.

"Well . . ." Her cheeks flushed a lovely shade of pink. "I was hoping to bring a little style to the island. A little class. I was thinking of opening an exclusive women's boutique."

Kate nodded her approval. "That would save me a lot of trips to the mainland," she admitted.

"And it would attract the tourists, that's for sure," Luella added without bothering to mention that she was probably the last person on the island who would ever shop anywhere that called itself a boutique.

"Clothing?" Chandra asked, and I was

grateful. Apparently, shopping was a subject nearer and dearer to her heart even than murder. "And jewelry, too?"

"Clothing, jewelry, shoes, purses." Mariah laughed. "It's not that I'm saying those of you who live here don't have style . . ." She took us all in with one regal glance. "But let's face it, ladies, when it comes to fashion, enough is never enough. I know I should have started looking for retail space last fall, but . . . well, it's complicated and I won't bore you with the details. Let's just say that I didn't have the financing then, and I do now. That's why I came to the island so early in the spring, to see if I could find an available storefront. Speaking of which . . ." She turned her full attention and a simmering smile on Ted. "That space will become available, won't it? The place that was the Orient Express? Renting it quickly would surely be advantageous for you, and it's an ideal spot. I remember seeing it as I walked around downtown the other day. I bet there's plenty of foot traffic that passes there on busy summer weekends."

The tips of Ted's ears turned red. "We might be able to arrange something, sure. Now that Peter Chan is dead, I imagine that invalidates his lease agreement, and you're right, getting another tenant in there fast would be ideal."

"You can't do that!" Chandra's hands flew to her cheeks. "Not without proper preparation."

Like the rest of us, Ted was at a loss. He cleared his throat. "Preparation? I'm not sure what you're talking about."

Chandra buzzed with excitement. Or maybe that was her aura getting all revved up. "A cleansing. You can't expect to walk into a building where there's been a murder and have life just go on as if nothing ever happened."

"Well, I suppose there will be some cleanup," Ted admitted.

Chandra was in her element now, and the center of attention, to boot, and she sat up tall, murder all but forgotten in the face of Mystical Matters. "I'm not talking about physically cleaning up the place," she said, and thinking about it, she wrinkled her nose. "Though I suppose someone will need to do that. But what I'm talking about is a spiritual cleansing. You know, a ritual."

Ted hesitated. Like anyone could blame him?

"It couldn't hurt," Luella said. "And who knows, it actually might help!"

"Might?" One corner of Chandra's mouth pulled into a cynical smile when she looked at Mariah. "If I were you, I wouldn't want to take a chance with that building otherwise. Imagine all the bad energy that was unleashed in the instant of Peter's murder."

Even I couldn't argue with that.

Call it karma. Call it vibes. Call it just plain spooky. Murder is an ugly business, and whether it actually helped or was purely symbolic, making an effort to dispel its shadows made sense to me.

Apparently, it did to Ted, too.

"It might not hurt to have somebody go in there and say a few prayers or something," he admitted. "You know, to sort of —"

"Cleanse the spiritual environment and readjust the feng shui. Of course!" Chandra hid her grin behind a expression that was supposed to be serene and oh-so spiritual. "I'd be happy to help. Of course, I suppose we'll have to wait until the police are done with the building."

Honestly, could we have asked for a more perfect cue?

No sooner had Chandra spoken the words than my door-bell rang.

When I answered it, police chief Hank Florentine stepped into the house.

"Exactly the man I need to talk to." Chandra didn't miss a trick. The moment she saw it was Hank, she sashayed into the entryway, her chin in the air. "I've been asked to do a cleansing," she informed him. "Of the place where the recent Unfortunate Incident occurred. You will let me know when your people have vacated the premises." This last bit was not a question, which was just as well, because Hank didn't look especially inclined to answer it.

In fact, cap in hand, he ignored Chandra completely and turned to me. "Any rooms?" he asked.

"Here?" Of course he was talking about Bea & Bees. I just wasn't used to being this much in demand.

"We've got a generator at the station," Hank went on to explain, "so there's electricity there, and heat. But the other guys on the force have all brought their families in. The place is crawling with people, and I'll tell you what, I don't really like the thought of sharing the floor in my office with a bunch of twelve-year-olds. I thought if you had an extra room . . ."

I did a quick mental tabulation. My guest rooms were full, but if Kate moved out of Suite #5 and into my suite with me, she could have the pull-out couch in my sitting room, and I could put Hank up in Kate's former room. It was good PR, what with me being new to South Bass and Hank knowing everyone there was to know on the island. And besides, if the little tingle on the back of my neck was right and Ted Brooks did know more about Peter's murder than he let on, it sure wouldn't hurt to have a man in blue under my roof.

Kate was still sitting at the dining room table, but she'd apparently done all the same calculations I had. She popped out of her chair. "I'll move my stuff down to your suite," she told me when she sauntered by.

"And I'll be back later this evening," Hank said. He plopped his cap on his head and opened the door and a fierce blast of wind rattled the chandelier in the hallway. "Hard to believe it could possibly be getting worse," he said, and he disappeared into the storm.

I turned to find Chandra with her arms crossed over her chest, aiming a death look at the closed door. "I can't believe you'd let that snake in the grass stay here with me."

"He's not staying with you. He's staying with us. And it might not hurt to have him around."

"Oh, you mean . . ." Chandra's gaze wandered (not subtly, I might add) into the dining room where our guests were digging into the oatmeal cookies. She gave me a broad wink. "I get it. Protection."

"We're not going to call it that." I wound an arm through hers and piloted her into the kitchen. "We're going to treat Hank just like any other guest."

"Guest?" Her *tsk* was one of epic proportions. "Just keep that son-of-a-bitch out of my way, or I'll tell you what, there's going to be another murder."

9

By late afternoon, the lunch dishes were cleaned up and Luella and Meg had started in on making dinner. That's not as easy as it sounds. I do, after all, technically live alone, and when there are other people in the house, they are people to whom I have promised only breakfast. I'm not at all sure how they managed, but after a great deal of digging through the freezer and poking through cupboards, the mother/daughter dynamic duo not only found the right ingredients for pizza for that Tuesday evening, but they put on a pot of beef vegetable soup to simmer the rest of the day so we could serve it for lunch on Wednesday.

I left them at their work in the kitchen and had just stepped out into the hallway when Ted walked down the steps bundled in his trenchcoat and wearing his fedora and a heavy black wool scarf that was triple-wrapped around his neck.

"You're not going out?" Okay, so not exactly a polite question, considering I said it in a tone of voice I might have used if I asked if he'd decided to walk to the moon. Before he could answer, I pointed to the window. "It's worse than ever out there. If you're going for a walk, you could get lost, and if you're planning on driving —"

"I've got four-wheel drive on my SUV." He sounded confident, but the look he gave the window and the weather beyond was anything but. "I can't just sit here and do nothing. I've got to check on my properties. They could be getting damaged."

"And there's nothing you can do about it. Not until after the storm lets up." Yes, I was the voice of reason.

And Ted still moved toward the door. "I know you're right." He shivered and he wasn't even outside yet. "But I can't stand the thought that there might be something bad happening and I don't know about it. If I get stranded someplace —"

"You'll need to call the police and hope for the best." I couldn't be any clearer. I might have turned into a full-service inn when it came to rooms and meals, but I was not the ski patrol. I wouldn't risk my safety or the safety of any of my guests who might pitch in and try to help, not when Ted should have known better and stayed put.

Unless the real reason he wanted to leave had nothing to do with his rental properties.

I was going to say that the thought stopped me cold, but cold was something I didn't want to think about, especially when the heavy oak front door rattled in the wind. I will say that considering the possibility brought me up short. And made me wonder if Ted had more on his mind than just checking out the condition of the buildings he owned.

If he was fleeing from the long arm of the law, who was I to stop him? There was no way he was going to be able to leave the island, anyway, and honestly, I knew I'd rest a little easier if, until we knew who was who and what was what when it came to Peter's murder, he wasn't under my roof.

I stepped away from the door. "Bon voyage," I told him.

Ted gulped down a breath for courage and headed outside.

"Oh my, it is terrible out there." No sooner had he left than Amanda came down the steps, still wrapped in her thick chenille robe and shivering in the blast of cold air that came in when Ted went out. "I'm so grateful you're letting me stay here," she said, glancing out the window. Together, we watched Ted retreat into the storm. Once he was down the front steps, we lost sight of him completely in the swirling snow. "It's bad enough being in a strange place, but then to not feel well . . ."

"You're obviously better. You came downstairs."

"Yes." She drew in a deep breath and let it out slowly. "I don't want to push too hard, but I thought I'd watch a little TV, maybe make a cup of tea."

I motioned in the direction of the parlor. "Put up your feet and make yourself at home. I was just going into the kitchen. I'll put on the kettle for you."

When I got into the kitchen, I found Meg stirring the soup pot and her girls next to her, both busy with coloring books. Kate, Chandra, and Luella all had their noses pressed against the back window that looked out over the driveway.

"He's leaving? He's going out in this weather?" Shaking her head, Kate turned and walked back over to the breakfast bar. She slipped onto one of the high stools there. "What do you suppose he's up to?"

I sat down next to Kate, and Luella and Chandra came over. I told them what Ted had told me. "I'm not sure I believe him," I made sure to add. "But there's not much I can do about it. I can say this: if he gets stuck, I'm not going to get him."

"If he gets stuck . . ." Chandra plopped down on the stool next to mine, her head propped in one hand. She drummed her nails against the granite counter. They were purple, studded with gold stars, and when she beat her fingers up and down, the stars winked at me. "If he gets stuck . . . not that I'd wish that kind of thing on anybody, mind you . . . but if he did get stuck out in the snow somewhere, we'd have more time to search his room," she said.

I'm not sure mortified quite covers the feeling that washed through me.

The sensation didn't last long. But then, that's because it was instantly followed by appalled and astounded when Kate and Luella got right on board.

Kate was off the stool so fast, I'd bet anything she didn't even hear me voice an objection. By the time I was on my feet, my fists on my hips, my fellow book discussion group members were already at the door that led into the hallway.

"Ladies!" I didn't dare speak too loudly. Amanda was in the parlor. "We just can't go through a guest's room. That would be —"

"It's all in the name of our investigation," Chandra said, so jazzed by the prospect, she shifted from foot to foot.

"And it couldn't hurt, could it?" Luella asked.

I swung my gaze to Kate. "And you? What kind of a cockamamie excuse are you going to give me?"

"No excuse." Kate was all business, ticking off her reasons on her fingers. "First of all, you don't need one, because this is your house and you have every right to go anywhere in it that you want. Second, well . . ." A grin broke through her somber expression. "Heck, I don't need an excuse and neither do you. We're investigating. That gives us all the excuse we need to be just plain old nosey."

They piled out of the room, and after I asked Meg to pour tea for Amanda, I went along. Honestly, I didn't have much choice. Kate was right; it was my house, and if anyone saw me going into or out of Ted's room, at least I could explain myself. The other three? Not so much.

As soon as we were out of the kitchen, I shushed them and pointed to the parlor.

Chandra clamped her hand over her mouth. Kate and Luella nodded their understanding. Like thieves in the night, we

151

tiptoed upstairs.

Outside Mariah's room, I paused long enough to listen at her door and caught the faint strains of classical music. A finger to my lips, I signaled my confederates to keep on keeping quiet and we shuffled and shushed our way to Ted's door.

He'd locked it when he left, but I had a master key. Just to be sure he hadn't come to his senses and doubled back into the house while we were in the kitchen, I knocked.

"Ted, it's me, Bea. I've got . . ." I've got what? A lot of nerve? Rather than admit it, I scurried over to the linen closet and grabbed a pile of fresh towels. I rapped my knuckles on the door again. "I'm bringing in fresh towels," I said, and unlocked the door.

Ted hadn't returned, and don't ask me how I knew it would be so, but it was no big surprise that he wasn't the world's most tidy guest. There was a duffel bag open on the chair near the windows, and clothes spilled out of it. When Chandra made a beeline over there, I cautioned her not to touch anything, and watched as she leaned in nice and close with her hands behind her back, peering at what she could see of Ted's possessions like a nearsighted owl.

Luella went to check out the bathroom.

Kate and I did a quick turn around the bedroom.

"He reads the newspaper." There was a small pile next to the bed, and Kate shuffled through it. "The *Toledo Blade* from a couple days ago, and a *Cleveland Plain Dealer* from last week." While she set the newspapers aside, I took a gander at the bedside table.

Ted had left an iPod there along with a pair of reading glasses and a folded sheet of paper. Being careful to note exactly where I'd gotten it so I knew precisely where to put it back, I picked up the paper and unfolded it.

"It's a takeout menu," I said. "From the Orient Express."

Chandra, Kate, and Luella gathered around.

"That proves it," Chandra cooed. "He's our killer."

I restrained myself and didn't give her the look I wanted to give her. Then again, I was pretty sure Chandra wouldn't have noticed, anyway. Just like subtle doesn't work on people like Chandra, they're impervious to obvious, too.

"Of course he has a menu." Kate said what I was thinking. "He admitted he owns the building."

"And that he ordered lunch there on

153

Sunday," Luella said. "He must have picked up the menu at the grocery store. I saw a stack of them near the door."

That all made perfect sense, and in spite of Chandra's runaway imagination, I knew it didn't mean a thing when it came to alibis, motives, or murder. What did strike me as odd was . . .

Ted had turned off the lights in the room before he left, and I went over to the wall near the door and flicked the switch to turn on the ceiling fan and light, the better to take a closer look at the menu.

"This is weird," I said, and for the second time in as many minutes, the ladies gathered around me to see what I was talking about. I pointed. "Ted has one of the lunch specials circled. Look. It's the one for orange chicken."

Turns out, the League of Literary Ladies members are nothing if not plucky. There may have been a ripple of enraptured delight, but three cheers for us; rather than salivate at the very mention of orange chicken, we soldiered on.

"That's not so strange," Kate said, stepping back with her arms crossed over her chest. "Ted said he wanted to make sure there were no peanuts in his lunch, and see, Peter's menu lists the peanuts right there."

She pointed. "Right in the description of the dish."

"But that's the weird thing," I pointed out. "Remember, I used to live in New York, and that means I've had my share of takeaway. In my experience, you don't mark off the dishes you don't want to order on a menu. You star or underline or circle the ones you do want to order."

Luella stared at the menu. "So what does it mean?"

Leave it to Chandra to have the answer to that. She threw an arm in the air, one finger pointed to the ceiling, and her words were edged with what I suppose she thought was a Poirot-like accent. Honestly, she sounded more like Ozzy Osborne. "It means he has been lying," she announced. "From the start. The orange chicken, it was surely poisoned."

"Peter wasn't poisoned," I reminded her. "He was stabbed. And the orange chicken has nothing to do with it."

"Oh." Chandra's expression fell along with her arm. "Then what does it mean?"

I shrugged. It was as honest as I could be, and if nothing else, I figured I owed my coconspirators that. "If Ted is allergic to peanuts, I can't see why he'd want to order a dish that clearly has peanuts in it."

"So he didn't do it," Chandra said.

"So we don't know if he did it or not," I told her.

"So we have to keep investigating," Kate said, and before I could stop her, she was on her way out the door and headed for Mariah's room.

I scrambled to turn off the lights and lock Ted's door behind me.

"You just can't walk in there," I said in my best stage whisper, scampering over to join them outside Mariah's room. "She's in there."

"And you . . ." Since I hadn't needed the diversion, I was still holding that pile of towels, and Kate gave them a pat. "You have the perfect excuse to go in."

"But . . ." I should have known they wouldn't accept what I'd hoped was a valid excuse to abort the mission. Before I could, Chandra pushed me to the door and Luella knocked on it for me.

"Yes!" Mariah's voice floated from what sounded like a long way off, and I realized she must be in the bathroom with the door closed. I unlocked the bedroom door and stuck my head inside. The rest of me followed fast enough when the other ladies pushed into the room behind me.

"I've got clean towels," I called out to Mariah. I had to do it loudly. She had opera playing in the bathroom, and at that moment, the music crescendoed and some woman with a voice like a startled hawk joined in, holding a particularly high note for an incredibly long time. The resulting racket floated out to us along with the overpowering scent of flowery bubble bath. "I'll just leave the towels here on your bed," I called.

To which Mariah didn't answer at all, but I did hear splashing.

Before I even set down the towels, I realized the other ladies had wasted no time. They were already taking a quick look around.

"Nothing here," Chandra whispered, pointing to the empty suitcase that stood open near the closet. I recognized it as the one Mariah had risked her life to retrieve from her car after lunch.

"And nothing much here, either," Kate said. To my horror, she had a dresser drawer open and was poking around in it.

I made a frantic *shut-it* motion for all I was worth. "She might come out at any minute," I hissed.

"And if she does, she sure won't want to find us with these." I turned to find Luella holding up a package of condoms.

More splashing from the bathroom.

Was Mariah an enthusiastic bather? Or was she getting out of the tub?

I didn't want to take the chance of finding out.

I set the towels on the foot of the bed and signaled to Luella to put the box of Trojans back where she found them, and we high-tailed it out of there.

Out in the hallway, our whispered voices washed over each other.

"What does it mean?"

"Could it be that she's meeting someone here?"

"She didn't smuggle a boyfriend in with her, did she?"

I shushed them all. "It probably means she's not as much of a stranger here as she pretends to be." I wasn't sure of it, but I offered the theory. "Maybe she came here to meet somebody."

"Oh, an assignation!" Like it was suddenly too hot out there in the hallway, Chandra waved a hand in front of her face.

"Or it could mean she's as much of a stranger as she says she is," Kate added. "Maybe she's just hoping to get lucky."

I gave my ponytail a tug. "Maybe."

"Maybe, what?" Chandra asked. "Maybe she knows someone? Or maybe she was hoping for a wild and crazy weekend?"

My shrug said it all. "Maybe."

While I was busy pondering this, Luella had already moved on to Suite #1, where Amanda was staying.

This suite was at the front of the house and got soft light all day long. As least, when there weren't snowstorms in progress. I'd had it decorated in a pretty cream-colored wallpaper dusted with flowers in shades of mauve, pink, and purple.

"Make it fast," I said, unlocking the door and standing back so the others could go inside while I kept an eye on the stairway. "She's right downstairs, and if she hears us —"

Chandra poked her head into — and out of — the closet. "She's got pretty basic taste when it comes to clothes," she announced.

"And pretty basic habits when it comes to cosmetics and toiletries," Luella said from the bathroom. "Nothing fancy there."

Kate looked over the secretary desk in the far corner of the room where Amanda had set out a paperback with a dark cover I recognized even before she held it up and I saw the title *Evil Creeps* in red letters that ran like blood.

"Hey, look!" She waved the book. "Amanda's reading FX O'Grady. And you were too scared to even try a book from the master of horror, Bea."

"You've got that right." I sought to prove exactly how much I didn't care that I was a weenie by scooting into the room so I could take a quick look around.

Just as the ladies reported, Amanda's possessions were pretty basic. In fact, aside from the wonders I'd accomplished with the help of dozens of lacy doilies, three pretty little oil landscapes in gilt frames, and the assistance of a decorator who charged an exorbitant amount, there was nothing distinctive or unusual about the room at all.

I had just told the ladies this and stepped aside so they could exit the room before me when something caught my eye, a single sheet of paper lying facedown on the floor, one corner of it sticking out from under the frilly bed skirt. I would have ignored it altogether except for two things: I feared my cleaning crew might be getting a tad careless, and we'd just found what might be a clue — that menu from the Orient Express — in Ted's room.

With Kate, Chandra, and Luella already out in the hall, I stooped to retrieve the paper, flipped it over, and read the message that had been cobbled together from a mish-mash of matte newspaper headlines and glossy magazine pages.

YOU WON'T GET AWAY WITH THIS.
I'LL NEVER FORGET.
I SWEAR I'LL MAKE YOU PAY.

I read the message under my breath. But then, it's hard to find anything in the way of a voice when you feel as if you've been punched in the stomach.

Eager to see the note, the other women scudded back into the room and gathered around me.

" 'You'll never get away with this. I'll never forget. I swear I'll make you pay.' " From over my shoulder, Kate read the message and pointed to the block letters with one finger. "Bea, this sounds like —"

"The note I saw at Peter's." I nodded. "It's exactly the same. The paper . . ." As if it would reveal some secret to me, I turned over the note in my hands. "The lettering . . ." I flipped it back the right way and reread the threatening message. "It's all the same."

Chandra's voice was choked. "What does it mean?"

Carefully, I put the paper back where I'd found it and ushered the ladies out of the room. "It means . . ." I closed the door and faced them in the hallway. "It means Amanda is receiving threatening notes, too," I said, my stomach souring. "And that means . . ." The terrible reality of the situation settled over me like a scratchy wool blanket. "It means Peter wasn't the only one whose life was in danger."

10

So what did we know at this point?

Well, for one thing, I knew for certain that I never wanted to have to deal with this kind of snowstorm again.

No sooner had this thought occurred to me than my right boot got stuck in a snow-drift nearly as tall as me that had piled up at the bottom of my front steps. I gritted my teeth, yanked, and hoped that when my foot came out of the icy mound, my boot would still be on it. The snow had lessened from driving-downhill-with-foot-on-accelerator to something more like coasting. Teacup-sized flakes whirled in the sky above me, lacy Frisbees, then plopped to earth to add to the eighteen inches of wet, heavy snow already on the ground. It was bitterly cold, and I hunkered down inside my jacket, my eyes on the prize that was Chandra's vintage Volkswagen van idling in my drive-way.

What was I doing outside?

Wondering if I needed my head examined, for one thing.

For another . . . well, the answer was really quite simple, even if it wasn't all that smart.

First thing that Wednesday morning over steaming mugs of coffee and the oatmeal breakfast cake Meg had rustled up seemingly out of thin air, Hank Florentine had informed Ted that the cops were done with the Orient Express and he was free to get back into the building.

Don't think Chandra didn't glom on to that little nugget of information like a vampire hanging on to the neck of a swooning victim.

Remember, she was itching to do a cleansing at the restaurant. Truth be told, I was on the fence about that part of the plan. Might not help, but I guess it couldn't hurt.

And it really didn't matter. See, I knew an opportunity when I saw one. And this was an opportunity for us to get a there-might-not-be-a-second-chance look at the scene of the crime.

To anyone who might have happened to peek out their window that morning, we must have looked like a peculiar line of bundled-up ducks. Chandra had offered her van, insisting that, like the Little Engine

That Could, it would surely be able to plow through the snow and get us to our destination. She led the way, her purple coat a bright slap of color against the white landscape.

Kate followed behind, her arms firmly wrapped around herself against the cold. Luella, on the other hand, seemed impervious to the weather. Unlike the rest of us, her head was bare and she wasn't wearing gloves. When she looked over her shoulder to make sure I'd gotten my foot safely out of the snowbank, her cheeks were burnished red, like pomegranates.

Ted was behind me, huffing and puffing just like that Little Engine. He'd insisted on coming along, and since the building belonged to him, it was a little hard to say no. He'd returned safely from his foray into the storm the day before, and he was confident he could negotiate the nearly impassable streets one more time. One look at Chandra's van painted in an array of bright colors with a brilliant yellow hippie peace sign airbrushed on the side, and I could understand his decision to drive his own vehicle and meet us at the Orient Express.

Chandra got behind the steering wheel and Luella climbed into the front passenger seat. Kate and I piled into the backseat of the van, and one by one, we exhaled sighs of contentment. The heater was making a sound that reminded me of the pained squeal of an old dump truck's hydraulic system, but thank goodness, it spit out plenty of heat. There couldn't have been more than thirty feet between the house and the van, but it was a thirty cold feet. The warmth was heavenly!

Chandra's driving skills, not so much.

"Watch out for the lamppost!"

"You're going to end up in that drift if you don't turn the wheel. Now! Now!"

"If you try to go that fast, your tires aren't going to get any traction and you're going to slide!"

Our backseat driver advice didn't help matters.

Chandra held the steering wheel in a death grip, yanking it first one way, then the other, trying to negotiate a driveway none of us could see. When she finally got out onto what we took on faith was the road and straightened the van, I imagined two whispered prayers of thanksgiving. I didn't have to imagine my own, that one was real enough.

"Slow now," Luella advised. "Take it slow. We're not in any hurry."

We inched along.

Fortunately, it was a pretty straight shot into town, and by the time we were halfway there, I finally felt the knot of tension in my stomach loosen.

"I was thinking about Peter last night," I told them.

"You mean, about our case." Chandra looked over her shoulder at me and I curled my fingers into my palms.

I think the way I also clenched my teeth sent the proper message: I wasn't going to say another thing until she turned around and kept her eyes on the road.

She turned around and kept her eyes on the road.

"I was just going over it all in my head," I continued. "Trying to get things straight. Trying to figure out what we know."

"We know Ted might have lied about the peanuts," Luella said.

"And that it looks for sure like he's the killer," Chandra added, though I was pretty certain we'd actually never come to that conclusion.

"We know our Princess has got a wild side," Kate said, grinning at the thought of that box of condoms in Mariah's room.

"And that Amanda might be in danger." This was me, giving voice to the thought that had kept me tossing and turning all night. "You don't suppose . . ." Was I letting my imagination run away with me? It wouldn't be the first time. I took the chance of looking foolish. "You don't suppose she's just been pretending, do you? I mean, about being sick. Maybe after she got that note —"

"She's hiding out! From the person who killed Peter!" Chandra was so sure she'd hit the proverbial nail on the head, her hands flew to her mouth.

The van did a fishtail slide from one side of the road to the other, barely missed a huge stone planter at the end of somebody's driveway, and swooped so close to a big old oak tree, I swear if I'd had the window open (and if I weren't so busy screeching), I could have reached out and grabbed a piece of bark.

Beside me, Kate was plastered against the backseat, her mouth hanging open and one hand clamped to her heart. Chandra, it should be noted, still had her hands off the wheel, the better to throw them in the air while she howled like a banshee.

Yet even through my panic and the scenes of my all-too-short life flashing through my mind, I registered the fact that Luella kept her head. She turned slightly in her seat, her voice calm and so quiet, it was a wonder

Chandra could hear it at all above her own demented squawking.

"Turn into the spin," Luella advised, her eyes on Chandra in a way that reminded me of a trainer trying to get through to a Jack Russell. "Both hands. Come on, Sandy, deep breaths. There you go. Hands on the wheel. Turn. A little more."

We slowed down. We stopped sliding. One by one, all our spines went from scared stiff to slack.

Something told me no one was more relieved to see the Orient Express come into view than Chandra. Maybe a little too much so. No sooner were we outside the building that housed the restaurant than she slammed her foot on the brake. The van wobbled, righted itself, and skidded another thirty feet. It came to a stop inches from the front of the grocery store and the big square cooler that sat just outside the door, the word *Ice* written on it in red letters accented with blue frost.

Irony if I ever saw it.

"We're here." Chandra might have been smiling, but her voice bumped along to the same rhythm as my heart.

"My stomach's still back there," Kate said under her breath and with a look over her shoulder.

We tumbled out and into the snow, automatically gathering close together in hopes of keeping warm. We were still pressed into a tight little knot in front of the Orient Express when Ted pulled up in his SUV.

Not as dramatic an entrance as Chandra's, but I gave him big points for being careful.

A cold wind picked that particular moment to come whistling around the corner of the building and smack us in the face, and as one, we turned away and waited for it to die down. When it did and we turned around again, Ted had the door open and he was standing back to let us inside.

Cold. Snow. Knees still rubbery from the adventure that was Chandra's driving.

And still, we hesitated.

It didn't take my overactive imagination to know why.

"The last time we were here . . ." Chandra's voice reminded me of the drawn-out, mewling sound the wind made through the branches of a nearby tree.

"It was the night we found Peter." Luella, so brave in the face of the danger so short a time ago, eyed the door of the restaurant as if it were a snake, reared up and ready to strike.

Kate took a step back. "We could —"

"This was your idea." I glanced around at

them all so they got the message that the *your* was plural. Ted was already inside, but I wasn't taking any chances. I hissed out a whisper. "You're the ones who wanted to investigate. That means we're going to go inside and —"

If Luella's laugh hadn't stopped me, the friendly hand she clapped on my shoulder would have. "Look who's braver than the rest of us. The woman who won't read a scary book!"

"Maybe." How's that for a weenie way to respond? I knew if I didn't make the first move, they'd stand there forever, so I pushed open the door and went inside the Orient Express.

That morning, it looked the same as it always had, and something about the mere fact that nothing had changed made anger boil up inside me.

Everything had changed!

Didn't the Universe recognize that?

There in the restaurant with its red paper lanterns hanging above the three tables near the windows, and its Chinese calendar on the wall, featuring a gorgeous young woman in traditional clothing, everything was different.

It wasn't just the Orient Express anymore. Peter had died there.

A chill snaked its way up my back. I chalked it up to the storm, and when I felt Kate step up behind me in the doorway, I ventured a few steps farther inside.

"So . . ." Ted already had his coat off. He stood behind the front counter and rubbed his hands together, and I couldn't tell whether he was anxious for Chandra to get started or just plain nervous. "You sure you want to go ahead with this, Chandra? It isn't necessary. Not as far as I'm concerned. But if you're ready to get started . . ."

She was.

Oh, how she was!

Chandra had brought a tote bag in with her from the car, and now, she hoisted it up on the counter and dug through it. In less than a minute, she had three bundles of herbs and a white candle set up in the space between the cash register and the takeaway packets of soy sauce and hot mustard. Chandra slipped off her coat and handed it to me. I tossed it on the nearest chair and, curious, stood back to watch.

When Chandra took a few deep breaths, lit the candle, and mumbled something about the energy of the light washing over her, I guess Ted had had enough.

"I'm just going to . . ." He poked a thumb over his shoulder and disappeared into the kitchen.

With Ted gone, Chandra engrossed, and Luella pretending to be paying attention, I made my move. Kate stood on my right, and I poked her in the ribs with my elbow and motioned to the stairs that led up to Peter's apartment.

We were in luck; the door at the top of the stairs wasn't locked. We went right inside.

"The woman's off her rocker. You know that, don't you?" Kate grumbled as soon as we had the door closed behind us. "I think this pretty much proves it. Maybe I should go back down and record the show with my cell. Then maybe Alvin could see what I put up with all summer. The chanting! The weird rituals!" She shivered. "You'll see once the weather gets nice and she starts burning smelly things in her garden. Then you'll know what a saint I am for putting up with it all these years."

I restrained myself. But then, I wasn't as interested in Kate's woes as I was in Peter's living space. We were in the kitchen, a tiny room with a blue Formica counter, white cabinets, and a blue and white floor made up of those one-foot-by-one-foot tiles that anybody can stick down and install on their own.

Pretty basic.

Well, except for the cabinet that was ripped off the wall near the refrigerator and the hole in the wall behind it.

I went over for a better look.

"What?" Kate was right behind me, peering over my shoulder, her question barely louder than the chanting that floated up from the restaurant. "You're looking at it like it's some big deal. Peter was remodeling, remember. He must have told you that. He told everyone who came into the Orient Express how he was redoing the apartment. That's why he was always wearing a surgical mask. You know, because of the plaster dust."

I made a noise she might have interpreted as agreement, then decided that, like it or not, it was only fair to tell her what I was thinking. "If you were remodeling, why would you take down just one cabinet?"

One hand to her cheek, Kate considered this for a moment while from below us, Chandra's voice rose and fell to the tempo of a guttural noise that sounded more like really bad rap than actual singing. "It was damaged? He got a new refrigerator and it was bigger than the old one and the cabinet wouldn't fit? He decided to put up one of those microwave shelves and didn't have room so one cabinet had to go?"

All logical.

Still, the missing cabinet didn't sit well with me.

Neither did the hole in the living room wall. Or the carpet that was ripped from the floor in the bedroom.

"It doesn't look like remodeling to me," I said once we'd finished a turn around the entire apartment and were back in the kitchen. "It looks more like demolition."

"And it means . . ."

I didn't have an answer. And even if I did, I had no idea how that answer might dovetail with the details of Peter's untimely demise. I did, however, know when it was time to hightail it back downstairs. It was suddenly quiet down in the restaurant, and I didn't want to take the chance that Ted might go back in there now that the coast was clear, spiritually speaking. As quietly as we'd gone upstairs, Kate and I snuck back down. When I peeked into the restaurant, Ted was still nowhere to be seen. Chandra, on the other hand, was lying on the floor.

"She's grounding her energy," Luella informed us. And with a straight face, too.

"So . . ." Done doing what she'd been doing, Chandra popped up. "Does everyone's aura feel better? And . . ." She gave me a conspiratorial wink. "Any clues upstairs?"

So, in spite of the chanting and the burning — I waved a wisp of sweet-smelling smoke away from my nose — she had been paying attention.

"Nothing interesting," Kate answered for me.

Which was just as well. I wanted to have a good look around the restaurant before Ted decided it was time to lock up and head out. I paced the area in front of the counter, picturing everything that had happened on Sunday when I stopped in for lunch. There was no sign of the threatening note on the counter where I'd put it when I picked it up off the floor, but whether that meant the cops had found it and considered it evidence, or Peter had disposed of it long before his death the next day, I couldn't say.

As for the rest of the Orient Express . . .

With Kate, Chandra, and Luella standing back and watching, I walked around the restaurant. If there had been evidence left behind by the killer, the cops (of course) had it in their possession. Which meant there was little to go by other than impressions. And my imagination.

With that thought in mind, I stepped behind the counter and stood exactly where Peter usually did when he greeted patrons.

Just to the right of the cash register. Within easy reach of the takeaway menus, the carry bags, and the free fortune cookies he included with each order.

"This must have been where he was standing when he was attacked," I commented, and watched Kate's face pale, Chandra's blanch, and Luella give me a knowing nod. "He was right here." I glanced down at the floor. "And you saw exactly what I saw. It didn't look like there had been a struggle. Either Peter knew and trusted the person who killed him, or someone came at him from behind. Someone he didn't know was in the building."

I took another look around. The doorway that led out into the little hallway and the stairway to the apartment was to my right. "If someone was upstairs . . ." In my mind, I paced out the scene.

If Peter was standing where I was now and someone snuck down the stairs, he could have easily been surprised.

"He spun around." I did, just to keep the action straight in my head. "He was surprised." I stepped back like I imagined Peter had. "And the murderer —"

"Plunged that knife straight into his heart." Leave it to Luella not to sugarcoat the facts.

I drummed my fingers on the countertop and looked across the twelve feet or so that separated the counter from the windows that looked out on the street. The other ladies did the same, and saw exactly what I saw.

From this vantage point, I could clearly see the sidewalk and the four café tables that Peter had already set up out there in anticipation of warm weather. Beyond the waist-high wrought iron railing that separated the tables from the sidewalk was the street, and across it was an empty storefront with a "For Lease" sign in the window. To its right was a souvenir shop that wouldn't open until the beginning of May, and to its left, a place with a newly painted sign over the front door.

I read the bold, painted word. "Levi's."

Kate looked over her shoulder. "Levi Kozlov. He bought out that old bar. What was the name of it, Chandra? The place that was owned by the old guy who died last year."

"Last Drop Inn. That was it," Chandra supplied the information. "It was kind of a dive."

I'd already walked around the counter and taken a couple steps toward the window, my gaze on the bar. "Is the new place a dive, too?"

"The owner sure isn't." Kate's voice shivered with laughter. "Levi Kozlov has already got a reputation in town. Hot, hot, hot."

Interesting.

But hardly helpful.

"Do you suppose Levi's was open on Monday night?" I asked no one in particular.

I got shrugs for an answer, but that was pretty much what I expected, and it didn't matter, anyway. I'd already made up my mind. I told Ted we were leaving, pulled my gloves out of my pocket, slapped my hat on my head, and headed across the street to Levi's.

11

The front door of Levi's was unlocked, but except for the jar candles burning on the bar and a few more that had been lit and scattered on tables around the room, the place was dark and so cold I didn't take off my gloves or my hat once we were inside.

"Open, huh?" Through the gloom, I looked around at the empty tables, the silent jukebox, and the bar with no bartender. "Are you sure?"

"Sure, I'm sure." Perfectly at home, Luella hopped up onto a barstool and banged a fist on the bar. "Hey, Levi!" she called out. "You got customers."

A second later, a door that led into a back room swung open, and Levi Kozlov walked out carrying a case of beer.

Dark, remember, but that didn't mean I didn't catch the pertinent details: tall, blond, broad shoulders. I didn't notice the blue eyes until he slipped behind the bar, set down the case of beer, and stepped closer. When it bounced from Luella, to Chandra, to me, then Kate, his gaze was as bright as one of those candle flames and, yes, it looked as if Kate was right on the money when she let slip the word *hot.* From the chipped-from-granite chin to the tiny scar just above his left eyebrow, *hot* was the right word.

I might actually have been impressed if *cocky* didn't go along with the package.

"Now this makes it worthwhile staying open during the storm." Levi's voice matched the whole tall-and-gorgeous bundle, deep with just a trace of huskiness. Like we just woke him up. "Four beautiful women. What more could a guy ask for on a cold and blustery morning!"

Maybe it was me. Or the cold. Or the fact that we'd just left the scene of a murder. I was so not in the mood for *hey, look at me, girls.* I chafed my hands up and down my arms. "A little heat would be nice."

"You . . ." At the same time Levi dragged a candle closer to where I was standing, he leaned over the bar, the better to peer into my face. I could only imagine what he saw, and what I imagined wasn't pretty. My hat was pulled down all the way onto my forehead, and my bangs were wedged behind my glasses and poked my eyes. When I realized Chandra was hell-bent on heading out to the Orient Express that morning, I'd scrambled to clean up the breakfast dishes and get ready, and I'd grabbed the first scarf I could get my hands on. It was yellow and it didn't looked particularly good with my mouse gray parka, my green hat, or my navy mittens. I could feel the frostbite setting in, so I didn't need a mirror to know the tip of my nose was red. I was afraid it might be running, too.

Levi stepped back and crossed his arms over his chest, studying me carefully, and for one panicked moment, I thought I saw something very much like recognition register in his eyes. It passed in a heartbeat and a smile softened his chiseled expression, the kind of smile a saintly person might turn on a particularly ugly mutt.

"You, I don't know." He stuck out his hand and I hesitated, but then, I anticipated one of those too-warm handshakes guys sometimes give women: a little too long, a little too intimate for first contact. Fortunately, I was wrong about that. His handshake was quick and firm. Maybe my mittens were scratchy. "You must be new to the island. Like me."

"This is Bea."

The introduction came from Chandra, who put both her hands on my shoulders and pushed me forward with so much oomph, if there hadn't been a bar between us, I imagined I would have found myself with my nose pressed against Levi's sculpted chest.

Not a bad visual.

No sooner did the thought occur than I gave myself a mental swift kick in the pants. It's not that I get all weak-kneed when it comes to gorgeous guys. Let's face it, New York is full of them, and I'd met — and handled — my share. It wasn't the hunk himself I was reluctant to get closer to; it was anything that even smacked of a relationship. Of any kind. Especially when the male in question was studying me with interest and, for the second time in as many minutes, I swore I saw his eyes light as if he knew more about me than he let on.

Imagination, I told myself. A case of the nerves brought on by our stealthy visit to Peter's apartment. A momentary weakness I could — and would — conquer the way I'd always bested the things that stood in my way: through grit and determination and talent.

Right after I excused myself and headed into the ladies' room.

There was only one candle burning in there, and the water from the tap was icy. I took care of my drippy nose and made my way back to the bar as quickly as I could, eager to fool myself into believing that the company of other people might help warm me. And I guess it was a good thing I did. I was just in time to hear Chandra fill Levi in on the details of my life. Or at least on some version of it that existed in Chandra's scrambled brain.

"He was a lot older than her, you know. Marty Cartwright, that is. And poor Bea, she was heartbroken when he died. Just heartbroken. In fact, I heard she could barely get off the couch for months. But then, theirs was a passion that was doomed from the start."

I didn't bother to let Chandra know I was right behind her. I'd always loved a good story, and I was eager to see what she'd make of the one I'd told the ladies as we sat around the fire the night of the murder. She didn't disappoint me.

"He left her in pretty good shape. Oh, yes." At the same time Chandra nodded like a bobblehead, Levi glanced at me over her shoulder, apparently sizing up what he saw against what he was hearing. Something in his eyes told me Chandra's use of the word *passion* didn't exactly tally with the woman swaddled in mouse gray standing before him.

"That B and B of hers is all refurbished and redecorated and she doesn't have a care in the world," Chandra went on. "Not money-wise, anyway. But she is young and pretty, and of course, she's terribly lonely. She didn't notice me watching her when she told us the story, but I don't miss a thing, remember. When she talked about Martin, there was a certain wistfulness in her eyes. And she had such a bittersweet smile."

She would have gone right on and, truth be told, I was kind of anxious to hear it. Nothing hooks me like a juicy plot! Unfortunately, Luella threw me a sidelong glance, and Chandra caught on. She spun around, but it came as no big surprise that she didn't spend any time at all looking guilty for gossiping about me.

"I was just telling Levi . . ." She grabbed my arm to pull me closer. "His lights and heat are off, too, and he's tried to stay open, but he just decided this morning that he's going to have to throw in the towel. He's about to shut off the water so the pipes don't burst, and I was just telling him, he really shouldn't stay upstairs in his apart-

185

ment because it must be freezing up there, too. He should come to the B and B. We have plenty of room there."

We didn't have anything. Including room at the B and B. What *I* did have were some questions I wanted answered, and I was willing to ignore Chandra's chatter — and the spark of amusement in Levi's eyes — if it meant I could get to the bottom of things.

With that thought in mind, I hopped up on a barstool and watched Levi uncork a bottle of Riesling from the Wilder Winery. He poured it into glasses and passed them around, and when he handed the last one to Kate, he stood near her at the end of the bar, his elbow comfortably close to her hand.

In the dancing glow of the firelight, I realized how perfect they looked together. Him with those Slavic good looks, one lock of golden hair drooping over his forehead, the generous mouth, the strong chin. Kate, as usual, was all rosy and glossy, her cheeks a pretty shade of pink and her eyes smiling their approval when she sipped, then set down her glass. I wondered how long the two of them had been lovers.

Right before I told myself it was none of my business and I didn't care, anyway.

"We were just talking," I blurted out,

eager to dispel the images that popped into my head, "about the murder on Monday."

The bar wasn't the least bit dirty, but Levi grabbed a rag and swiped it all around. "You and everybody else. That's one of the reasons I stayed open during the storm. When something like a murder happens in a close-knit town like this, people need a place to gather and talk so they can try to make sense of it. You know, like a community wake."

It was a surprisingly insightful remark from a bartender. Or was it? Aren't pithy observations what bartenders are supposed to be all about?

"One of the reasons." It was still before noon, but it had already been a long morning, and hey, living through a drive with Chandra behind the wheel was definitely something to celebrate. I sipped my wine. The Riesling was nice and crisp, and I tasted pears and a hint of citrus. To show my appreciation, I raised my glass in Kate's direction. "You said giving people the opportunity to talk about the murder was one of the reasons you stayed open. What was the other one?"

Levi had a glass of water on the back of the bar, and he reached for it, took a drink, and set it back down. "The locals need someplace to gather," he said. "Someplace they can go for a change of scenery. You know, to relieve the cabin fever. I've actually had a pretty good crowd in here since the storm started. Until this morning, that is. Word must have gone around that my lights are finally out, too, and the heat's gone. I can't even cook anything. Tell me" — his eyes gleamed — "do you think they were coming in here just for the burgers? Because I kind of thought it was all on account of my sparkling wit."

Oh yes, as sure as I was sitting there, I was convinced that this little bit of gleaming (not to mention the schmoozing) was designed to distract me from the topic of murder. Truth be told, it almost did. But then, I'd always been a sucker for a guy with blue eyes. Call me shallow. The broad shoulders didn't hurt, either.

But hey, if I'd learned nothing else since my life in New York had turned upside down, it was that I was the one in control.

Of my life.

Of my emotions.

And of this investigation.

As if the Universe was reminding me of exactly that, the mailman walked in the front door, a pleasant man named Charles whom I'd met a couple times, but who, of course, knew Luella, Chandra, and Kate well. He stopped to chat with them.

And I closed in on what I wanted to talk about in the first place.

Which, just for the record, had nothing to do with gleaming blue eyes.

"Did you have a pretty good crowd here on Monday night?" I asked.

It obviously wasn't a question Levi expected from a woman with a recently drippy nose and her hat pulled down to her eyes. His gaze snapped to mine and don't think I didn't notice that his dreamy smile turned a little icy around the edges.

"Are you asking me if I saw anything the night of the murder?"

With one gloved finger, I traced an invisible pattern against the bar. "Yeah. I mean . . ." I turned on the barstool so that I could look beyond where Charles and the ladies were talking about the storm and see out the front window. "It's a pretty straight shot from here over to the Orient Express. If the lights were on over there — and they must have been since Peter was still open for business and they were on when we arrived after our book discussion group — and if you were behind the bar, standing where you are now . . ." I wondered if he even picked up on my casual shrug, seeing as how it was encased in layers of wooly clothing and topped off with a parka. "It seems to me you would have seen exactly what was going on over there."

It wasn't my imagination; he hesitated. Just long enough to get his story straight in his own head. "Too bad I didn't, or I might be able to do something to help the police. But you're forgetting, it was snowing like a son of a gun, and that made visibility practically nonexistent. Besides, I didn't have a moment's peace that night. From dinnertime on, I was slammed."

I leaned an elbow on the bar and propped my chin in my hand. "On a night when it was snowing like a son of a gun?"

He cocked an eyebrow at me. It was a nonchalant sort of gesture, and as sexy as sin. No doubt he'd perfected it on a thousand women before me, and just as certainly, every single one of them had succumbed. It was another shot at distraction on his part and he was way off base if he thought there was a snowball's chance in hell of it working. Then again, this distraction was far more interesting than the last. The first time he may have just wanted to divert the conversation from the unpleasant topic of murder. This time, he was definitely trying to avoid talking about what he may or may not have seen on the night of the crime.

"Like I said, the locals like a place to escape, and on Monday night, the heat was still working. We had pool players . . ." When I followed his gaze into the darkness on the other side of the room, I made out the shapes of two hulking pool tables. "We had people at the bar. We had plenty of dinner orders, too."

"And you were so busy, you didn't notice a thing that happened across the street."

It wasn't a question. Which was why I wasn't surprised when Levi didn't answer. There was a tad more wine in the bottle, and he divided it among our four glasses, starting with Kate and working his way back down the bar to me. He drained the bottle into my glass. "The cook I hired for the summer hasn't come over to the island yet," he said, setting down the bottle and meeting my gaze straight on. "Good thing I'm really good at a whole lot of things." He paused here long enough to make it clear that, just for a second, we weren't talking about running a bar any longer. When he was sure I got the message, he got back on track. "I was pouring drinks and flipping burgers in the kitchen. If there was anything to see . . ." His gaze drifted to the Orient

Express before it moved again to mine "Whatever happened over there, I didn't see a thing."

I didn't so much give him a smile as I tried to move my lips, just to make sure they weren't frozen. "I bet that's what you told the cops."

"How do you know the cops talked to me?"

"They would have been stupid not to, and don't tell Chandra, but Hank Florentine doesn't strike me as a stupid man."

"But I do."

"I never said that."

"But you expected me to tell you something I didn't tell the cops."

"Did I?" I drained the wine in my glass. "And here I thought I just stopped in to be part of the communal wake."

I slid off the barstool and prayed the other ladies got the message. Whatever we'd hoped to find at Levi's, it wasn't forthcoming. Neither was Levi himself. There was no use prolonging the visit or the agony of being so carefully studied by that steady, molten gaze.

Tugging down hats and rebuttoning coats, our little group shuffled to the door.

"We'll see you later?" Chandra called back to Levi. "Remember, Bea's got a generator and lots of heat."

I had my back turned, but there was a mirror nearby, so I could see that Levi's teeth were clenched. From this distance, I couldn't be sure, but I swear his answer was something like, "The Ice Queen? That's hard to believe."

Me? Get angry at the slight? Not to worry. When he turned his back on the door and hoisted up another case of beer, I got a good look at his butt.

So I mean, really, who had the last laugh?

"I brought burgers."

The last person I expected to see at my back door later that Wednesday afternoon was Levi, so it was only natural that I'd stand there with my mouth opening and closing like the walleye I'd heard the fishermen in these parts loved to catch.

If he held it against me, he didn't show it. Without being invited, he stepped into the house, and just inside the door, he dropped the bedroll that had been under his arm. I stepped back, he stepped forward, and we did a little backward shuffle all the way into the kitchen, where he set down a couple overflowing shopping bags. "I've got fries, too," he said, unloading the bags onto the counter top. "And chicken wings for lunch tomorrow. And onion rings. Do you like onion rings?"

I love onion rings. I didn't bother to mention this. But then, I was a little busy stepping back so I could cross my arms over my black sweater and say, "Wow, it must have gotten as cold as hell at the bar. Otherwise, you wouldn't be desperate enough to opt for the Ice Queen's palace."

Good thing Chandra picked that moment to come waltzing in because, really, I was pretty sure he was going to pretend he didn't know what I was talking about, and that would have been a major disappointment.

"Oh, this is perfect," Chandra crooned. "I'll set another place at the table. Oh . . ." Her mouth dropped open and I could see that she was doing some quick mental calculations. "If we only had one more," she purred, "there would be thirteen. Thirteen suspects gathered together in the snow. Just like in the book!"

I didn't give Levi the opportunity to ask what she was talking about. I suggested he leave his sleeping bag in the parlor until we figured out a more permanent place to house him, and told him dinner would be served at six.

Yeah, it was cruel to leave him hanging

like that.

But then, two could play the game.

12

As it turned out, Chandra got her wish. Just as we were about to sit down to dinner, Jayce Martin, the owner of the local ferryboat fleet, showed up at my door. By this time it should have come as no surprise that he was looking for a place to stay.

Thirteen.

There were thirteen of us in the house.

But not thirteen for dinner.

I was waiting at the door to the dining room, directing my guests to their seats, when Amanda came down.

"Oh." She stopped just short of the dining room, one hand on the wall to steady herself. "I think maybe . . ." She pushed off and back toward the steps. "I'm not feeling well again. I think I'll just go back upstairs and relax."

I couldn't imagine it was the fabulous aroma of the burgers wafting from the kitchen that caused her cheeks to pale and her hands to shake, and after I promised her a bowl of soup once we were done eating and watched her go back upstairs, I went into the dining room, wondering if I'd been right about Amanda all along.

Maybe that threatening note she received meant she wasn't ill, but was hiding from someone.

Maybe when she came down to dinner, she saw that someone seated at my table?

With a cold chill on the back of my neck, I stood at the head of the table until everyone else was seated, using the opportunity to take stock of my guests. Her back to where I stood, Kate was at the far end of the table nearest the windows with Chandra to her left. Levi was next to Chandra, Hank was next to Levi. Ted had automatically grabbed the chair here at the head of the table, and there was an empty seat to his left that I would slip into as soon as everyone else settled in. That would put Meg next to me, but not her kids. They had chosen to eat in the kitchen. Luella was next to Meg, and Mariah (who was dressed to the nines in slinky black pants and a gorgeous red cashmere sweater) was next to her. Jayce was at the far end of the table. He was a rugged, dark-haired guy about our age, and it didn't take a rocket scientist to see that no lights and no heat were the least of his problems.

Two minutes into dinner I realized Jayce couldn't take his eyes off Kate. Fifteen minutes later, and the story was no different. The poor guy was head over heels.

Kate might have noticed if she weren't so busy checking her text messages.

"So, what do you think, Bea?" Luella passed a plate heaped with the burgers Levi had donated to the feast to Meg, and from Meg, it came to me. Since I already had a burger on my plate, I passed it on to Ted, who eagerly took a second. "I know it's not my place to decide, but I couldn't help but wonder about the logistics. If we all stay in the rooms we're in, and Jayce and Levi bunk together in the parlor —"

It was exactly what I had been thinking, so I told her, "That's the simplest solution, though it's not going to give you a whole lot of privacy." I glanced down the table toward Jayce, but since he was so fixated on Kate, he hadn't even heard me. I had no choice but to look across the table at Levi. No skin off my nose, especially when I had the chance to add so very sweetly, "There's a fireplace in the parlor. You should be plenty warm."

I wondered if anyone else noticed that the

smile Levi gave me was just a little too tight around the edges. In addition to the burgers and onion rings, he'd also brought salads that he said he didn't want to see go to waste. He reached for the bowl, took another helping, and drizzled on blue cheese dressing. "I appreciate it," he said with a nod toward me. "The floor to sleep on as well as the warmth."

Was it his way of apologizing for the dig back at the bar?

I didn't have a chance to find out.

Chandra finished the last of her burger and spoke with her mouth full. "This is perfect. Now that we're all gathered in one place, we can talk about the murder."

Hank Florentine was seated directly across from me, so I couldn't miss the way one corner of his mouth pulled into a grimace. Or the fact that he rolled his eyes. "That's not a polite topic for a casual gathering," he growled. "You should know better than that, Sandy. Nobody wants to talk about the murder."

"Shows what you know." I wasn't sure if Chandra was referring to the subject of murder or his use of her legal name. Either way, she shot a look down the table at her ex. "It's news, isn't it? And people always want to talk about the news. Especially around here. Murder is sensational, and let's face it, life here on the island can sometimes be a little dull after winter's over and before the tourists arrive."

"I like dull." When Jayce spoke up and Kate looked across the table at him as if it was the first she realized he was there, the tips of his ears turned red. "I mean, dull as in a routine. Routine is good. It makes me feel comfortable and in control."

Poor Jayce. I could have told him it was the wrong opening gambit. Dull and Kate were not words that were commonly used in the same sentence.

I bet Levi knew that.

I slapped the thought from my head. Though they were seated near each other, Kate and Levi had barely exchanged a word throughout dinner, much less a glance. But then, if they didn't want anyone to know they were involved . . .

Once again, I shook the thought aside. I had more important things to think about than . . . well, than that.

Like how to corral Chandra when she started in again. "I bet Jayce knows more than he's letting on," she said, jiggling her eyebrows to emphasize her point. "After all, he gets a first look at everybody who comes and goes. You know exactly who's come to the island in the last few days, don't you, Jayce?"

Jayce was finishing up a bite of salad and he held up a finger as a way of indicating he'd answer as soon as he swallowed. I couldn't blame him for not catching on to the subtext of Chandra's question. After all, who in their right mind would actually think that we were looking to solve Peter's murder?

"The weather's been pretty mild this spring," Jayce said, "and some of the summer residents have been showing up to get their cottages ready. A few of the restaurants are open, too. Places like Levi's. So there have been a few tourists, too. So the answer . . ." He sat back. "Who's been coming? Plenty of people."

"But who hasn't left?"

I could have kicked myself the moment the words were out of my mouth. I hadn't meant to say them out loud.

Hank's gaze shot to me. But then, so did Ted's. And Mariah's. None of that was nearly as unnerving as the look I got from Levi. Cold? Those blue eyes of his were suddenly icicles.

"Who hasn't left?" Completely oblivious to the fact that this was one question I shouldn't have asked in a houseful of strangers, Chandra laughed. "Well, all of us. That's for sure!"

A couple heartbeats later, the gravity of the question and all it meant finally struck and Chandra's eyes went wide. She took one moment to glance around the table, her gaze flitting from one guest to the next. That is, before she fixed it on her empty plate.

"Levi brought apple cobbler." I popped out of my chair and headed into the kitchen to get it, grateful that I remembered and thankful for the diversion.

Apparently, so was everyone else. A murmur of anticipation went around the table along with a couple heartfelt thank-yous to Levi for his generosity.

"It's no big deal." His voice rumbled its way to me in the kitchen. "I'm happy to share. Besides, I didn't want to have to throw any food out. Ever since the storm started, it's been really slow at the restaurant."

Chandra and Kate helped me clean up the dishes. Luella took dinner up to Amanda. Now that the parlor was officially a guest room and not a place for gathering, my other guests disappeared into their respective suites. Once our chores were finished, so did Chandra, Luella, and Kate. Fine by me. I poured a cup of coffee and turned off all the lights in the kitchen except for the one above the breakfast bar, where I sat down.

By this time, the howling wind had become nothing more than background music, and I looked out the window and saw that once again, the snow had picked up. Since we'd gotten home from our foray into town, there were another couple new inches of the white stuff on the back porch. Freezing outside, but warm inside, thank goodness. I wrapped my hands around my coffee mug, enjoying the heat seeping through to my fingers and the comfortable quiet inside the house.

Alone time.

That's what I needed to get my thoughts in order.

I reached over to the nearby built-in desk, grabbed a legal pad, and made a list. If anyone happened to see it, I could always say I was trying to get everyone's bill straight.

What I was really doing was trying to figure out if any of my guests had a motive for murder.

I'd gotten as far as writing down everyone's names when the door swung open and Levi stepped into the kitchen.

Since his name was at the top of my list, I flipped the legal pad facedown on the counter. "Kate's in my suite," I told him. "Last I saw her, she was surfing the Net. I'm sure she's still awake."

He pursed his lips. "And I care about that . . . why?"

It wasn't a question I expected. I sucked in a breath and sat up straight. "I thought that —"

"Me and Kate?" He took a couple steps farther into the kitchen and, damn, but I wished I could see his eyes better through the gloom. Something told me they were sparkling, but whether with amusement or derision . . . well, that remained to be seen. "Interesting. I mean, the fact that you spent that much time thinking about me."

The sensation that scooted up my back wasn't a thrill. It was a bristle. That pretty much sealed the deal. We were talking derision here. "Trust me, I hardly spent any time on it at all," I said, my voice as tight as my smile. "Sometimes, I just get a gut feeling. You know, an impression. I'm usually right."

"Not this time."

I did not sigh with relief. I swear.

What I did do was try not to look like a complete moron. I went for a smile, and this one actually might have convinced both Levi and me if it didn't wobble around the edges. "Sorry. I just thought —"

"Sure you did."

"That is, I didn't —"

"No, I mean, why would you?"

I couldn't exactly tell him it was because both he and Kate were so attractive and they seemed so comfortable together and so I just naturally assumed . . .

When I realized my voice was actually shaking, I could have crawled in a hole and died. "I just naturally assumed —"

"You were sort of on the right track. Kate and I, we met right after I arrived on the island and opened the bar. I went out to the winery to do a tasting and place an order. She's easy to talk to. That is, when you're talking business. We hit it off, and I actually met her for coffee once." Levi poked his hands into the pockets of his jeans and rocked back on his heels. "Once was all it took. But then, I'm kind of a gut-instinct guy myself. It didn't take long for me to re-alize that Kate is —"

"Beautiful, accomplished, and success-ful?" At times like this, it is best to show that jealousy — or sour grapes — has no place in the conversation.

Levi chuckled. "I was going to say uncomplicated."

"And that's a bad thing?"

He slid onto the empty stool next to mine at the breakfast bar, his knees and mine nearly touching. The only polite thing to do was turn slightly in my seat, the better to keep his space his and my space personal. I knew this. For some reason I couldn't explain, though, I couldn't move a muscle.

"With Kate," he said, "what you see is what you get. She's ambitious, smart, and, yes, very pretty. Some guys wouldn't complain. That's exactly what they're looking for."

"You mean some guys like Jayce?"

Another chuckle, this one as warm as the darkness that surrounded us. "Poor sucker. He has no idea how out of his league he is. Then again, if he's looking for a woman like Kate . . ."

"You're not." It wasn't a question, so technically, I couldn't be accused of sticking my nose where it absolutely, positively, totally had no business.

Levi didn't so much lean forward as he shifted just slightly in his seat. The air stirred and I caught the combined scents of burgers and onion rings that clung to his jeans and red wool sweater. Have I mentioned that I'm nuts about onion rings?

He fixed his gaze to mine. "I like a woman who keeps me guessing," he said.

I grabbed my coffee cup and took a sip, and while I was at it, I told him there was more coffee in the pot. He declined with a shake of his head that caused one honey-colored curl of hair to brush his forehead.

The coffee was supposed to distract me, and it would have worked if it weren't for that damned little curl!

"I'm not sure you're going to find that kind of woman up here on the island," I said, and three cheers for me, I called on all the experience I'd garnered from years of attending cocktail parties, and made it sound like we were having the most normal small-talk conversation in the world.

Even though something about Levi's tall and gorgeous presence made me feel anything but normal.

But then, a sizzling bloodstream and a pounding heart have a way of doing that to a girl.

"The people I've met here on the island are pretty up-front and not very mysterious," I said. "They're good people. Honest people."

"I didn't say I was looking for dishonest." With a tiny smile on his lips, Levi pushed a hand through his hair. "Besides, if I listen to everything Chandra says, it sounds like some people around here have lives that are plenty interesting. You know . . ." He raised his eyebrows. "Dramatic and passionate."

I felt my cheeks flame and set down my coffee cup, the better to drop my face in my hands and groan, "I hope you don't believe everything you hear from Chandra."

He laughed and I came out of hiding to find his smile warming the space between us for one second. Two.

A gust of wind rattled the branches of the tree outside the kitchen window and we both flinched. Levi got up and poured himself a glass of water. He brought it back to the counter, but he didn't sit down.

That was a good thing, I told myself. I could switch positions in my chair. I did . . . thus assuring a little more room to breathe, and a lot less of the heat that inconveniently erupted when Levi was sitting too close.

He set his glass on the counter. "No worries," he said. "About Chandra, that is. I haven't lived here more than a couple months, but hey, Levi's is nothing if not the center of island gossip. Even before I met Chandra, I'd heard about her. I know she's . . ."

Searching for the right words, he hesitated, so I filled in the blanks. "Inventive. Imaginative. Funny. Funky." These were not bad qualities, I realized with a start. In fact, they were the very personality traits I admired in so many of my friends back in New York. "Chandra's not a bad person," I announced, and no one was more surprised to hear it than me. Which didn't mean I'd completely lost my mind. "Now if she'd only do something about Jerry Garcia."

I expected Levi to ask what the heck I was talking about, but instead, he laughed. "Alvin Littlejohn loves my Caesar salad," he explained. "I know all about you and Kate and Chandra and your coerced book club."

"Then I guess some of that stuff Chandra was talking about at dinner . . . about thirteen suspects and being snowed in, and the way she was asking questions . . . I guess it all makes sense. We just read *Murder on the Orient Express.*" Oh yes, this was subtle of me, and I congratulated myself. I had successfully nudged the conversation to where I knew it had to go. Even if I didn't want to see it arrive there.

"It's only natural everybody on the island would be talking about the murder." Levi stated the obvious. "And like you said, Chandra has quite an imagination."

"I guess she's not the only one." I clutched my hands together in my lap. "When we stopped at the bar this morning —"

"And you grilled me about what I saw the night of the murder."

I pursed my lips. "That wasn't grilling. It was polite conversation. And like you said, only natural. Of course I'm as curious as everyone else about what happened to Peter."

"Hence, the grilling. About what I saw."

I poked my glasses up to the bridge of my nose. "Only you didn't see anything. Remember, that's what you told me. You didn't notice what was happening across the street because you were so busy in the kitchen and behind the bar."

Levi didn't need to confirm or deny. I have an excellent memory.

He downed his water and took the glass over to the sink.

Dumb luck? Or a calculated move?

It was hard to say.

I only know that it was dark over by the sink, and when Levi turned around, his face was lost in the shadows. "Like I told you back at the bar, we were slammed."

The warmth had been nice, but sometimes — like it or not — it's impossible to ignore the cold, hard facts. "Except tonight," I reminded him, "when I came in here to get dessert, I heard you tell everyone in the dining room that you brought the apple cobbler because you didn't want it to go to waste. You said that since the storm started, it's been slow at the restaurant."

Honestly, I think I would have thought less of him if he'd scrambled to come up with some half-baked explanation.

But I wouldn't have been as disappointed as I was when he headed for the door.

"It's getting late," he said before he walked out of the kitchen. "I think I'll turn in."

After he was gone, I spilled the rest of my coffee into the sink and watched it go down the drain.

Just like my hopes.

No, no, no . . . not those kinds of hopes! Like I said before, I wasn't looking for a relationship with anybody. Even if the anybody in question was tall, gorgeous, and honey-colored.

I was talking about murder.

And how I'd hoped that Levi would slip up and tell me why he'd lied about what he saw the night Peter was killed at the Orient Express.

I woke up at 3:17.

My first thought was to blame the coffee, but I knew that wasn't true. It must have been years of living in New York that inured me to caffeine; I often drank coffee late at night, and it never made me toss and turn.

No, something else was bothering me. Something I couldn't put a finger on.

Until I realized it was deathly quiet outside.

No wind.

As if moving would break the spell and call back the storm, I lay perfectly still in my queen-sized bed, listening for the all-too-familiar sounds of creaking trees and scraping branches.

Instead, all I heard was the distant drumming of waves on the beach. For the last few days, their tempo had been pounding, furious. Now, it reminded me of the gentle rhythm of a lullaby.

One, two. One, two.

I closed my eyes, and let the sound lull me back to la-la land.

One, two. One, two.

Thud, thud, thud.

My eyes flew open.

That wasn't an outside sound. It came from inside the house.

I propped myself on my elbows and held my breath, and I was just about to tell myself that I was imagining the sound of footsteps — or dreaming — when the sound echoed through the silent house again.

Thud, thud, thud.

Someone was walking around upstairs.

No sooner had the thought occurred to me than I told myself to get a grip. There were thirteen adults and two kids in the house, after all, and no rules against getting up in the middle of the night to use the bathroom.

Except I didn't hear any water running.

Thud, thud, thud.

I swung my feet over the side of the bed, poked them into my slippers, and reached for my robe.

My private suite is at the back of the house, parallel to the kitchen. It's not nearly as big as my condo back in New York, but it's plenty roomy enough for me. I had the door closed between my bedroom and the living/reading/den area where Kate was sleeping on the pull-out couch, and I inched it open and bent my head to listen.

The only sound I heard was the muffled rhythm of Kate's breathing.

And more footsteps from overhead.

As quickly and quietly as I could, I slipped through the living room and out into the hallway. From here, the sounds were more defined, and there was no doubt they were coming from the upstairs hallway.

I stood frozen at the bottom of the steps,

and when I realized my stomach was in my throat and my hands were suddenly shaking, I grabbed the banister and tried the calming exercises I'd practiced nonstop with the therapist who'd helped me get from one day to the next in those final, chaotic months in New York.

"Stop being stupid, Bea," I reminded myself. "Stop being a wussie." These were not words Dr. Byncrest ever used. He was supportive, positive.

"It's your house, Bea," he'd remind me, and I reminded myself of the fact right now. "It's your life. Nobody can keep you from being in charge and in control. Nobody can take your power unless you let them."

Brave words, and thank goodness, I finally came to believe them. Dr. Byncrest saved my life. And my sanity.

But then, all this sounds a little crazy, doesn't it? That's because I've never confessed about what happened in New York.

And about the stalker who turned my world upside down.

13

His name was George Mattingly, but of course, I didn't know that. Not at first. Back when it all began — three years before I moved to South Bass Island — all I knew was that I sometimes felt as if someone was watching me, that I sometimes was sure someone was following me, that I often felt as if my life was under a microscope, every moment of it dissected and examined.

My friends said it was only natural. I was young, reasonably good looking, and pretty darned successful in a career I hadn't chosen as much as it had chosen me. Of course people were watching me.

For a while, I actually fell for the story.

But when strange notes and gifts began to arrive . . . When I got the heavy-breathing phone calls . . . When I heard someone walking through the condo at night when I was the only one there . . .

The thought crackled through me like a

jolt of electricity, and I snapped out of it. And though I didn't remember my knees giving out, I found myself sitting on the bottommost of the steps that led up to my guest suites.

"South Bass Island, Bea," I reminded myself, shaking myself back to reality, my voice entirely too small and breathy for my own liking. "All that is yesterday's news, and George Mattlingly is in prison."

At least that's where I'd last heard he was.

My hands began to shake again, and I clutched them together and reminded myself that since the trial and Mattingly's conviction, I'd taken every precaution humanly possible to keep my movements private and my life, a secret. I'd thrown off all the trappings of my old life. I'd left New York. In an effort to disguise myself, I'd even taken to hiding behind these silly glasses . . .

I put a hand to my face and realized I'd left my black-rimmed glasses next to my bed.

No matter, I didn't need them, anyway; the lenses were nothing more than window glass.

I was good. I was covered. No one knew I was here on the island, and the people who did know knew because they were here on the island with me, but they didn't know I was me.

Trust me, this little bit of twisted logic made perfect sense inside my cannonballing mind.

Besides, I reminded myself, if Mattingly wasn't right where he was supposed to be for the next six years, I certainly would have heard the news from Jason Arbuckle, my attorney. Jason would never lie to me. Not about the man who'd made my life hell.

Soothed by the thought, I pulled myself to my feet, ignored my Silly Putty knees, and started up the stairs. At the top, I paused, bending my ear, waiting for the sounds of footsteps to come again.

I wasn't disappointed. This time, the shuffling footsteps were followed by a smooth, mechanical sound, like a doorknob turning.

There was a nightlight on outside the bathroom, but really, it didn't help much. I squinted, and looked from door to door, and when I thought I saw the door of Suite #5 inch open, all my hard-won logic went right out the window and I careened from nervous straight to panic mode.

Suite #5 was Hank Florentine's room.

Yes, of course I told myself to get a grip, but it was kind of hard considering that my mind was suddenly racing through the possibilities, all of them bad.

If one of my guests didn't like the subject of murder being brought up at the dinner table because that guest had killed Peter . . .

If that person thought his (or her) secret wasn't safe with a cop in the house . . .

If that someone decided Hank had to be kept quiet — or worse . . .

Before I even realized I was moving that way, I was outside the door of Suite #5. There was a table nearby, with a brass candlestick on it, and I grabbed it and wrapped my sweaty fingers around the base. When the door finally opened, I was ready, candlestick raised over my head.

Good thing I had the presence of mind not to bonk Chandra with it!

"Oh my goodness! Bea!" She gasped and pressed a hand to her heart and the unbuttoned blouse she was holding closed with one hand. "What on earth are you doing?"

"What am *I* doing?" My heart was pounding so hard, I could barely hear my own rough whispers, what with all the noise. "Chandra, you scared me to death! What are *you* doing?"

Her grin was the only answer I needed.

That, and a glimpse of Hank through the open door. He was lying in bed, one arm bent behind his head. It was a good thing the lights in Suite #5 were off and I couldn't see much. I swear, the man was as naked as a jaybird.

"I thought you couldn't stand him."

That was me, my voice low. After all, my dining room was filled with guests eating breakfast, and one of those guests was Hank. I might still be reeling from the discovery of Chandra's midnight tryst, but I'm not completely without good sense. Tapping one toe, I stared at Chandra, who was plucking English muffins from the toaster and buttering them.

Carefully, carefully buttering each one.

Kate zoomed by. She'd just delivered the first dish of eggs to the dining room and she stopped at the stove and waited for Luella to reload the bowl. "Who hates who?" she asked.

"Whom." My correction was instinctive, and with a wave of one hand, I told Kate not to pay it any mind.

"Chandra." I pointed, and whispered, "Chandra said Hank was a snake in the grass."

Chandra's expression was deadpan. "He is a snake in the grass," she grumbled, carefully buttering another muffin. "He's a creep. A hard-headed jerk. A —"

"Then what were you doing in bed with him?"

Kate's mouth fell open. Luella turned off the stove and stared at Chandra. They both hurried over and we gathered in a tight knot around Chandra and the toaster.

"You? In bed with —"

"Sandy, I can't believe you. I remember the day you divorced the man. You said you'd never —"

"You were upset when he got here. You didn't want to be under the same roof as Hank." She'd finished with the last of the muffins and I plucked the plate out of her hands then hurried into the dining room with the muffins in one hand and the newly filled bowl of eggs in the other. "Don't try and talk your way out of this," I warned Chandra when I got back to the kitchen in record time. "When I heard you walking around upstairs, I thought there was a burglar in the house. You owe me an explanation. What were you doing?"

A tiny smile played around her lips. "What weren't we doing?"

I felt heat rise in my cheeks. "That's not what I meant. I mean, what were you thinking?"

Chandra rolled her eyes. "Oh, come on, girls. None of us is a kid. You know I wasn't thinking. Except to think about how good the sex always was with Hank."

"But you hate the man!" Yes, this declaration came out just a little too loud. I clapped a hand over my mouth.

Chandra puckered. "I hate certain things about Hank. That's for sure. But there are other things . . ." Her face split with a grin. "Besides," she added with a look at the closed dining room door, "Hank and I, we were talking. I mean, when we weren't doing other stuff." She added a wink for dramatic effect. "And guess what, ladies? I found out something interesting. You know, about Peter's murder."

Chandra scooted over to the kitchen table with Kate and Luella right behind her. It took me a moment to shake myself out of my surprise-induced stupor and follow.

While they sat down, I stood at the head of the table, my fists on my hips. "Are you saying that you had sex with Hank just to try and get him to talk about the murder?" I asked.

Chandra's laugh ricocheted against the ceiling fan above the table. She grabbed my arm and pulled me into the seat next to hers. "That's not all I was trying to get him to do, and I have to say, honey, it worked like a charm." She laughed again, and when she was done, she smoothed a hand over the heavy sweater she'd pulled on earlier before she ducked next door to feed the cats.

"It's sweet of you to worry about my morals. Really." Chandra gave my arm a friendly pat before she burst into another laugh. "But don't be silly. I went to bed with Hank because I wanted to go to bed with Hank. Having him talk about the murder, that was just icing on a very sweet cake."

"So?" Luella leaned closer. "What did he say? About Peter?"

"And the murder?" Kate chimed in.

Chandra held up a hand, her index finger pointing to the ceiling, and in a really bad Belgian accent said, "Well, for one thing, mon ami, it was not, how you say, a robbery."

I ignored the literary reference. And the incorrect French. Since I wasn't sure Kate and Luella had picked up on the real significance of the statement, I filled them in. "If the Orient Express was robbed, that would mean it could have been a random crime. Somebody taking advantage of the fact that Peter was alone. Or thinking no one would discover the robbery for a while because the weather was so bad. But since nothing was taken —"

"It could be because we showed up,"

Luella said. "Maybe there wasn't time for the killer to ransack the cash register."

"Except that we didn't see anyone in the restaurant. Unless . . ." Thinking, I drummed my fingers against the table. "I suppose the killer could have escaped through the door in the kitchen."

"How can you say that so calmly?" Kate's complexion was green. "That means when we were walking in . . ." She didn't finish the thought. But then, she was busy swallowing hard.

I nodded. "He could have been right there, just walking out."

"So the fact that Peter wasn't robbed?" Chandra wrinkled her nose and shrugged. "Okay, I admit it. I don't really get it, either. Hank made it sound like it was some kind of big deal."

"Because it means the killer might have had another motive," I pointed out. "Something more personal."

As one, all our gazes traveled to the dining room.

I knew they were thinking what I was thinking. Which is also why I knew I had to cut off any panic at the knees. "We can't say for sure," I reminded them. "We don't know if it's one of my guests."

"But we know Amanda got the same kind

of threatening note Peter got," Luella said.

"And we know the Princess is here on the island to see a man," Kate put in. "What if that man was Peter?"

"And we know Ted and Peter had a fight," Chandra said.

"And we know Levi lied about being busy Monday night." This was a detail I had yet to report to the ladies, and though it gave me no pleasure (and yes, I was annoyed at myself when I realized it), I told them everything that happened with Levi the night before. Well, not exactly everything. I left out the stuff about the darkness and the warmth of his smile.

Taking it all in, Luella tipped her head. "So we know plenty."

Kate sighed. "But we don't know anything."

"Not anything about Peter." This was a new idea, and I wondered why it hadn't occurred to me sooner. I popped out of my chair and headed into the dining room, and the other ladies trailed behind.

Lucky for me, everyone but Ted was done with breakfast and had already left the room. That meant I didn't have to face Levi and wonder what was going on behind those gleaming blue eyes of his. Or face Hank, for that matter.

For one thing, I wasn't sure I could talk to Hank with a straight face, not after seeing him the way I'd seen him in the wee hours of the morning. For another, I wasn't sure I was all that comfortable interrogating Ted, not with a professional in the room.

Ted was just scooping up the last of the eggs from the serving bowl, and I sat down next to him.

"You were Peter's landlord."

We both knew this to be true. That would certainly explain the *no duh!* look he tossed my way while he tucked into the last English muffin.

I was in no mood to beat around the bush. "What can you tell me about him?" I asked.

Ted chewed and swallowed. "The man was an unprincipled creep," he said.

"Come on." Kate took the chair on the other side of Ted. "We all knew Peter. He was charming."

"Charming to customers, maybe. But that's because he wanted to keep you coming back and spending your money. In business dealings, he was underhanded, dishonest, and unscrupulous," Ted said.

Chandra shook her head. "But he was such a good cook!"

"Which doesn't mean he was an honest person." I can't say how the ketchup bottle ended up on the breakfast table, but it had been a busy morning and lots of people came and went in the kitchen; Ted grabbed the ketchup and doused his eggs. He shoveled up a mouthful.

"I first met Peter Chan twelve years ago back in Cleveland," he said, ketchup on his lips. "He rented a building from me and opened a restaurant, and it tanked. How do I know?" Ted stabbed another forkful of eggs. "Because I went around to collect the rent one day, and found that Peter had moved out. Took all his equipment. And left me in the lurch."

"He owed you money?" I asked.

Ted poured coffee from the carafe on the table and added two spoons of sugar and the last of the cream. Really, the last. I'd drained the carton when I set the table that morning. "Lots of money," he said.

"But then, why . . ." I wondered if I was missing something, so I thought through my question once, then again, before I gave voice to it. "Why would you rent him another place?" I asked. "If he owed you money and you didn't trust him, why lease him the building for the Orient Express?"

Ted was about to polish off the last of the eggs on his plate, and he tossed down his fork. "Well, that's just it, isn't it? That's why

I was so mad when I walked in there Sunday afternoon and found Peter behind the counter. I sure didn't expect to see him. And I bet he didn't think I'd just stop in out of nowhere, either. His jaw just about hit the floor when I walked through that door! I never would have rented another property to Peter Chan, and he knew it. We did the whole lease agreement months ago, worked through an attorney, and the only contact we had was via email. That lousy, no good son-of-a-gun had somebody else sign the lease agreement for him. Somebody named Amanda Gallagher."

That explained everything!

Well, part of everything, anyway.

"That's why she was pretending to be sick," I said, popping out of my chair and leading the way up the stairs to Suite #1. "Amanda was probably surprised to find out Ted was here. She didn't want to run into him."

"But why would she sign the lease, then try to avoid the man?" Chandra's question came from right behind me.

"And how did she know Peter?" Luella was in back of Chandra, but she asked her question, too.

"And why — ?"

At the top of the stairs, I stopped Kate's question with one hand out like a traffic cop, and led the way to the door of Amanda's room. I knocked. Three times.

There was no answer.

At least not from Amanda's room.

Across the hall, Mariah stuck her head out of her door. "I thought I heard someone knocking. Now that the storm is over, it's so wonderfully quiet here. I can see why you love this island, ladies. I'm thinking I'm really going to like it here, too." She stepped out into the hallway, resplendent as always, even if she was wearing the same black pants and red cashmere sweater I'd seen her in the day before. I forgave her the fashion faux pas. Even the most with-it princess can be forgiven for not packing every gorgeous outfit she owns when she doesn't know she's going to get stranded in a snowstorm.

"If you're looking for Amanda," the Princess said, "I think you're looking in the wrong place. While we were all at breakfast, I saw her tiptoe down the steps bundled to the teeth. It looked like she was going out."

Indeed.

We hurried into the kitchen and got on our coats and boots, and when we stepped outside, I paused for a moment, savoring the quiet and the blinding light of the sun glancing off the mounds of snow. The sky was clear and an amazing shade of blue, and somewhere nearby, a cardinal called out. Grateful we'd made it through the storm, I lifted my face to the sun. That is, right after I whisked off my glasses, got a pair of sunglasses out of my purse, and popped them on.

Thank goodness for a good pair of sunglasses that cut the glare. When Chandra whined, "How are we going to find her? We don't know where she was going," I was ready.

I held up a hand, my index finger pointed upward much like a Belgian detective. Or at least an incense-burning, crystal-reading cat spoiler who has dreams of being a Belgian detective. When I had everyone's attention, I slowly lowered my hand, pointing down to the snow.

"Footprints!" Kate was on it like . . . well, like white on snow.

Our heads down, we followed the trail Amanda had left, around the back porch and on to the front of the house. From there, the footprints led down the road toward town.

I was still studying them when I heard the

engine of the VW van cough into life behind me.

"Come on." Chandra stuck her head out the window of the van and waved us in. "There's no way I'm walking all the way into town. We can drive slow and still follow the footprints."

We did, and honestly, it wasn't any big surprise when we saw that they stopped right in front of the Orient Express.

Then again, Amanda was standing outside the front door, so that was pretty much a giveaway, too.

I popped out of the van before Chandra had it in park, and even before I was up to the door, I saw what Amanda was doing, and sucked in a breath. She had a nail file in her hands, and she was working on the lock of the door.

"What on earth are you up to?" I glanced around, grateful that the street was empty and that Levi's across the road was closed so no one could be watching from the window. "Give me that." I held out my hand and, red-faced, Amanda dropped the file in it. "Are you trying to get arrested?"

"I'm not trying . . . I mean, I am try-ing . . . That is, I'm not . . ." Amanda's shoulders heaved. By now, the other ladies were out of the car, and we closed in around

Amanda. "I just wanted to get inside," she said, her voice clogged with tears. "I just wanted to see the place."

"The place you signed the lease for?" For a warm and fuzzy tree hugger, Chandra can be pretty intimidating when she tries. She stood up straight, pulled back her shoulders, and leaned in nice and close to Amanda. "Why would you need to do that?"

"I didn't. I mean, I didn't know. I mean . . ." The blubbering didn't help Amanda's explanation.

It was time to regroup. I signaled the ladies to back up and give Amanda some room to breathe, then closed in on my own. Literally speaking, of course.

"We found out what was going on, Amanda," I told her. "You signed the lease for the Orient Express. Ted told us. Is that why you've been trying to avoid him?"

Amanda threw her hands in the air. "But that's just it, don't you see? The last person I expected to see here on the island was Ted. I know what happened back in Cleveland all those years ago. With Peter and the restaurant he had there. I knew if Ted ever saw me again he'd think I had something to do with Peter skipping out on his rent even though I didn't, and then Ted would be furious."

My mind working a mile a minute, I tried to make sense of the scenario. "If Ted knew you on sight, why did he lease the Orient Express to you?"

Amanda sniffed, and I found myself thinking that it was a good thing the sun was out and the air was warming bit by bit. Otherwise, her tears would have frozen to her cheeks. "Back then," she said, sniffling, "he didn't know me as Amanda Gallagher. Back then, I was using my married name, Amanda Chan."

I was the first who snapped out of stunned silence and voiced the question I was sure we were all thinking. "You were married to Peter?"

She shook her head. Not like I was wrong. Like just thinking about it disgusted her. "Biggest mistake I ever made in my life," she said. "And the best thing I ever did was divorce him. The man was a creep."

It was the same word Ted had used to describe Peter. And it didn't explain . . .

"But if you hated your ex—" I fought to make sense of everything she told us. "Then why did you lease the building for him?"

"Don't you get it?" Amanda's voice brimmed with tears. "I didn't lease the building. Peter forged my name on the lease. My maiden name. That's why Ted didn't recognize it. A few weeks ago, I ran one of those free credit checks. That's when I found out. That's why I came to the island. To have it out with Peter. The son-of-a-bitch didn't even let me have that much satisfaction. He died before I ever had the chance."

"Then you . . ." I took a step back, astounded by where my own deductions took me. "You didn't receive a threatening note like the one Peter got. You wrote those notes!"

She didn't look embarrassed. "As soon as I saw the building lease on my credit report, I knew Peter was behind it. That's when I sent the first letter. I thought I'd scare him, you know? Just to get even. And to let him know he wasn't going to get away with it. Then I sent another one, and another one. And then I came to the island. I figured by then, he'd be shaking in his shoes. He should have been, the lowlife. How dare he do something like that? It's got to be illegal. I mean, it's identity theft, right? Leave it to Peter." Her laugh contained exactly zero amusement. "If there was a sneaky way around a law or a quick way to make a buck — honest or not — Peter was the one to do it. To tell you the truth, that's actually why I came here today. I wanted to see the place where Peter died. You know, just to mark the occasion with a little happy dance."

"What Peter did was illegal, sure." I did my best to make sure I didn't sound like I was accusing her of anything. Not yet. "But so is murder."

Amanda's mouth fell open and color raced into her porcelain cheeks. "You don't think . . ." She lifted her chin. "I sure didn't kill Peter," she said, her teeth snapping out the words. "As much as I would have liked to, I hate to admit it, but I just didn't have the nerve."

14

We waited until Amanda walked away, and then we waited some more, just to be sure she didn't double back and try to break into the Orient Express again.

Guests with police records are bad for business.

Then again, having a guest who was a murderer wouldn't do much for the reputation of Bea & Bees, either.

"Ted and Amanda both have reasons to hate Peter." I thought the words were just playing around inside my head, but apparently, I spoke them out loud, because there outside the front door of the restaurant, Kate, Luella, and Chandra turned to me. I explained as simply as I could.

"They both have motives. I wonder about opportunity."

Chandra looked genuinely confused. "You mean . . ."

A leftover blast of wind raced down the

street, and though the sun was quickly warming the air, the breeze blew across the piled-up snow and created instant air-conditioning. I stuffed my hands in the pockets of my parka. "I mean do either one of them have an alibi?"

Kate's mouth thinned. "Well, they were both on the island that night. We know that because Amanda checked into your place on Sunday and Ted showed up Monday evening. By then the ferry wasn't running. So they both had to be on the island at the time Peter was killed."

"And Ted arrived late, remember." Luella started back toward the van. "That means he could have been anywhere before he came to your place."

"He said he was checking his properties." Chandra jumped behind the wheel. "But maybe that was just a story."

"And maybe . . ." Another memory from that night jumped up and slapped me like the leftover icy wind that blew off the lake. I climbed into the van and put on my seat belt. "Remember when Amanda came down and asked for tea the night of the murder? She was wearing boots. That means she must have gone out sometime that night."

"She said she forgot her slippers," Kate reminded me.

"Completely possible," I conceded. "But if you forgot your slippers, wouldn't you just walk around in your socks? Why boots? And why — ?"

It was the mention of socks that knocked another memory out from where it had been lodged in the deepest recesses of my brain. The night of the murder, after we came back to the B and B and built a fire, we left our boots by the door and padded around in our stocking feet. After Amanda went back upstairs —

"There was a wet patch on the carpet!" I was so upended by this dim memory, I grabbed the sleeve of Kate's jacket and gave her a shake. "Remember, Kate, you stepped in it. After Amanda came down, the floor was wet."

Chandra was backing out of the parking space, and in the rearview mirror, I saw her flash me a look. "Which means — ?"

"That her boots were wet, of course. She *had* been out." I shot a look down the street in the direction Amanda had gone, and saw her in the distance, plodding on toward the B and B. "Funny, she didn't mention that when she told us what a creep Peter was."

"So Ted and Amanda both have motive. And opportunity." Luella was sitting up front, and she turned in her seat. "What are the chances somebody else on the island did, too?"

I answered her with a question of my own. "What are the chances Marianne might be at the library today?"

Nobody bothered to ask why I was interested.

We drove straight to the library.

As it turned out, Marianne *was* at her post at the library's main desk that morning. She was surprised when we knocked and asked to be let in, but she didn't question it. Instead, she told us that she had stopped in to make sure nothing in the library had gotten damaged and was relieved, now that the electricity was coming back to the island bit by bit, that the library's lights were on and the heat was pumping.

"And with all this peace and quiet . . ." Marianne glanced around the library, which was smaller than the library room in my condo back in New York. She sighed with the contentment of a real book lover. "Before we officially reopen for business and our patrons return, I can do some serious shelving without being interrupted."

For our part (okay, truth be told, *my* part, because I was doing the talking for the group so I was the one who made up the story on the fly), we said that while we waited out the storm back at the B and B, we'd been discussing *Murder on the Orient Express* and wondering what it would be like to be real detectives. With Poirot's incomparable skills in mind, we'd given ourselves a challenge.

"We're going to put our own little gray cells to work." I was afraid I sparkled a little too much when I said this and that it might give us away, so I toned down my smile and opted for at least part of the truth. "We'd like to see how much we can find out about Peter Chan."

"Internet?" Marianne suggested with a gesture toward one of the library's computers.

I put Kate and Chandra on it.

But I had other ideas. "Microfilm," I said. "Cleveland newspapers."

Humming with the excitement of helping us explore the classic book in this new and different way, Marianne led the way to the library's one and only microfilm reader.

Luella poked me in the ribs. "If I didn't know better, I'd think you actually had some experience being a detective."

"Oh, or a secret past!" From over by the computer, Chandra practically swooned. She had just slipped out of her coat, and she clutched her hands to her heart. "Leave it to Bea to have some great, exciting double identity."

When everyone else laughed, I joined in. Not exactly as easy as it sounds when the emotion felt so hollow. "Actually," I said, skirting the subject as cleanly as I was able, "I've had some experience doing research. Newspapers are always a great place to start."

"But how do we know where to look?" By this time, I was sitting in front of the microfilm reader, and Luella was seated on my left. "It's not like we know much about Peter."

"We know he lived in Cleveland twelve years ago," I reminded her. "And we know he left suddenly. That means he might have had a very good reason to get out of town. A reason besides dodging his rent payments, that is."

With that in mind, we asked Marianne for the microfilm reels from the proper dates and got down to business.

It was slow going, and by the time we were all the way through May, my head pounded and my eyes felt as if they were going to pop out of my head. We started in on June and I rotated my shoulders, getting rid of a cramp.

"Baseball scores, hints of public corruption, oil prices, movie reviews." I scanned page after page, providing Luella with a running commentary, just in case she didn't read as fast as I did. "Recipes, letters to the editor, a lawsuit resulting from a death at a Chinese restaurant."

My own words echoed back at me and I sat up like a shot and pointed to the screen. "A lawsuit resulting from a death at a Chinese restaurant," I repeated.

I didn't need to. Luella was already out of her chair, leaning over my shoulder and reading the article along with me.

I skimmed, voicing the highlights. "Popular eatery . . . elderly woman . . . Anastasia Golubski . . . became ill immediately after eating there in early March . . . some question as to the cause of death . . . civil suit brought by family against owner . . ." I wasn't surprised and I don't think Luella was, either, when I read the man's name. "Peter Chan."

While I reread the article and hit the proper button on the machine to make it print, she flopped back down in her chair.

"What are the chances?" I asked.

"You mean the chances someone might have a grudge against Peter because of the woman's death?"

"That." I grabbed the article from the printer. "And what are the chances that person could be on the island?"

The most logical way back to the B and B from the library was down the road that ran parallel to the lake, but once we were on it, we realized village officials had called out the backhoes and dump trucks usually used for repairing roads and put them to work removing snow. The road was blocked, and rather than follow the trucks at a snail's pace, we endured a couple harrowing minutes of Chandra inching the van forward, then slamming it into reverse to get us turned around. We went back the way we came, right past the Orient Express.

"Hank," Chandra said just as we approached the building, and I was just about to lecture her about her love him/hate him relationship when I saw what she was talking about. Hank's patrol car was parked in front of the restaurant.

When Chandra parked the van, I didn't object. But then, I think my reasons for wanting to get another look at the Orient Express were different from Chandra's. (Hint, hint: Chandra ran a comb through her hair and slapped on some lipstick before we went inside.)

"Hey, Hank." Her hips swaying just enough to distract Hank's attention from the clipboard he was holding and the notes he was jotting, Chandra strolled into the restaurant as if she had every right to be there. And since she got away with it, the rest of us followed right along, sans hip swaying. "What are you doing here, big guy?"

We exchanged glances, wondering what, exactly, the nickname referred to. Maybe Hank was thinking what we were thinking, because color raced up his neck and into his face. "Just looking things over again," he said, ignoring her too-familiar greeting and setting down the clipboard on the front counter so he could run a hand through his buzzed hair. "I don't know why, but this case is making me crazy. It just doesn't make any sense. But then . . ." Hank's glance skipped over Chandra to the three of us standing right behind her. "I'm probably boring you ladies to death with talk of police work."

"Actually . . ." I figured I might not ever get a chance like this again. Besides, Hank owed me. If it weren't for Bea & Bees, he'd be sleeping on the couch at the station. And he would have missed out on his assignation with Chandra the night before. "We were here yesterday," I said, and reminded him, "You said Ted could get back in and Chandra came over to —"

"Yeah, yeah. I remember." He waved a hand as if he could still smell the herbs Chandra had burned during her cleansing ceremony. "It's up to the building's owner, after all, who he lets in and what they do when they get here. And if mumbo jumbo makes Ted Brooks happy, I suppose that's all that matters. But let's face it, all that hocus-pocus is nothing more than horse hockey!"

Chandra crossed her arms over the front of her purple coat, and in a voice filled with so much patience, I was sure she'd lectured Hank about this a thousand times before, she said, "Just because you can't see something doesn't mean it doesn't exist."

"Right." There was no doubt about how Hank felt about the subject, either. I mean, what with the way he split the word into two syllables. His chin came up. "How many times have I told you, if you'd get your fuzzy brain out of the clouds —"

Patience gone in a flash, Chandra's voice was sharp. "And if you'd try to see further than the end of your nose —"

"You'd realize that you're just kidding yourself." Bad move to bring it up in the first place, and punctuating the statement with a laugh didn't earn Hank any points. "Isn't that what I've been telling you for years, Sandy?"

"It's Chandra." Her jaw tightened. So did her fists. "And if you'd just take a little time to think less about yourself and more about the magical world around you . . ."

I left them at it. The sometimes lovebirds were too busy fighting to notice when I slipped up the stairs and back into the apartment. A second later, Luella and Kate followed me into Peter's kitchen.

Kate glanced around. "We've already been here. What are you looking for, Bea? Nothing's changed. Nothing's different."

My hands on my hips, I glanced around the kitchen, too. Of course, it looked exactly the same. Same blue counter. Same white cabinets. Same blue and white floor. "Something's still bugging me," I admitted. "Something about Peter saying he was remodeling."

Kate's smile was stiff. "You're not still worried about that cabinet being pulled off the wall, are you?" She pointed that way. After all, Luella had not made the trip upstairs with us on our last visit to the Orient Express, and apparently, Kate thought she might miss the white cabinet propped next to the refrigerator. "Bea thinks it's weird," she whispered, but loud enough to make sure I could hear.

My not-so-sweet smile told her I got her message. That didn't stop me from taking another stroll through the apartment. As Kate was so quick to point out, nothing had changed, and honestly, I hadn't expected that it would.

Maybe that's why I was so thrown for a loop when I realized there were two holes in the living room wall.

Since Kate was standing next to me, hers was the arm I rapped. "Two." I pointed, my finger vibrating with the excitement that coursed through me like the punch of a shot of Red Bull and vodka. "Two holes."

"Sloppy, but hardly telling," Kate commented.

Luella leaned between us, the better to see what we were talking about. "For such a neat man who took such pride in his cooking, you'd think Peter would have cleaned up after himself."

"That's the whole point!" Now my whole body was feeling the crazy cascade of exhilaration. Unable to keep still, I closed in on the wall. And the holes. "There was only one hole in the wall yesterday," I said.

"Oh, yeah?" Hank's question caromed

246

through the tiny room. I hadn't realized he'd come upstairs and was standing in the kitchen doorway. I spun that way, one hand clapped to my heart. "So yesterday when you said you were downstairs doing that goofy magic ceremony, you Nosey Norahs were really up here?"

My smile came and went. "We weren't all Nosey Norahs," I confessed. "Chandra and Luella stayed downstairs. And it was a good thing Kate and I came up here," I added, before he could start tossing around words like *trespassing* and *breaking and entering,* and before Kate could turn up the juice on the look she shot my way, the one that indicated that, clearly, I was a traitor. "Otherwise we wouldn't have seen the hole in the wall. The one hole in the wall" — I held up a finger — "that was here when we were here yesterday."

"But today there are two." Fingering the cleft in his chin, Hank nudged Luella and Kate aside and stepped closer to me and to the wall. Chandra had been in the kitchen, and with Hank out of the way, she moved into the living room, too. He studied the new hole, and when I made a move to get an even closer look, he held out an arm to stop me. "We need to get the crime scene guys in here to have a look around and see

247

if there's any evidence. Son of a gun." As if some amazing thought had just occurred to him, he shook his head. "It's not possible. It couldn't be."

"What?" we all asked in unison.

"Luella . . . Kate . . . You must remember, it happened about four years ago."

If that was the case, then whatever he was talking about, Chandra would remember it, too. Don't think I didn't notice that he'd purposely left her out of the conversation. Or that the very fact made her scrunch up her mouth as if she were about to spit nails.

"There was a guy here in town who we looked at in connection with a couple burglaries," Hank said. "Guy by the name of Chuck Anderson."

Luella's expression was thoughtful. "Chuck was a local boy, and always a bad one. Trouble at home. Trouble in school. I did some business with him back when he ran the bait and tackle shop," she said, strictly for my benefit.

So was Kate's next comment. "The bait and tackle shop." She pointed down to the floor and beyond, to the restaurant. "It was right here in this building. Right downstairs."

"And Chuck" — Hank took over the telling of the story — "lived up here. He was what we call a person of interest in any number of local burglaries, but we were never able to pin anything on him. A couple years back, he left here for a day on the mainland and was nabbed on some burglary charge over there. If you ask me, it was no coincidence that the burglaries stopped here on the island as soon as Chuck was behind bars. And you know what? I'm thinking it might be just about the time he'd come up for parole."

A piece of the puzzle clunked into place inside my head. Maybe. I told myself my theory was only that — a maybe. I wouldn't know more until I had more information. "What kinds of things were missing?" I asked Hank. "In those burglaries you were never able to pin on Chuck?"

Hank thought about it, but only for a minute. Like cops everywhere, he had an encyclopedic knowledge of the cases he'd worked. Especially the ones he hadn't been able to solve.

"Chuck had a good eye. And he only targeted the summer residents. One of the items that was never recovered was a diamond tennis bracelet. White gold, with a couple carats' worth of little diamonds on it, all told. I remember that burglary because the homeowners put up quite a stink. They were all for blaming the Department, said we didn't provide adequate protection, even though they'd left for a day of boating and hadn't locked their doors."

I looked at the hole in the wall. It was plenty big enough to stash a diamond tennis bracelet.

"And the other missing things?" I asked Hank.

"A couple rings. One emerald, one ruby, the way I remember it. And a set of gold cuff links. Had the owner's initials on them, which to me meant they weren't going to be easy to fence. But hey, gold prices have skyrocketed since then. I'm sure one of those dealers that pays you cash for your gold would gladly take them, no questions asked."

"And you never could link Chuck Anderson directly to any of these crimes?"

I don't think I was imagining it; when Hank swiveled his gaze from the hole to me, I had the distinct feeling he was about to ask why I thought any of this was my business.

I was ready with an answer before he could ask the question. "I was just thinking, that's all. If Chuck was back on the island —"

Hank cut me off with a brisk wave of one

hand. "No way. I'd know it. Chuck was a fixture around here. Everybody knew him, and anybody who saw him now would recognize him. If he came over on the ferry —"

"It was mild last week." Luella's reminder was gentle, but pointed. "I had my boat out."

I jumped on the suggestion. "Which means Chuck could have come over from the mainland on a boat of his own. Or he could have had someone bring him on a private boat, right?"

Hank wasn't convinced. "But if he did —"

"If he did, he could have been looking to collect something he didn't have a chance to take with him when he left the island." I gave the holes in the wall a pointed look. "What if, all those years ago, he hid the jewelry up here in his apartment?"

"And you think Peter found it when he was remodeling?"

I couldn't say, so I didn't bother to answer Kate's question.

Chandra didn't give me a chance, anyway. "If Chuck came back," she said, stepping up so that Hank couldn't ignore her, "he might have been the one who made this mess."

"But if Chuck hid the jewelry in the first

place, he'd know exactly where it was. He wouldn't need all these holes." Yes, the realization smashed my Chuck-as-bad-guy theory to smithereens, but I had no choice but to voice it. "But . . ." I stopped before I spoke, and realized that Chandra, Kate, Luella, and Hank all had their eyes on me, waiting to hear more.

"What if someone else knew the jewelry was hidden somewhere in the building?" I suggested. "That would explain why no one spotted this Chuck character. Because Chuck wasn't here. We don't even know for sure that he's out of prison, do we?"

A muscle jumped at the base of Hank's jaw. "You can bet I'm going to find out, ASAP."

I went right on.

"Another unknown person would also explain why that person had to make so many holes in the walls. He knew the jewelry was here, he just didn't know where exactly. And that makes me think . . ." I took as good a look as I was able to at the closest hole. "He may not have found what he was looking for the first time he was here. That's why he had to come back. But the first time . . ." I was going out on a limb, and I waited to hear it crack beneath me. "The first time, my guess is that he ran into

Peter when he was here. Maybe that's why Peter was killed."

It all made so much sense, and I should have been happy about it.

After all, I was beginning to piece together a reasonable explanation for the crime.

But if that was true, why did my stomach feel as if it had been tied into a couple hundred Boy Scout knots?

Well, heck, that was easy! We'd just talked about it when we ran into Amanda outside the front door. That's when we figured out that Ted and Amanda both had reasons to kill Peter, and the opportunity to do it, too. Then we'd just determined that some unnamed friend or relative of Anastasia Golubski, the woman who died after eating at Peter's restaurant, might be seeking revenge. After that, we tied the building and the destruction inside it to a known burglar who might be looking for the valuable jewels he'd been forced to leave behind when he went to jail.

Heck, I should have been jumping for joy. But all I could think of was how much we were in over our heads.

See, instead of having no suspects? We suddenly had too many.

15

When I opened my eyes the next morning, the sun was just creeping over the horizon, and for a moment, I allowed myself to wallow in the pristine perfection of dawn's early light. No snow clouds. No wind. No pounding waves. For a couple days there, I'd started to question the wisdom of moving to the island, but now that the storm was over and life was back to normal —

Hardly.

Not with an unsolved murder tainting the atmosphere, the reputation, and, yes (don't tell Chandra I said this), the aura of the island.

The realization hit like the touch of an icy hand, and I pushed myself up on my elbows. That's also when I realized that it wasn't the sunlight that woke me up in the first place — it was the sound of footsteps in the hallway upstairs.

Chandra and Hank.

Marveling at the convoluted machinations of the human psyche, I smiled. Whatever the heck was going on with those two, I guess it was fair to say that they'd gotten over their differences in regard to what Hank called *mumbo jumbo.*

Or at least they put those differences aside for as long as it took to get it on.

I plumped my pillow and plopped back down, but as hard as I tried, I couldn't get back to sleep. Not with thinking about everything we'd discovered in our last couple days of investigating and — on a more mundane note — everything that needed to get done in time for breakfast. After twenty minutes of trying to coax back the Sandman and failing completely, I gave up on the idea of dozing for a little while longer. With a sigh, I swung my legs over the side of the bed, poked my feet into my slippers, grabbed my robe, and headed to the kitchen to make coffee.

"Oh." Just inside the kitchen door, I stopped cold. But then, I hadn't expected to find Levi sitting at the kitchen counter.

Did I care that I looked (literally) like I'd just gotten out of bed? That my hair was a fright? That my robe was the red plaid flannel one I'd bought on a summer trip to Maine that I never expected to be quite as chilly? And that my feet were encased in pink bunny slippers?

I shouldn't have.

I didn't, I told myself.

That didn't keep me from cringing.

Not that it mattered. My mortification dissolved in a flash when I saw what Levi was doing. He had a checkbook open on the counter in front of him and he was writing out a check. To me. His sleeping bag was rolled and tied. It was on the floor near the back door.

"You're leaving."

Not a question, but then, it was pretty obvious, so why pretend?

He ripped the check out of his checkbook and set it on the counter. "I figured it was time to see what's happening back at the bar."

"That makes sense." It did, and had this been any other guy — and had I been thinking about anything other than murder — I would have left it at that. "It would make even more sense if you planned to check the building then come back here to sleep where it's warm and where we have electricity. And if you weren't doing it so early. You know, so you could slip out without anyone seeing you."

"Slip out? Is that what you think I'm doing?"

It was a no-brainer, but still, he'd asked the question. He deserved a straight answer.

I strolled over so I could glance at the check, cursing the fuzzy pink bunnies who blazed the path with heads bobbing. "You paid me too much. I guess you wanted to be sure there was no question about what you owed me. That way, you could be certain you wouldn't have to see me again."

"That's not it at all." His answer was a little too sharp, a little too quick. Levi knew it. He stood and reached for the navy peacoat he'd left hanging on one of the chairs at the table, and yes, I noticed him noticing the bunny slippers. He was smart enough not to comment. "I wanted you to know how grateful I am to you for taking me in. That's why I gave you more than the amount we agreed on."

"I don't need charity. Yours, or anyone else's."

"I can see that." Another glance at the bunny couple, and in addition to being smart, I learned Levi had a poker face. I stored away the information for a time I might need it. "And I'm not just saying that because the B and B is nice," he said. "Or because of all that stuff Chandra said about how much money your late husband left you." He put on his coat and stepped away from me and toward the door. "You have a good head for business. And you're a gracious hostess, even in the face of what could have been an accommodation disaster. You handled it well." Another glance down, and this time, I learned one more thing about him: he could only keep a straight face so long. A smile tickled the corners of his mouth. "I predict you're going to be successful at this B and B thing. In spite of the pink bunnies."

I was not in the mood to join in the fun. "But you're going to make sure you're not around to see it."

Levi smile disappeared. "I honestly can't see that you'd care."

"Honestly, I'm not sure I do."

"Then why — ?"

"I've got a lot of unanswered questions, and it seems to me, you're trying your darnedest to make sure they stay that way. Truth be told, that leaves me with another question — why?"

"Why do you have questions? I can't say. Unless it's questions about you and me."

Oh, yeah. I could see how a woman could fall under his spell. It was the voice, as smooth and intoxicating as really good bourbon, and the face that would make the gods weep with appreciation. It was the whole, delicious package that was Levi Kozlov.

And I wasn't buying it.

I crossed my arms over my chest. Defensive? Yes. But it didn't hurt to send the signal: You're not battering down these walls, buster. I don't care how cute you are.

"There is no you and me," I reminded him, though I shouldn't have had to. "We hardly know each other."

"And you want to keep it that way."

"I'm not the one sneaking out before it's barely light."

"You're not the one with a building where there might be burst pipes."

"A building across the street from the scene of a murder."

Like a sniper with a target in his sights, he went perfectly still, poised to make the next move. One second. Two. If there was any vacillation going on behind that gorgeous face, it didn't show. He wasn't unsure about what he wanted to do next. I knew that instinctively. He knew it as surely as he knew his own name. He just didn't want to do it.

"There's nothing I know that you need to know," he said. "Trust me."

259

"I wish I could."

He lifted his bedroll and tucked it under his arm. "You know what, Bea? I wish you could, too."

Levi already had his hand on the back door when it popped open.

"My goodness!" Mariah stepped into the kitchen, her cheeks pink, but whether it was from the temperatures outside or the surprise at finding us there, I couldn't say. Her smile was bright, and a little apologetic. "I hope I'm not interrupting anything."

After hearing Levi call me a gracious hostess, I figured I had a reputation to live up to, but still, Mariah didn't strike me as the up-early-and-out-the-door type. "It must be awfully cold out there," I said, glancing to where her hands were stuffed in her pockets. "Is anything wrong?"

"You mean, why was I out of the house so early?" She laughed and moved another couple steps past Levi and into the kitchen. "No, no, nothing's wrong. I woke up early and watched the sunrise, and I realized I've been cooped up for so many days, I felt as if I'd just burst if I didn't get outside and get some air. I took the opportunity to put a few things I wasn't using in the car. And I took a walk. A very short walk. It looks like it's going to turn into a beautiful day, but right now . . ." She shivered. "It's still plenty cold out there."

"Just what I was thinking!" It was the morning for early risers. A spring in his step (I knew exactly why), Hank came into the kitchen, already dressed in his uniform. "Cold," he said, "and I was just on the phone with the station. The block where your place is . . ." He looked at Levi and at his bedroll. "There's still no power. We're asking people to stay away from those buildings. No use going into a dark place and getting hurt. Right now, all our resources are being diverted to snow removal. We'd rather not have to deal with residents having accidents."

Levi dropped his bedroll back on the floor. "Then it looks like I'm staying."

I wished he would have said it with a little more enthusiasm (why, I couldn't say, or maybe I could and I didn't want to think about it), but hey, at this point I'd take anything I could get. All I was hoping for out of Levi was some answers. With a few more hours to try and a little bit of luck, maybe I'd get them.

He shrugged out of his coat. "I make a mean cheese omelet," he said.

I wanted to tell him I didn't need the help, but let's face it, I am not one to look a gift horse in the mouth. Especially one who can cook. No sooner had Levi stuck his head in the fridge to search for ingredients and I'd moved over to the coffee maker, than I heard Hank talking to Mariah. Talk about moves!

"Let me help you with your coat, honey," Hank said. "A woman as pretty as you shouldn't have to do things for herself."

I was tempted to turn around and give him a piece of my mind, along with the news flash that, yes, I'd heard him with Chandra not an hour earlier, but I held my tongue and measured out the coffee. It was none of my business, and besides, Mariah didn't seem to mind.

In fact, she giggled, and in a low, seductive voice, told him she'd take care of her coat herself. "If you'd just be a darling," she purred, "and get me the very first cup of coffee out of that pot, I'd be eternally grateful."

Apparently, Hank liked the idea of eternally grateful and all it might imply. Before I knew it, he was standing right behind me, an empty coffee mug in his hand.

I poured the first cup for Mariah, another one for Hank, and grabbed one for myself while I was at it. When Mariah and Hank trailed into the dining room together, I poured another cup for Levi and took it over to where he was standing near the sink, cracking eggs into a bowl.

He didn't look my way. "Peace offering?" he asked.

I set his down so I could wrap my hands around my own mug. "Do we need one?"

He leaned over and turned on the disposal to get rid of the eggshells, and he didn't bother saying a thing until it was done whirring. "We do if you think I had anything to do with Peter's murder," he said.

"I never said you did."

He dug around in the nearest drawer for a whisk and gave the eggs a thorough beating. "You never had to."

"It's not like I think you killed the man."

"Really?" Levi left the whisk in the bowl and turned to me. "Then why are you trying to grill me every chance you get?"

"I'm just —"

"Being nosey?"

"Trying to solve a mystery."

"Why? Because you want to be some kind of hero again?"

It didn't take more than a second for his meaning to sink in, and I swear, in that one heartbeat, the coffee in my mug went from piping hot to icy cold. But then, my veins suddenly filled with ice water, and my hands

263

were glacial.

Hero.

I'd been called a hero — by the media, by the bloggers, by the cops — when I stood up to George Mattingly. When I testified against him in court.

"What do you . . ." My mouth was filled with sand; the words wouldn't come out. I cleared my throat and tried again. "What do you know about it?" I asked.

Levi had already gone back to the eggs. I'm not much of a cook, but even I knew there wasn't an egg on earth that needed to be beaten that hard. "What do I know about what?" he asked.

I couldn't play games. Not when it came to this. I laid a hand over Levi's and he froze. "You said *again.* You said I was trying to be a hero again."

"Did I?" As if it was the most normal thing in the world, he slipped away from me so he could grab a dish towel and wipe his hands. He leaned his back against the sink and shrugged.

"I guess I meant you were a hero for taking us all in when we didn't have anyplace else to stay. Is there something wrong with that?"

"No." The word came out along with the breath I didn't realize I was holding. My heartbeat ratcheted back. "I just thought —"

"What?"

"Nothing." I whizzed past him, determined to get dishes from the cupboard before he could notice that my hands were trembling. I would have made it if he hadn't grabbed my arm, holding me in place at the same time he spun me to face him.

"Bea —"

My gaze went from where he held on to me to his face. "What?"

He didn't answer. Not right away, anyway. Not until our gazes locked, and my breath caught again. Not until he dropped his hand as if my arm were on fire. He backed away. "Just tell me when you want me to start cooking."

When breakfast was finally on the table, I found I wasn't very hungry, so I retreated into my private suite and took care of some paperwork. It would have been easier to concentrate if I could knock the conversation with Levi out of my head. The way it was, the words played round and round. It's no wonder that by lunchtime, my stomach growled and my nerves were frayed.

"We're out of milk." I banged the carton — the carton someone had emptied, then put back in the fridge — on the counter. "Why didn't someone tell me we were out of milk?"

"It's not like it would have mattered." Chandra said this so matter-of-factly, I knew she was the guilty party. "The grocery store hasn't opened back up yet. We couldn't run out and get more milk, anyway."

"That's a great excuse for not throwing the carton away." I did just that.

"You're a tad cranky." Kate was at the desk in the kitchen, checking her text messages, and she glanced over her shoulder at me. "That doesn't have anything to do with a certain handsome bartender, does it?"

I gritted my teeth. "The certain handsome bartender —"

"Always has his eyes on you." Kate got up and went over to the cupboard. I'd put her in charge of finding something that would go along with the chili we'd be serving for lunch, and she rooted around until she found a box of crackers. "Every time I look at him —"

"Oh, come on!" I was so not in the mood to hear this kind of hogwash. Not when Levi and I were always at odds with each other. Not when he'd made that off-the-cuff *hero* remark that still had my stomach tied in knots. "Why on earth would you notice what Levi is up to?" I asked Kate. "You never pay attention to anything but that phone of yours. Sorry. I just can't believe you get that many messages. Nobody's that important."

"Maybe she's just pretending to check her messages." Chandra slid by, a bag of grated cheese in one hand, a bottle of hot sauce in the other, and a sly smile on her face "So she doesn't have to notice that Jayce Martin can't take his eyes off her."

"Please!" Kate pursed her lips. "You can't possibly think —"

"That he's not good enough for you?" Chandra snorted. "Is that what you're saying, Kate? Jayce is a fine man. And he comes from a good family. But then, I guess the rest of us common folk here on the island just can't measure up to the great Wilders."

Kate dumped crackers into a bowl. "*Common* being the operative word."

Chandra made a face. "Oh, yeah?"

"Yeah." Kate propped her fists on her hips. "As a matter of fact, if you weren't so busy bonking your ex, you might notice —"

"Girls!" Luella walked into the kitchen after calling everyone down for lunch. She aimed a laser look on each of us. "What the heck is wrong with you? It's just like the old days, you three sniping at each other like there's no tomorrow."

"I was not sniping," I pointed out, because it was the truth, and because this was my house to begin with and I shouldn't have to defend myself. "If Kate wasn't so busy —"

"Oh, no!" Kate threw a hand in the air. "Don't pin this on me. You were fine until I mentioned Levi. Then you got all prickly and all hell broke loose."

I stepped up to her. "You haven't seen hell yet. And if you don't mind your own business —"

"Kate Wilder? Mind her own business?" Chandra cackled. "If she could do that, we never would have met in the first place. If she didn't keep dragging me into court —"

Kate swung around to face her. "If you didn't keep burning those stinky fires."

"And playing that stupid opera."

"And has anyone mentioned the cat?"

"Oh, no!" For a woman in her seventies, Luella could move pretty darned fast. In the blink of an eye, she was standing in the center of our little showdown. Her face screwed up and one eye narrowed, she glanced from Kate to Chandra to me. "I'm not going to let this happen," she said.

I knew what she was talking about. That didn't keep me from getting defensive. "What?"

"You know what." Since I asked the question, I deserved the full brunt of her anger, and I got it. "You three." She pointed at each of us in turn. "You three were finally getting along. And now you're going to start again. On account of what? Because we've been cooped up together too long? Because we can't get to the bottom of what happened to Peter? Those aren't good excuses. I will not have you acting like toddlers who need a time-out. Not again."

Chandra grunted. "I don't see how you can stop it," she grumbled. "If Kate would just —"

"Oh, no." Kate backed away, distancing herself not from the argument, but from any criticism Chandra might level. "Don't you blame me, Sandy."

Oh yeah, she emphasized the name. Just to twist the knife a little.

"Stop right now." Luella stomped one sneaker-clad foot. "We've come too far to backslide," she said. "And maybe the three of you don't care, but I'll tell you what; I sure do. Lord knows how much longer we're going to be stuck here together, but I'm certainly not going to spend my time with the bunch of you going at each other. We've got to get back to the way things were. You know, when we were all working together.

When we were friends."

Were we?

Friends?

Right about then, I was too angry to debate her use of the word.

My guess was that Kate and Chandra were, too. They were both breathing hard, their jaws as stiff as mine.

I forced my muscles to relax, but I couldn't keep myself from sticking out my chin when, like the naughty toddler Luella had accused me of impersonating, I asked, "What are you going to do about it?"

Luella's slim shoulder shot back. "Do about it? I'm going to . . . I'm going to . . ." She glanced around the room and her gaze landed on my library copy of *Murder on the Orient Express,* still on the countertop where I'd tossed it. "I'll tell you what I'm going to do. I was just reading an old newspaper article about some group on the mainland that puts on mystery parties. You know, for fun. I'm going to go in there right now . . ." She stabbed one finger toward the dining room. "And I'm going to tell your guests that tonight, you three are hosting a murder mystery dinner."

"But —" I shouldn't have bothered trying to object. Luella was already on her way out of the room, and if there was one thing I knew about Luella, it was that she was as tough and unforgiving as the lake waters she navigated so expertly. "But it's already noon, and you're not giving us much time."

"Noon. Yeah." I was surprised the look Luella shot at the clock didn't stop its hands. "Then you three better get crackin'."

16

"This is good. Really good." Luella looked up from the dashed-off-at-the-speed-of-light-and-off-the-top-of-my-head script I'd handed her. "You should be a writer."

"No." I shooed the thought away with the wave of one hand and what I hoped was a convincing smile. "That's one thing I know for sure I don't want to be."

"But, isn't it good?" Luella looked to Kate and Chandra to support her position. Since Kate was staring at the pages in front of her, chewing her lower lip, and Chandra stood near the kitchen door with her back to us and her arms folded over her chest, I was pretty sure they weren't in the mood for Luella's not-so-subtle attempt at stirring up some kind of literary camaraderie.

Then again, I wasn't sure I was, either.

Frosty.

I guess that's the best way to describe the mood in the kitchen that late afternoon. I hadn't left the house all day, and something told me it was probably colder in there than it was outside. Just the way it had been since right before lunch.

Truth is, I wasn't exactly feeling warm and fuzzy, either. Not that I held a grudge or anything. I'd gotten rid of most of my anger at having it out with Kate and Chandra earlier with an hour of frantic writing at the computer.

But that didn't mean I was ready to forgive or to forget.

In fact, I'd only gone along with Luella's crazy idea about a murder mystery dinner as a way to thank her for all the help she'd provided over the last days. It wasn't Luella's fault that the two most difficult neighbors in the world just so happened to be stuck in the house — and the book discussion group — with us.

"I guess it's okay." A copy of the script was on the table in front of Kate, and with thumb and index finger, she nudged it aside, convinced — I was sure — that keeping it too close would be nonverbal confirmation of the fact that I was not as big a nuisance to the neighborhood as she'd always said.

Fine by me.

I was a nuisance?

Well, she was a stick-in-the-mud. And a self-important snob, to boot.

She was also, as it turned out, willing to give credit where credit was due. Even when it was obviously painful. Until that moment — until I watched Kate's spine stiffen and the muscles in her shoulders tighten so much, just seeing them made mine ache — I don't think I'd ever completely understood all the nuances of the word *begrudging*.

Kate made them roaringly clear. "You've taken the entire story of *Murder on the Orient Express* and distilled it down to its essence." Was this a compliment I heard forming on her lips? I braced myself, wondering, if that were the case, if I could be gracious.

"It's just enough to get people interested," Kate went on, her voice thawing just a tad. "Just enough to get them involved. But not so much that it's going to drag out forever and everybody's going to end up bored."

Okay, so not exactly a compliment. Not an effusive one, anyway. And not exactly groveling, either.

I took what I could get. This was as close to an apology as a woman like Kate was ever likely to give.

Or maybe not.

The next second, she sat up as if she'd touched an electrical line and a smile eased the obstinate set of her chin. "Hey!" She turned in her chair to look at me. "What if we did mystery dinners at the winery this summer? The tourists would love it, and we could do it in conjunction with wine tastings. With you writing the scripts —"

I didn't know of any other way to say *no* than just to say it, even if it meant getting on her bad side — again. I never had a chance. Chandra, who was apparently not the fastest reader in the world, had just gotten to what I knew would be the most significant aspect of the script, at least for her.

"Bea!" When she spun around, her eyes were bright with what I was afraid were tears of thanks. "After all those terrible things I said. You still . . ." She cleared her throat, and when she spoke, her accent was as heavy as that fat lady who's said to end the opera. "It is I! I who am playing the great Hercule Poirot!"

"But of course." I slipped into the accent without even thinking, gave myself a mental slap, and dropped it pronto. "I knew you'd want to be Poirot," I told Chandra. Then, because I couldn't stand the fact that it looked like she was about to cry, I turned to Luella.

"And it only makes sense that you're playing Mrs. Hubbard," I told her. "She was a dear friend of the mother of the murder victim, and she's the lynchpin of the piece."

"And me?" Kate did another quick read through. "I'm the countess and the count is . . ." Her mouth thinned, but her cheeks flushed. "Jayce? Really? He's not exactly the count type."

"Why not? Because he's not good enough for you?" Chandra stepped forward, but I placed one hand on her arm and gently urged her to stay put.

I could be sweet when I wanted to be (which wasn't often), so I pasted on a smile. "Come on, Kate," I said. "Think of poor Jayce. Because that's what I was thinking when I gave him the part. His business has really suffered with the ferry being shut down. He's been cooped up here, and every time I see him, he's either got his nose buried in some fishing magazine or he's staring at you. Cut the guy some slack. Besides . . ." I had more pages waiting on the computer printer and I went and got them. "Maybe if you two actually got to know each other, you'd decide Jayce isn't so bad after all."

"He's a mighty fine man." This from Luella. "Reminds me of his father. Good man, Daniel Martin, honest and hard working. Good family man, too. You could do worse, Kate. Much worse."

"And that Jayce . . ." Chandra jiggled her shoulders. "He's cute, too!"

"All right, already!" Kate surrendered so quickly, I couldn't help but wonder if this was the opportunity she'd been waiting for, an excuse to be thrown together (figuratively speaking, of course) with the strapping ferryboat captain. "Stop with the matchmaking." I was more convinced than ever that she was keeping her real feelings for Jayce buried when she tapped the pages of the script into a too-neat pile and set them down precisely in front of her. "It's not going to work, but that doesn't mean I can't get along with the man. I'll play the countess to his count."

"That's all we ask." I gave three more sheets of paper to each of the ladies. "I found roles for every one of our guests. We'll hand out the roles as they come down to dinner. I've tried to keep everything nice and simple, just what they're supposed to say when Poirot interviews them."

"Meg is playing the cook. Brilliant!" Looking over her pages, Luella laughed. "And Hank is the bodyguard, a retired policeman. And Princess Dragomiroff —"

"Let me guess!" Chandra edged up behind

Luella so she could read over her shoulder and squealed with laughter when she saw her hunch was right. "Think she'll get it?" she asked. "When we tell Mariah she's playing the part of the Russian princess, do you think she'll get it?"

"I'm not trying to be mean," I assured them. "And I'm certainly not poking fun at Mariah. I just figured she's got the right wardrobe. Everybody else's parts are pretty self-explanatory."

"Oh look, Levi's playing the victim's secretary. And Bea is the Swedish nurse." Chandra's wink was over-exaggerated. "Think they'll have a scene together?"

I ignored this comment because, let's face it, Levi and I had already had a few scenes together, and none of them were what I'd call well written. Precisely why I'd made sure to cast us in roles that absolutely, positively did not interact.

"Next . . ." The printer spit out another round of pages, and I handed them around. "Props," I explained. "We'll need to get it all collected before everyone comes down to dinner. Nothing should be hard to find."

"Blanket, coat, wineglasses, matchbook," Chandra read under her breath. "Most of it should be easy enough. Do you care where we get it?"

"*Mi casa es su casa!* Except if you're going to use something that belongs to one of our guests. Then you should probably ask first." I checked the clock. "We've got thirty minutes until dinner hits the table. As the guests come down, give them their roles and make sure they stick to the script or this could go on forever."

"So no ad-libbing." Kate nodded her understanding and stood.

"Like I said, short and sweet. I've pretty much limited everyone's role to things like saying they didn't know Ratchett, the victim. Or they had no motive for killing him," I said.

"Maybe unlike one of our dinner guests." Leave it to Luella to be the thoughtful one.

I crossed a finger over my heart. "I'm not thinking we can use this little play to somehow expose Peter's killer," I said. "Honest."

"But it would be terrific." Kate gathered her papers. "If we play our cards right —"

"I'm no Shakespeare and this isn't Hamlet. What murderer in his right mind is just going to confess just because of some silly play?"

I was right and they knew it. I mean, that's the only possible reason no one argued with me, right? One by one, they filed out of the kitchen to get busy.

"Good work." When she went by, Luella patted me on the back.

"Thanks." I collected the pages of my own script and the list of props I needed to collect. "But you already said that. You said you liked my little play."

"I did." Chandra and Kate had gone out into the hallway, and from the kitchen, we heard them talking and laughing. "But this time," Luella grinned, "I wasn't talking about the script."

Dinner was a tad late being served.

Who would have imagined it!

No sooner had my guests come down and Kate and Chandra began passing out their parts for our version of the classic mystery, than a hum of excitement started up. Blame it on cabin fever and the weather that had us stuck inside together all these days. My guests (well, except for Levi, who stayed in the parlor until the very last minute; little Isabelle, who wasn't feeling well; and Amanda, who refused to come down on the grounds that she didn't want to face Ted) were actually eager to assume their roles in our little production and insisted on returning to their rooms to cobble together costumes.

As we'd predicted, Mariah was all about playing Princess Dragomiroff. She disappeared upstairs and when she came down again, she was wearing a shimmering purple caftan and a dozen gold bracelets. Ted didn't have to stretch too much to play Foscarelli, the car salesman. When he walked into the dining room in a plaid sportcoat that was probably as old as me, I had a feeling he'd brought it along to the island just in case he happened upon a special occasion. In spite of Kate's protestations, she and Jayce must have actually put their heads together long enough to coordinate their outfits. Kate trudged home to grab an elegant black suit and wore it with a cream-colored cami and a string of pearls, and Jayce slicked back his hair and wore a black sweater tied artfully over his shoulders. He looked so darned Continental, it took me a minute to notice that the sweater was mine.

When he finally did make an appearance, Levi . . .

I'd given him the role of Hector MacQueen, the victim's secretary, and maybe he knew the book and knew that Hector was one of Poirot's chief suspects from the start.

Maybe that explained why he sat at the farthest end of the table from where I took a seat and didn't look my way the entire evening.

Ask me if I cared.

Go on, ask.

Because I didn't. So there. As far as I could tell, Levi Kozlov and I had nothing in common, nothing we needed to say to each other, and nothing else to talk about. Unless we were talking about what he wasn't talking about when we were talking about Peter's murder.

So why should I possibly care?

While those thoughts played through my head, I listened to the excited burr of conversation around the table, and when the dishes were cleared (we were really scraping the bottom when it came to groceries, so it was turkey sandwiches and potato chips that night), we got down to the business of having a little fun.

"Ladies and gentlemen!" I stood. For my role as Greta Ohlsson, the Swedish missionary, I'd chosen a black skirt and the only white blouse in my closet. Unfortunately, it had short sleeves and an un-missionary-like V-neck, but I'd topped it off with a brown jacket. My hair was in a bun. My glasses were right where they belonged, on the tip of my nose. Oh yeah, I looked plenty prudish, and just a little frumpy, too.

Maybe that's why Levi wasn't giving me the time of day.

Ask me if I cared.

"Before we get started, I thought I should give you a little background about the book we've based our little dinner mystery on," I said. Yeah, bad grammar. No one batted an eye. They were all sitting on the edges of their seats, eyes turned toward me and bright with excitement. Well, except for —

Never mind.

"Because we didn't want to take up too much of your time, we cut down the original story considerably. In fact, we're going to skip the beginning altogether. What you need to know at this point is that the body of Samuel Ratchett has been found in his compartment on the Orient Express. The train is stranded because of a snowstorm." My audience appreciated this as only people stranded in a snowstorm could and a smattering of applause went up. I waited until it died down before I said, "That means the murderer is still on the train. What that murderer didn't count on, though . . ." Call me a geek, I drew out the suspense, just a little. What the heck, if you're going for fun, you might as go all the way. "Is that there's a famous Belgian detective on board. Ladies and gentlemen, I give you Hercule Poirot!"

That was Chandra's cue and she worked it like a pro, stepping out from the hallway and into the dining room just as I'd instructed her. Never one to shrink from the limelight, she struck a pose, one arm tossed in the air, one finger pointed to the ceiling. She'd found a raincoat somewhere and she wore it over dark pants and a shirt I was pretty sure didn't belong to her. But then, before she slipped on the raincoat, I saw the Put-in-Bay Police Department emblem on the sleeve.

"It is *moi*! Hercule Poirot. The famous detective." Sometime after she'd left the dinner table, Chandra had painted on a curling mustache, and now she stroked a finger along her upper lip. "I have come to . . . how you say . . . investigate. Yes, I have come to investigate this body you say you have found."

Because I didn't want to relegate any of our guests to the part of Ratchett, I figured the most delicate way to handle the problem of a dead body was just to hint at it. Chandra stepped into the hallway, peeked around the partially closed parlor door, then jumped back, her mouth open in horror.

"Mon Dieu!" she cried. Only it came out sounding more like, *"Mon Die-ee-you."*

"It is Ratchett, and he has been stabbed

many times. Quick, Pierre Michel." I'd given the part of the train conductor to Meg's little daughter, Mila, and beaming, she stepped up right when she was supposed to. "Give to me the blanket so that I can cover up this horrible sight."

Mila did just as instructed, and I saw that when Kate and Chandra had gone out to collect props, they'd picked up Levi's bedroll to use as a blanket.

Our Poirot untied the bedroll, flapped it open and declared, "Voila!"

Voila, indeed.

Chandra couldn't see it from where she stood, but the rest of us in the dining room did, and a collective gasp went up.

But then, it was the only natural response, considering that when Chandra fluffed Levi's bedroll open, a diamond tennis bracelet fell out of it and landed on the floor.

17

Remember what I said about Levi and me and the scenes we'd already played out together? Poorly plotted, average dialogue, and when it came to suspense (not to mention a satisfying denouement), they pretty much fizzled.

Well, the next morning, I found myself smack in the middle of another one, only this time, it was straight out of a noir crime novel.

Me, not so bundled since it was early and the temperature was already nudging into the forties, walking into the Put-in-Bay police station, thermal coffee mug in one hand and my heart in my throat. No shrinking violet, I, but I fully expected that the moment he saw me, Levi would tell me to mind my own business. And get the hell out of his life while I was at it.

At the front desk, Hank didn't bother to check to see what was inside the coffee mug.

But then, I don't suppose I look like the type who'd try to smuggle in a file. Or a weapon. It was the dark curls. And the way my eyes looked so big behind the clear lenses of my Coke-bottle glasses.

Besides, Hank was no fool. Word on the street was that the ferry wouldn't be running again until the next day. Even if I were crazy enough to try and help Levi break out of jail, there was no place he could run. Even if I believed passionately in his innocence and knew this was the only way for him to gain his freedom, there was no place for him to hide.

Just for the record, I'm not crazy.

And I wasn't sure I believed Levi was innocent.

I had never actually seen a jail cell before, but I have to say, after years of watching *Law & Order,* this one was pretty much what I expected. Basic. Spartan. Gray and depressing.

When the door that led down the corridor to the town's three cells clunked closed behind me, Levi glanced up from where he was sitting on a built-into-the-wall cot with a too-thin mattress.

"Hey." Okay, so it wasn't sparkling conversation, but it's not exactly easy to think of repartee at a time like this. Grateful I'd brought the tall, skinny one instead of the short, roly-poly one, I poked the thermal mug through the bars. "I brought you coffee."

Levi eyed the cup as if it were an alien that had just stepped out of the mother ship. Or maybe it was me he wasn't sure about.

He scraped a hand through his hair and got up to accept the offering. "Thanks." He sipped carefully and, finding the coffee wasn't too hot, took a long drink. "Hank brought me some earlier, but it wasn't nearly this good."

"French roast."

"Yeah."

I shifted from one boot-clad foot to the other. "Have you called a lawyer?"

Levi took another drink before he answered. "I honestly haven't had time to think about it. After what happened at dinner last night . . ."

Yeah, dinner last night.

Like a video on fast-forward, the incident played through my head, and once again, I saw that bracelet spill out of Levi's bedroll and onto the floor. The diamonds caught the light of the chandelier over the dining room table and threw it back at us in a rainbow palette that winked and twinkled and blinded us so that, for a few, stupefied seconds, we all simply stared as if we'd been hypnotized.

And then the room erupted.

A couple people jumped out of their chairs. A few wondered out loud if this was somehow part of the play and what diamonds had to do with *Murder on the Orient Express.* Through the sudden, deafening rush of blood in my ears, I heard voices overlap.

"What on earth is that?"

"Are those diamonds?"

"Why would Levi be hiding a diamond bracelet in his sleeping bag?"

A few people around the table didn't say anything at all. They just sat there with their mouths hanging open. I was, I admit, one of them.

Through it all, Levi was stone-faced and silent.

Hank, not so much. After all, Hank might have questionable ethics when it came to what he did with his ex, but he was a good cop through and through. He clearly remembered the story he'd told us in Peter's apartment just a couple days earlier. Yeah, that one. The one about Chuck Anderson and how Hank had always suspected him in connection with the theft of a tennis bracelet covered with a couple carats of small diamonds.

A couple carats of small diamonds that flashed up at us from my dining room floor.

Talk about ending a scene on a cliffhanger. Before any of us regained our composure, Levi was being led out to Hank's cruiser, stone-faced and silent.

He still was.

He shook his head. "I don't have an attorney. Not one who handles criminal cases."

"The court will appoint —"

"Yeah, I know all that. I guess I just need some time to think about it."

"They questioned you?"

Levi's look was so sharp, I thought this might be the *get the hell out of my life* moment I'd been waiting for. I held my breath and watched him curl one hand around the coffee mug.

"Hank tells me that bracelet was stolen," he said.

"Yeah, I know. The man who stole it was wanted for questioning in connection with a number of burglaries on the island. He used to live in the apartment above the Orient Express and we think . . ." I bit off the words. This wasn't the time — or the place — to look like a fool. "Hank thinks that the jewelry and the murder might be connected."

Levi nodded. "That explains a lot, I suppose."

"But you can't be Chuck Anderson." It wasn't like I'd ever seen this Anderson character, but I studied Levi, anyway. There were smudges of sleeplessness under his eyes and a curl of honey-colored hair stuck up at a funny angle over his right ear. I resisted the urge to reach through the bars and smooth it down.

"If you were Chuck Anderson, Hank would have recognized you right away. Chuck ran the bait and tackle shop where the Orient Express is now."

"Hank asked me about him."

"And you told him?"

Levi finished his coffee and handed the cup back to me. "I told him the truth. I have no idea who he's talking about. I don't know anyone named Chuck Anderson."

"But you had the bracelet Chuck Anderson stole."

He pulled in a long breath. Unlike my other guests, Levi had done nothing in the way of assembling a costume for the murder mystery dinner. Even though he was playing the role of Hector MacQueen, a man I pictured in an understated suit and carefully arranged tie, Levi was wearing jeans along with a green flannel that was open over a black T-shirt. The vivid color of his shirt was a stark contrast to his pale face.

"I can only tell you what I told Hank," he said. "I don't know how the bracelet got in my bedroll."

I wanted to believe him. But then, I bet Hank did, too. Innocent until proven guilty. That is what our entire legal system is based on, right? If I could keep that in mind, maybe my stomach would stop jumping like a Sea World porpoise. Then again, maybe it would never settle down until I got the answers to my questions.

"You were all set to leave the B and B yesterday morning."

Okay, not a question, but it didn't hurt to line up the facts.

Levi's gaze snapped to mine. "And you think that's because I wanted to get out with the bracelet."

"I didn't say that."

"It's what you were thinking."

"It doesn't matter what I think. But you know it's what Hank thinks."

"Then he's wrong."

"Then why were you leaving?"

"I told you. I wanted to check on the bar."

"And get the bracelet out of the house."

With one hand, he slapped the bars. "If that's what you think, why did you bother to come here?"

Turnabout is fair play. Or at least that's what they say, though who they are and why they think they should have the last word in things like this is beyond me. What I did know was that if I expected answers to my questions, it was only fair to meet Levi halfway.

Then again, I'm not sure shrugging counts as an answer.

"I couldn't stand the thought that you'd spent the night in jail," I admitted, because that much was true, and the only thing I was sure of when it came to Levi. "It couldn't have been comfortable."

"You coming here didn't make it any more or less comfortable. Still, you came."

"I wanted some answers." I stepped back and eyed him. "I'll admit that. I want to understand what's going on. Maybe . . ." I turned this thought over in my head, the better to try to see it from all angles. "Maybe I'm not willing to let the system take over and just tell me what happened. Maybe I need to prove it all for myself. All I can think about right now is that you were all set to walk out my door, and that Hank is the one who came into the kitchen and told you to stay put."

The briefest of smiles flickered over Levi's lips. "Hank has reminded me of that. More than a few times. What he hasn't come right out and done — not yet, anyway — is connected the dots. I guess it's up to us to do that, Bea, so let's just lay it on the line. Hank thinks the fact that I had that bracelet means I had something to do with Peter Chan's murder."

Yes, of course, I knew that was exactly what Hank was thinking. I just never expected that hearing the terrible thought put into words would have such an impact. It hit somewhere between my heart and my stomach, and I grabbed onto one of the bars of the cell and held on tight. All along, I'd wondered if one of my guests was connected with Peter's murder. I just never thought . . .

Hyperventilating did little for the cool, calm image I was hoping to project. When the next breath rushed into my lungs, I clamped my lips shut and forced it to stay there. One heartbeat. Two. I told myself to get a grip. Panic would only make Levi feel worse. And it wouldn't get me the answers I was looking for.

I forced a composure I didn't feel. "Well, Hank will think whatever Hank is going to think. But he's going to have to prove his theory. You might have had the bracelet, but at least you don't have a motive for killing Peter."

"Well, about that . . ." Levi turned to pace the confines of the cell, and automatically, I found myself leaning forward, hoping for a glimpse of his face. I wanted to know what he was thinking. I wanted to look into his eyes. I didn't get a chance until he came back to face me, and when he did, my stomach went cold even before he said, "I did have a reason to want Peter Chan dead."

Lucky for me, there was a chair nearby, because when I dragged it in front of the cell and flopped into it, my legs were rubber. "Why?"

Levi scrubbed his hands over his face. "I suppose you'll find out eventually, anyway. So will the police if they don't know already. It happened back in Cleveland twelve years ago."

"Anastasia Golubski?"

The name rushed out of me, and like a cattle prod, it hit Levi in the stomach. He flinched and wrapped both hands around the bars. "You know?"

"I know . . ." There was so much to tell, and honestly, I didn't know what might help and what might be off-limits, especially considering that I didn't know if I could believe anything Levi said. I stuck to the facts and hoped for the best. "She died after eating at Peter's restaurant. Her family filed a civil suit, but —"

"It was a shaky case from the start." Levi's voice was husky. "She was an old woman and the fish wasn't as fresh as it should have been. Anyone else would have felt icky for a couple days, then been fine. But she had a compromised immune system. Every time we tried to get the word out and tell the world what happened to her, we got shut down by Chan's team of lawyers. They said we were slandering him. They said we were putting his business at risk. A civil suit was our only course of action. We just thought the public needed to know."

"We." I didn't miss out on the single, all-important word.

"Anastasia was my grandmother."

I let the information sink in, but if I had any hopes of it making me feel better, they were dashed. The more I thought about it, the more guilty Levi looked.

"I didn't know Peter Chan was here on the island," he said, as if he were following my train of thought as it veered from one track to the next. "I moved up here last fall to get the building ready and get everything in line. He never showed up until a couple months ago. When I saw who'd opened the restaurant across the street from mine . . . well, I couldn't have been more surprised."

"That's not what the cops will think. They'll think you moved here to keep an eye on Peter."

"There's not much I can do about that. They're going to think what they're going to think. If they look at when I bought my building and when Chan opened his place . . . well, I guess that would tell them I was here first."

It was the only piece of good news I'd heard since I walked in, and a tiny one at that, but I was ridiculously comforted by it. Just so I didn't get carried away by the euphoria, I needed to know more. "Peter must have seen you around. He didn't know you?"

Levi shook his head. "Back when Gram died, I was just a college kid, and of course, my last name is different from hers. I knew he wouldn't recognize me. Besides, just from the times I saw Peter in court, I knew he was so full of himself, he never would have even remembered Gram. I'm sure he put her out of his mind the moment she was wheeled out of his restaurant by EMS."

"You never forgave him."

"Would you?"

My own grandmother is the doyen of lunching ladies in a small town along the Hudson River, a patroness of the arts, and charming enough to talk the birds down from the trees. That is, unless you cross her. Then she's so terrifying, she can drop a grown man at twenty paces with just one icy glare.

"I adore my grandmother," I admitted.

I hadn't realized I'd grabbed hold of the bars again until Levi's hand closed over mine. "Then you know how I feel."

I might, if the touch of his hand didn't have a crazy sort of effect on my brain that made it impossible for me to think about anything but how warm his skin felt against mine. The next second, I told myself to get a grip, slipped my fingers out from under his, and clutched my hands in my lap.

"That's why you told me you were busy last Monday night when you weren't. That's why you said you didn't see anything happening across the street. You wanted to stay as far away from the investigation as you possibly could. So Hank wouldn't find out that you knew Peter." Since he didn't argue with me, I knew I was right. That also meant . . .

I was afraid I swallowed a little too hard and that it sounded a little too much like relief when I said, "That's why you were leaving the B and B. You weren't leaving —"

"To get away from you?" For the first time since I'd arrived, Levi smiled. "First you thought Kate and I had a thing going, then you figured I couldn't wait to put some distance between you and me. What I said the other day, Bea, about how I thought you'd be a success at running the B and B, that was the truth. You're a good business-woman. But I'll tell you what, you're a lousy judge of people."

I wasn't sure what I was supposed to say, I only know that whatever it was, it wouldn't make its way past the sudden tightness in my throat.

Maybe Levi realized it, because he went right on. "Back at the B and B, there was a little too much talk about Peter's murder. A few too many questions. I thought if I steered clear —"

"Did you see something the night of the murder?"

The question brought Levi up short, and again, I braced myself. I'd all but come out and called him a liar, so if there was ever a *get the hell out of here* moment, this was probably it. I guess that's why when he said, "I saw someone leave the restaurant," I replied with a intelligent and levelheaded, "Huh?"

"I saw someone leave the restaurant."

"And you never bothered to mention that to the cops?" I was already out of my chair before I realized this sounded way too confrontational, but by then, it was too late. "If you saw the murderer —"

"I saw someone. And I couldn't describe that someone if you paid me. It was snowing hard, remember. And visibility was lousy, even from just across the street. At one point in the evening, I looked over there and I saw Peter leave the building. He was carrying a couple big shopping bags, like he was making a delivery. A few minutes later, I saw him come back with what looked like the same shopping bags."

"That's odd."

Apparently, Levi didn't think so. But then, he was in the food service business, too. He'd probably seen all sorts of variations on the same theme and he explained it away with a, "It happens. You get to the place where you're making a delivery and the person doesn't have the money to pay for it. Or they tell you you brought the wrong stuff. Or —"

"Or someone wanted to get Peter out of the restaurant. Because that same someone wanted to get into the apartment upstairs and get the jewelry."

Levi's brows dipped low over his eyes. "You think —"

"It's a possibility. More than a possibility. Someone wanted him gone, but maybe he didn't stay gone long enough. Then when he came back —"

"I didn't see anyone walk in there while Chan was gone, but then, I really did have a couple customers." The steady way he looked at me when he said this dared me to challenge him. "Then, a while later, I was behind the bar and I happened to notice someone walking out. Like I said," he added before I could jump in with the same ol' questions, "I couldn't tell who it was. I couldn't say if it was a man or a woman. All I saw was a figure. Bundled. You know, like the person was wearing a heavy coat. And one of those colorful knit hats. You know, the kind with the earflaps. That person walked out of the restaurant right before you and your friends arrived."

I plunked back in the chair. "You saw the murderer?"

"I saw someone." Levi emphasized that last word.

"And you didn't bother mentioning this to the cops?"

Was my voice really that sharp and accusatory? Apparently, because Levi shot me a look that said he wasn't wounded, just disappointed. "As a matter of fact, I told Hank about it last night," he said.

"But before that —"

"What difference would it have made?" His question bounced off the institutional gray walls. "I couldn't describe the person, so that wasn't going to help. And it's not like the cops needed to know there had been a murderer in the restaurant. They already knew that because they had Chan's body. So maybe I should have said something. I just didn't want to get too close to the situation."

"It's a little late for that now. Now you're plenty close."

"Yeah." He sat back down on the little bunk, his head in his hands.

Close, huh?

It may have been what we were talking about, but right about then, I'd never felt further from anyone in all my life.

18

"Well, if you ask me, he couldn't have done it." Chandra's chin jutted at a stubborn angle. "That Levi is far too cute to be a murderer."

I'd been looking over the bills I was making out for my guests, and I glanced up at her over the rims of my glasses. "I'm thinking the court isn't going to take that into consideration."

"But he is cute. You do finally admit that?" Kate sidled by. With all the excitement at dinner the night before, we hadn't had a chance to clean up, and slowly, the props were being returned to their owners. Well, except for Levi's bedroll. That had been confiscated by the police.

Kate put a wineglass in the dishwasher and a matchbook that we'd never had a chance to use as a clue back up in the cupboard where it belonged. For now, Luella was up in Suite #6 taking care of little Isabelle while Meg went home to check on the house and pick up some pediatric fever reducer.

"Cute has nothing to do with any of this," I reminded Kate and Chandra. "The facts do. And the facts —"

"Is he gone?" Amanda peeked around the kitchen door and, seeing that the coast was clear, walked into the room. "Ted isn't around, is he? I thought I heard him go out."

"You can't hide from him forever." She looked so relieved, I'm pretty sure she didn't care about this, and I guess that's why I took pity on Amanda and told her, "Ted said he'd be gone at least a couple of hours."

Amanda's bottom lip puckered. "I just don't know what I'm going to say to him when I see him. How I'm going to explain."

"Well, explain is something you're going to have to do." Hank strode into the room just in time to join in the conversation. "The fact that your ex-husband forged your name on the lease papers for the restaurant, that's something you're going to have to discuss with the county prosecutor over on the mainland. It may be relevant to our murder case."

She didn't look enthusiastic about it, but Amanda nodded. Right before she stuck her head in the refrigerator to root around for something to eat.

"That's the whole thing, isn't it?" I asked everyone, and no one in particular. "What's relevant, what isn't. It's all so confusing. All these little bits and pieces, and none of them seem to lead anywhere."

"Or they lead somewhere you don't want to go," Hank suggested.

Did everyone on the island think I had some burning love for Levi Kozlov? It was ridiculous. I hardly knew him, and what I did know, I wasn't even sure I liked. Apparently, I was going to have to take out an ad in the local newspaper, disavowing myself of the man — and the crazy tingling sensations he conjured up as if by magic.

I gave Hank a level look just so he'd know he was barking up the wrong romantic tree. "I'm not ducking the truth," I told him. "I'm just saying —"

"That Levi's too cute to be a murderer," Chandra piped in.

I sighed. "That all the pieces just don't line up. Levi says he never knew anyone named Chuck Anderson. So if Chuck really did steal the bracelet and hide it in the apartment, how could Levi have known it was there?"

"Well . . ." Hank scratched his chin.

"Maybe Levi's not telling the truth. Or maybe he has some other connection. I asked him about it, of course, and he denied it, just like he denied knowing Chuck. But I'm thinking that maybe Levi knew a guy by the name of Wally Rowe."

Her eyes wide and her mouth hanging open, Amanda whirled away from the fridge and promptly dropped what she'd gathered into her arms. A glass jar of pickles hit the ceramic tile and shattered. A plastic jar of mayo rolled my way. A package of American cheese hit the floor with a *thwack.*

"Wally?" Amanda's breaths came hard and fast. "How do you . . . What do you know about Wally?"

After the initial moment of shock, we all sprang into action. Kate picked up shards of glass. Chandra got paper towels and sopped up pickles and brine. The mayo jar wheeled to a stop at my feet and I grabbed it.

Hank . . .

His head cocked, Hank eyed Amanda just long enough to make her nervous, and once he was sure he had, he stooped, picked up the cheese, and set it on the nearest counter.

"What do you know about Wally Rowe?"

Hank echoed Amanda's question, and that was all it took. Her expression dissolved from surprise to *oh boy, I stepped in that one,* and, hoping to hide it, she stared at her shoes.

Silent, his expression blank, Hank crossed his arms over his chest and waited. Long enough for Chandra and Kate to finish the cleanup. Longer. Until the atmosphere around us felt as it were a rubber band being pulled tight. Tighter.

It snapped when Amanda said, "Wally . . . Wally used to work for Peter. At the restaurant Peter owned in Toledo. The place he ran last year."

"Really?" Thinking this over, Hank narrowed his eyes. "Well, a few years ago, Wally lived up here, and when he did, he was a known associate of a guy named Chuck Anderson."

I listened to all this along with the *kerchunk* of the pieces falling into place inside my head. "That means if Wally knew Chuck and Wally knew that Chuck stole that jewelry, Wally might have said something to Peter, right? And if he mentioned it to Peter —" I sucked in a breath as the fog lifted.

Her already pale face suddenly ashen, Amanda burst into tears and her voice bumped over the story. "One night back at the restaurant, I was helping to clean up, and Wally and Peter were having a couple

307

drinks. I heard Wally . . . I heard him tell Peter that he knew about buried treasure. It sounded crazy." Amanda's laugh was filled with nervousness, not amusement. "I mean, really, who talks about stuff like that, right? And later, I asked Peter about it, and Peter, he told me I was nuts, that I'd heard Wally all wrong. I knew he was lying. But then, that was something Peter was really good at."

I slapped a hand against the table. "Then I was right. About the apartment!" I sat back and, yes, I looked right at Kate. There's no time like a murder investigation for a little one-upsmanship. "Peter wasn't remodeling. He was searching. He was tearing apart the apartment to find the jewelry. But if Wally knew it was there —"

Amanda shook her head. "He knew there was jewelry. He didn't know where it was."

She didn't need us to ask what I was sure both Hank and I were about to ask; Amanda went right on. "If he knew where to find the jewelry, Wally would have come for it. And if Peter knew where it was . . . I'll tell you what, he wouldn't have wasted a single minute, the low-down, no-good scumbag. He would have been up here on the island and in that apartment in a heartbeat."

"But he waited." This really wasn't as big

a mystery as it seemed, and after I had another moment to consider it, I knew why. "Wally knew the jewelry was hidden, but not where, and he told Peter the story. Like you said, Peter would never let something like that alone. So he did some digging. It couldn't have been any big stretch for Peter to find out Wally used to live up here. Or that Wally knew Chuck."

Hank confirmed this. "That was mentioned in the local papers because once, we charged Chuck and Wally as accomplices in a robbery." His face twisted. "Had to drop the charges when we couldn't get enough evidence."

"So that's it!" I rubbed my hands together. "Peter did some research. He found out Wally and Chuck were connected, and of course, once he knew that, he would have known Chuck ran the bait and tackle. And that he lived upstairs. I'd bet anything that's why Peter came to the island, and why he opened the Orient Express."

Amanda's voice was sour. "Well, that would certainly explain it. Peter always thought of himself as some big city restaurateur. When I heard he came up here, I thought it was fishy. Then I remembered the story about the jewelry."

I made sure I caught Amanda's eye before

I said, "So that's why you showed up here, too."

She hung her head. "To look for the jewelry. Okay, I admit it. Once I heard Peter was here, I figured out what he was up to. I thought maybe I'd come have a look. Then when I found out how that no-good lowlife signed my name to the lease . . . well, it just made me madder than ever. I wanted to scare him. But I'm telling you . . ." She looked up at Hank, her eyes pleading. "I didn't kill Peter."

"But you did go out the night of the murder." Oh yes, I said this as if it were common knowledge, but it surprised Amanda, all right. Just in case she was going to deny what I knew to be true, I reminded her, "That night when you came down for tea, you were wearing your boots. They left a wet spot on the carpet."

"That doesn't mean anything," she insisted, even though she knew it did, and caved instantly. "All right, I did go out. I was going to leave another note for Peter. I thought maybe I'd sneak into the kitchen while he was up front with a customer. I figured that would really scare him, you know, walking back into the kitchen and realizing somebody had been there, somebody who didn't like him. I waited across the street in front of that empty store, the one that's for lease, and I watched for a while. I didn't see Peter behind the counter so I figured he was in the kitchen, and so I waited some more. I never did see Peter, but I saw . . ."

She glanced up at Hank, then looked away again, unsure of how he'd take this piece of news that she'd never bothered to share with the police. "I saw somebody leave. Somebody big, all bundled up in a coat. And wearing one of those bright knit hats. You know, the kind with the earflaps."

It was exactly what Levi told had me, and what I knew he'd told Hank when he was questioned at the station.

Hank and I exchanged glances. We didn't have to say a word because we both knew what the other was thinking: Amanda couldn't have known what Levi told us. It looked like Amanda was telling the truth.

"The person you saw . . ." I stared at her in an effort to get her to concentrate. "Could it have been Ted?"

She wrinkled her nose. "It could have been. Maybe. I guess. But . . . I dunno." She gave up with a frustrated sigh.

"And when you went back the other day to try and break into the restaurant, you were there to look for the jewelry?" Amanda didn't really need to confirm; I knew it was true even before I asked, and she nodded in response.

"And Wally?" Hank asked. "Could he be the one who showed up here last week? The guy you saw walking out of the restaurant that night?" He didn't add *and who killed Peter while he was at it,* but Amanda dismissed the idea instantly, anyway.

"Wally's dead," she said. "He has been for nearly a year. One night when he was leaving the restaurant, he stepped out in front of a bus."

"So Peter thought he was the only one who knew the secret." I thought this over. "Which means he probably wouldn't have shared it with anyone. That still doesn't explain how Levi ended up with the bracelet."

"Or what happened to the other stuff Chuck Anderson swiped." Hank shook his head. "I've had my guys go over that apartment with the fine-tooth comb. If the rest of that jewelry was ever there, it sure isn't there now. And it's not in Levi's things, or back at his bar. Believe me, we know. We looked there, too."

"So maybe Levi was telling the truth when he said he had no idea how the bracelet ended up in his bedroll." This was nothing more than a simple statement of fact, so it shouldn't have earned me three pointed looks from three different directions.

"What?" I threw my hands in the air. "I'm just trying to look at this thing from as many angles as possible."

"Uh-huh." Kate nodded.

"You bet." Chandra grinned.

"If you're talking about what I think you're talking about, I want in on it." Luella sailed into the room with Mariah's sable coat over one arm. "Whether it's murder or our hunky bartender friend, I really don't care. Anything's better than cleaning up after a sick little girl."

"Actually . . ." Kate couldn't keep a straight face. "We were talking about Bea and Levi."

"We were talking about the murder," I corrected her. "And trying to stay sane and rational and see everything that's happened from every possible point of view."

"Well, here's another mystery for you." Luella set the coat on the chair in the corner. "While I was upstairs checking on Isabelle, I figured I might as well return the Princess's coat. You know, the one we took to use as a prop in the play last night. And guess what, ladies. Our Princess Drago-miroff is gone."

It isn't often that we can put a finger on the truly important moments in our lives. Days come and go. Incidents that seem ordinary turn out to have significance, and often, those events that seem earthshaking at the time turn out to be nothing in the long run but a big ho-hum.

But this moment, I recognized as momentous.

This was the moment when I realized I truly was an innkeeper, because I looked over at the accounts I'd been working on and wailed, "She can't be gone. She hasn't paid her bill!"

Kate gave me the thumbs-up, then laughed when she saw the look of horror on my face when I realized I was suddenly looking at the world through the same mercenary glasses she wore.

Kate patted my arm. "Sane and rational, remember, you're the one who said that, Bea. Our Princess probably just stepped out to the car or went for a walk. That's the sane and rational answer."

Sane and rational, yeah.

Which didn't jibe with Mariah going out for a walk without her coat.

It would be my last evening with guests packed into the house cheek by jowl.

The thought hit me sometime that Saturday afternoon, and honestly, I can't say whether I was happy, sad, or just plain relieved.

As of the next morning, the ferry would be up and running, and my guests would pack up and leave. Like on the Orient Express, the stranded travelers would settle their business and go their own ways.

Unlike the Orient Express, where Hercule Poirot used those brilliant little gray cells of his, we had no solution to our murder.

"Well, what did you expect?" I was outside and headed for the garage, grumbling to myself while I mushed through the calf-high slush that was all that was left of the piles of snow. "You think you're as bright as Poirot? Or as smart as Christie?" I didn't need to step in a puddle of mush and get a bootful of icy slop to wake up to the cold reality.

I told myself not to forget it and kept on with my mission. In honor of sunshine, blue skies, and the last night we'd spend together under one roof, I'd decided on a looking-forward-to-better-weather cookout, and I got to the garage and dragged out the propane grill that I bought with thoughts of warm summer nights dancing through my head. There were still some of the frozen burgers left that Levi had brought over, and now that the grocery store was open again for business, Kate and Chandra had gone for hot dogs, buns, and the makings for s'mores.

"If you can't make summer come to you, at least you can make it summery."

The sound of the voice behind me made me whirl around, and my heart bumped to a stop.

"Levi! You didn't —"

"Escape?" He laughed, though how he was able to after all he'd been through in the last twenty-four hours, I wasn't sure. "Scout's honor!" He held up one hand. "Hank says he's not sure what to charge me with, and there's nowhere for me to go, anyway, so I might as well spend the night at home. I thought I'd stop by" — he poked his thumb over his shoulder and toward the house — "and pick up my things. At least the stuff the police haven't collected as evidence."

"And tomorrow when the ferry's running?"

"Jayce Martin has strict orders. I am not to board the ferry. No matter what."

"Well, good. I mean about you not being in jail anymore." I was pretty sure this was true, so I don't know why I sounded like I couldn't make up my mind. I patted the vinyl cover on the grill. "We're having a cookout."

"I see that." Levi was wearing his peacoat open over that same green plaid shirt and black T-shirt I'd seen him in earlier that morning when I'd visited him at the police station. The bright sunshine emphasized the bags under his eyes, but I didn't have long to study them. He turned and headed toward the house. "I won't be long. I'll just get my stuff and get out of your way. I can understand that your guests would be uncomfortable having me here."

"Did Hank tell you? About what Amanda said?"

My question stopped him and he turned back around. "About the man she saw coming out of the Orient Express? Yeah, he mentioned it. I've never spoken to Amanda. You should know that. We didn't put our heads together and concoct the story."

"I didn't think you did."

"I can't tell what Hank thinks."

I tried for light and casual and hoped my smile proved it. "I'm pretty sure that's a cop thing. You know, cryptic and stone-faced."

He stuffed his hands in the pockets of his coat. "There's a lot of that going around."

"There are a lot of questions that we still

haven't answered."

"I get it." He backstepped away. "Like I said, until those questions are answered, I'll make myself scarce. I don't want anyone to be nervous or worried just because I'm hanging around."

He didn't have to put it into words. I knew that *anyone* included me.

I took a step forward. "I've been thinking . . ."

Levi stopped.

"About your bedroll," I explained. "And the bracelet. Your bedroll was in the parlor all day long. Anybody could have put that bracelet in it."

It wasn't my imagination, though it may have been a trick of the bright sunlight glancing off the last of the snow; I swear I saw some of the ice in his shoulders thaw, and the lines of stress in his face melt. "That's pretty much what I told Hank. Unfortunately, neither of us could figure out why someone would want to do that."

"To deflect suspicion away from himself — whoever that is — and onto you, I suppose." In the time since the realization had occurred to me, it was the only valid explanation I could come up with. "My guess is whoever did it, that person figured he'd have time to go back and get the bracelet. I mean, obviously. Unless he wanted you to have it."

"You mean as a kind of substitute for the legal settlement my family didn't get in Gram's death."

I twitched my shoulders. "It does sound kind of wacky, doesn't it? Like we've got some sort of Robin Hood killer on our hands. But that would mean someone knew who you were, and knew about your connection with Peter. That doesn't seem likely since it's something you've kept under wraps."

"Not anymore, since Hank knows." He took another step back.

"Stranger things have happened, I suppose."

"Yeah, stranger."

It was one of those awkward moments when you realize your conversation has run out of so much gas, you can't even figure out a way to put on the brakes and bring it to a stop.

Levi knew it as well as I did. Still facing me, his gaze fixed to my face, he moved toward the house. "So, I'm just going to —"

"Levi?" Oblivious to another soaking from an even bigger puddle than I'd stepped in the first time, and all too aware of the symbolism, I took two impetuous steps toward him. When he stopped to find out what I wanted, I found myself suddenly tongue-tied.

"I was just thinking." I wasn't the least bit cold, but I poked my hands in my pockets, too, my body language a mirror of his. "What I mean to say is, how about if you stay for dinner?"

19

By dinnertime that night, Mariah had still not returned to the B and B. I was worried, and not just about her unpaid bill. Hank had already left for home, and I called him there and told him what was troubling me. I didn't need to mention the condoms. Chandra had already told him about that.

And he'd already made up his mind about what Mariah was up to.

I wasn't convinced, and Hank took pity on me. He said he'd tell the officers on duty to be on the lookout for Mariah. Other than that, he claimed there wasn't much they could do. She was an adult, and except for skipping out on her bill, there was no reason for the cops to look for her.

The next morning, Sunday, my guests slowly drifted away. Ted said he wanted to be on the first ferry off the island and assured us that he'd left all his contact information with Hank. Amanda said exactly the same thing. Jayce had been up long before the sun, itching to get back on his ferry and back to the lake. And convinced that Isabelle would finally feel better once she was sleeping in her own bed, Meg had bundled up the girls and taken them home.

Levi, it should be noted, left the night before. In fact, he was gone as soon as he helped clean up the dishes. Frankly, I didn't blame him. For one thing, he got more than one nervous sidelong glance from my guests during dinner. For another, well, there was only so long a person could be comfortable sleeping on the floor, even if it is on an antique Oriental rug and in front of a fireplace.

Levi didn't thank me before he left, and for this, I was grateful. I wasn't looking for his gratitude, only for the truth. Since neither of us seemed to know how to find our way there, it seemed simpler just to say good night and wonder if it might also be good-bye.

None of this made me feel any more upbeat when Kate, Chandra, Luella, and I walked into Suite #4 to have a look around. I glanced from Mariah's tote bag, to her slinky black pants draped over the foot of the bed, to the red cashmere sweater that had been neatly folded and left on a chair.

"She left and didn't take anything with her. That's just strange. I don't understand why the cops don't think it's strange."

"Because she's an adult. And she can do whatever she wants to do," Kate reminded me.

"Yeah, but with a murderer on the island . . ." There was no use going over it all again, but honestly, I just couldn't help myself. I plunked down on the bed that was still neatly made from Saturday morning. "We need to go over the clues again," I said.

Kate had just come out of the bathroom after looking around in there. "So you don't think Levi did it?"

"Do you?" When she didn't answer, I moved on to Chandra and Luella. "Do any of you? Because I'll tell you what, I'm thinking someone set him up."

"But why?" Chandra poked through the dresser drawers and found nothing interesting. She gave up with a sigh. "Why would someone want to make Levi look guilty?"

Luella finished looking over the other side of the room. "To make themselves look innocent, of course," she said.

"Except there's no one who really looks guilty. And no one who really looked innocent," I grumbled. "It's all so darned frustrating. Let's look at the clues again."

"You mean like the frilly glove we found at the Orient Express?" Chandra asked.

"Or the pack of chewing tobacco the cops picked up there?" Kate put in.

"And the threatening notes from Amanda?" Luella asked.

"And don't forget the diamond bracelet," Chandra added.

This time, the sound that erupted from me was more screech than grumble. "See? It's just what I was saying. It's almost like there are too many clues."

"Like more than one person did it!" Chandra's mouth dropped open. "It's just like in the book. They all got together and —"

"Really?" Kate's sour smile told us she wasn't convinced. "Don't you think we're taking this whole *Murder on the Orient Express* thing too far? That sort of conspiracy might work in a book, but think about the logistics of it in real life. Ted would have had to work with Amanda, who would have had to plot with Mariah, who would have had to plan with Levi. And they all would have had to have motive."

"Well, Ted and Amanda and Levi did," I reminded them. "But if there was some bundled person who left the Orient Express the night of the murder, and if it was the killer, then that person had to have had a motive, too. That brings us right back to —"

"The jewelry," we all answered in unison.

"And Levi's bedroll on the floor of the parlor all day long," I reminded them before anybody could try and convince me he was suspect numero uno again. "I dunno . . ." I got up from the bed and walked out into the hallway, closing the door to the suite behind me. In spite of the fact that I was more than a little miffed about getting stiffed for the bill, I prayed nothing had happened to Mariah. But just in case it had and the police would need to look through her things, I locked the door. I didn't have another guest scheduled to come in for a couple weeks; I didn't need the room.

We started down the steps.

"It's the frilly glove and the chewing tobacco that have me confused," Luella said.

"It's like a man did it," Chandra commented.

"And like a woman did it," Kate added.

"And then to top it all off . . ." At the bottom of the stairs, I paused and looked back up to the second-floor landing. "Our Princess has vanished. She can't have gotten to the mainland. Not before this morning, anyway, and if she did that, Jayce would have seen her. It's like she just poofed off the island. Or like she worked some kind of magic and became someone else."

I had a lot to do to get the B and B back to pre-snowstorm shape, and I'd just taken a step toward the parlor with the thought of fluffing couch pillows, folding used afghans, and seeing how desperately and how soon I'd need my cleaning people in, when I pulled up short.

"She became someone else."

I repeated the words, and when all Chandra, Kate, and Luella did was look at me with blank expressions on their faces, I said them a little louder. "She became someone else. Our Princess Dragomiroff."

"Uh, okay." Chandra nodded. But then, I'm pretty sure that's how a person's supposed to respond when a mentally not-so-stable person starts carrying on. So that person — in this case a curly-haired woman who was jumping up and down and flapping her hands in front of her friends — doesn't go completely off the deep end.

They didn't get it.

Or maybe it was me who was so far off base she wasn't even in the realm of reality.

I tried again anyway.

"Dragomiroff," I said, pronouncing each syllable slowly and carefully. "It explains everything. The gorgeous clothes, the perfect makeup, the hair that was never mussed. Drag-o-mir-off."

Chandra caught on first, and I knew exactly when it happened because her cheeks shot through with color. "That explains why the bitch had better eyebrows than me!"

"You don't think . . ." Kate waited for me to jump in and tell her I was only kidding. "You do think. Chuck Anderson?"

"Chuck Anderson," I said, and because I knew they would stand there with their mouths hanging open and stare at me for the rest of the day, I grabbed Chandra's arm, threw open the front door, and raced to her van. "We've got to get to the ferry," I said. "Before Chuck gets away."

"So let me get this straight." Hank was wearing sunglasses, but I really didn't need to see his eyes. He was stationed on the dock, carefully watching the ferry plow through the waters and back to the island after its most recent trip to the mainland. "You're telling me that Mariah . . ." Even a cop can only keep a stony expression for so long. He screwed up his mouth and his cheeks puffed out. I can't imagine cops are squeamish about much. Except maybe something like this.

"You're telling me that beautiful woman was actually a man?"

"Dragomiroff. That's what gave me the clue." I don't know why I bothered to mention this, except that it was the truth, even if it obviously didn't mean much to Hank. "The pieces fit," I told him just as I told him on the phone when I called on the way to the ferry dock. "The person who both Levi and Amanda saw walk out of the Orient Express —"

"They weren't sure if it was a man or a woman." Hank nodded.

"And the frilly glove and chewing tobacco . . ."

"Could have both belonged to Chuck." He darted me a sidelong look. "If that was Chuck." Hank yanked his hat off his head and scratched a hand along the top of his buzz cut. "It's not possible," he said. "I mean, a man would know something like that, wouldn't he? And I —"

"Admit it Hank, you thought she was hot." Chandra laughed. "You never had a clue."

"It doesn't mean a thing." The ferry docked, and Hank pushed off from his post. As soon as the gangway was down, he hopped onto the boat.

"Oh, this is going to be delicious, teasing him about Mariah." Chandra chuckled. "I guarantee you, Hank Florentine," she called after him, "you're never going to hear the end of this!"

"If we're right," I reminded her. "If we're way off base —"

"Then it was worth a few chuckles, anyway." Luella clapped me on the back.

But no one was laughing when Hank marched off the boat. "Third trip of the day," he grumbled. "And Jayce says first thing this morning, there was a big guy on the boat, all right, and he looked vaguely familiar, except that he was bundled up and wearing a scarf and hat so it was hard to tell. It might have been Chuck Anderson, all right. I showed Jayce a photo of him. He's not sure. But maybe. I've already called the cops in Catawba, but if that was Anderson" — he emphasized the *if* — "he's long gone by now."

"And if it was Chuck Anderson?" I didn't want to beat a dead horse, but I wondered if Hank was thinking what I was thinking.

"Then he sure could be our killer," he said, confirming my suspicion. "He knew where the jewelry was hidden, because he was the one who hid it."

"And he called Peter to place that takeout

order and never expected him to come back so soon," I added, just in case anyone forgot about this. "He was there to get the jewelry, ran into Peter, and —"

No one needed to fill in the blanks; we all knew what happened after that.

We watched a few people get off the ferry and a line of people who'd been waiting on the dock filed on. Jayce gave the horn a toot.

"So now what?" I asked Hank.

When he looked south over the lake to the mainland, Hank's expression was grim. "Somebody will find him," he said. "We'll put out an APB and I guarantee, somebody over on the mainland will nail the son-of-a-bitch. For now . . . well, I guess the good news is that he's off our island."

"I guess the thing that really bothers me is that we weren't able to prove anything." Yes, I was grumbling. Could anyone blame me? It was Monday evening, and after the stressful week we'd all had, we decided to bend Alvin Littlejohn's rule just a tad. Our book discussion group was still meeting, only at the B and B. With a pitcher of margaritas.

Don't tell Alvin, but we weren't talking about *Murder on the Orient Express* as much as we were about Peter's murder.

"Hank hasn't heard a word from any

police department over on the mainland." Chandra crunched into a tortilla chip. "And until they find Chuck —"

"If they ever find Chuck." Leave it to Kate to be painfully honest, even when this was something none of us wanted to hear. She must have realized it, because she puckered like a prune. "I'm just sayin'. It doesn't hurt to look at things —"

"Through very un-rose-colored glasses." Luella apparently didn't hold this against Kate, because she gave her a quick hug. "It's okay, honey, we know. No one could make a success of a business like you have without being level-headed and willing to face facts head-on. Even if they're not the facts you like."

"You got that right." Chandra snapped another chip in two.

"So the facts are . . ." I trailed a chip through the bowl of salsa in front of me. "That Ted was mad at Peter because Ted got fooled and rented him the space even after Peter stiffed him back in Cleveland."

"Check." Kate made a mark in the air. "That's why Ted lied about the peanuts. He wanted us to think that was the reason he and Peter were fighting, when they were really fighting about the lease. He thought if word got out that they knew each other previously, it would make him look like a suspect."

"Does it?" I asked no one in particular. I hated second-guessing my own (if I do say so myself) brilliant deduction about Princess Dragomiroff, but as Luella had pointed out, sometimes there is no escaping the facts. "Ted doesn't have an alibi for the time of the murder, and he does have motive."

Chandra wrinkled her nose. "I thought we thought the murderer was —"

"We did. We do," I assured her. "I just want to get everything lined up and in order. Ted could have done it, though I think murder is a pretty drastic way to handle a lease dispute. My guess is that Ted's the type who would have used the courts, not a knife, to settle things with Peter. And then there's Amanda —"

"Well, can you blame her for hating her ex?" Chandra topped off her drink. "If there's one unalienable right every woman has, it's the right to hold a grudge against an ex-husband."

Even when each of us fixed her with a look, she went right on looking bitter. In a Chandra sort of way. Which meant her mouth was pulled into a thin line and her eyes were narrowed. But there was still a little smile that tickled the corners of her lips.

"Well, just because Hank and I sometimes get along doesn't mean I don't hold a grudge," she explained, and grinned. "Besides, when I think that Hank was actually flirting with Mariah . . ." She shivered.

And we all laughed.

"Chuck had us all fooled," I said. "The fact that Mariah was so perfect, that should have told us something."

"Maybe it did tell us something," Luella pointed out. "Maybe Mariah was just Mariah and this has nothing to do with Chuck. Maybe those condoms in her room —"

"Weren't because *she* was hoping to meet someone but because *he* was," Kate said. "I think Bea's right. Chuck and Mariah are the same person. After all, nobody's that perfect."

Of course, Kate was, and the fact that she didn't even realize it surprised me. And realizing that, I actually felt my opinion of Kate soften. Well, just a little bit, anyway.

Warm and fuzzy moment complete, I got back to the matter at hand. "Something tells me none of this would have happened if the real Poirot were around. No offense, Chandra," I added, and since she was sipping her margarita, she wiggled her fingers to tell me none was taken. "Our friend the Belgian detective would have seen right through Chuck's disguise. If," I added, just to be fair to all sides, "Chuck really was disguised."

"Maybe a detective would have caught on right away. In a book. But let's face it, life isn't a book."

How true! I nodded. "In so many novels, things are usually tied up nice and neat at the end. Authors have that luxury. Each author is in charge of the universe she creates. Christie was able to give us a satisfying solution to *Orient Express* because she set up the story in the first place. With all the clues lined up and all the pieces in place, the ending just flowed organically."

Luella had passed on a margarita. She finished her bottle of lite beer. "There you go, talking like an English teacher again!" She sat back and yawned. We'd convened our little meeting at the usual time, seven o'clock, but what with discussing the book (a little) and the events of the last week (a lot), it was almost eleven. "I've got to get a move on," she said. She pushed back her chair but she didn't get up from the table. "I've got a charter going out in a couple days and there's plenty of cleanup to do on the boat thanks to the snow."

"Back to reality." Kate finished the last of her drink, keeping her place.

"Yeah, time to get back to the real world." Chandra sat back, but she didn't get up, either.

"It's sure going to be quiet around here," I commented. "It's been —"

"A huge inconvenience for everybody," Kate said.

"A major hassle," Luella added, "what with all the work we've all had to do to keep everything up and running and everyone happy."

"A big old pain in the butt." Chandra grimaced, but when it came to hiding her true emotions, she wasn't much of a player. Her cheeks dimpled. "I mean, what with having to spend a week with the likes of my book discussion group and the world's two most annoying neighbors."

"Exactly what I was thinking." Kate reached for her purse.

"Which is exactly what I was thinking," I added, not to be outdone. "Which is why I was wondering if maybe you'd all like to stay for just another night."

Luella's eyes lit. "One more breakfast together."

"And a chance to discuss our case again in the morning," Kate added.

"Meg brought over a batch of frozen almond cranberry muffins this afternoon." Chandra's eyes twinkled. "I wasn't supposed to tell you about them, Bea. You were supposed to look in the freezer and find the surprise. But if we're all here in the morning . . ."

"My girl makes one heck of an almond cranberry muffin," Luella said.

It was all the encouragement we needed to make up our minds.

20

I woke up to the sounds of someone walking around upstairs.

"Big deal," I grumbled at the same time I punched my pillow and flipped over. "Guests in the house," I reminded myself. "Kate and Luella and Chandra." Only no Hank for Chandra to pay a clandestine visit to, and no sounds of water running in the bathroom, either.

With a mumbled curse, I rolled to my back so I could push myself up on my elbows and listen some more.

Footsteps, surely. And not like someone was just walking around to get a drink of water or a book to occupy the hours when sleep wouldn't come.

Slow footsteps.

Stealthy.

Like George Mattingly's the night I woke up back in my New York condo and found him in my kitchen.

That's all it took. That one thought.

My body froze and my mind went numb along with it. All that stuff about taking control of my life and owning my power was great in theory, and from the safety of my therapist's office. But when push came to shove and reality thumped to the sounds of furtive footsteps, I'm afraid it was a little hard to remember.

That is, until I heard something else — scuffling, and a muffled cry.

I was out of bed so fast, I didn't bother with my bunny slippers. I took the steps two at a time, and when I got upstairs to the hallway, Luella was already standing outside the door of her room. I didn't need to be a famous Belgian detective to know something was wrong. Her eyes were wide with fear and her face was as pale as her pink flannel nightgown.

But then, I could hardly blame her. There was a man standing right behind her. He had one of Luella's arms twisted behind her back. His other arm was around her. The gleam of the night-light outside the bathroom door glinted off the knife he held to her throat.

Dim light or not, I would have recognized those shoulders anywhere.

"Chuck Anderson." My voice hop-skipped, just like my heartbeat. "Or should I say Mariah Gilroy?"

He didn't so much smile as he flashed his teeth. "I wondered when someone would catch on. You gotta admit, it was inspired."

"If you hadn't left Mariah's clothes behind, no one ever would have caught on," I told him. "But you didn't need them anymore, did you? You arrived on the island as a woman, and you left as a man. It was the perfect cover."

Chuck inched out into the hallway, bending Luella's arm to get her to move, and instinctively, I lunged forward.

"Stay where you are." Chuck gave Luella's arm another twist and though she didn't call out, there were tears in her eyes. "You let me leave, and no one will get hurt," he said.

I made a sweeping gesture that would have done Vanna proud. "So leave."

With Luella in front of him like a shield, he took another couple steps out of the room.

"Only . . ." I moved forward to block the stairway. "Luella's staying here."

Mariah had a decidedly attractive smile. Chuck, not so much.

Aiming that predatory smirk my way, he inched closer to the stairs. "You think I'm that stupid?" he asked. Call me psychic, I don't think he was really looking for an answer. "All I have to do is leave the old lady behind and walk out of here and you'll be right on the phone to the cops."

"I can understand how you'd think that." I refused to budge. Chuck would have to go around me — or through me — to get to the stairs. "Let Luella stay and I won't call the cops. I promise."

His laugh sent a chill up my spine. "And I just fell off the turnip truck. No. If I'm going to get off this island, I'm going to need a little insurance." He tugged Luella's arm. "She's it."

"But taking Luella with you, that's not really going to make a difference as far as you leaving the island, is it?" There I was, trying to reason with a murderer. It might have been crazy, but it was my only option.

He inched the knife closer to Luella's bare neck, and in the blade flashed in the glow of the night-light. "It better make a difference, if you want to see her alive again," Chuck said. "Or maybe I should just take care of her right now. It's her fault I had to come all the way back here." With a grunt, he shoved Luella toward the steps.

Luella opened her mouth in a silent scream and threw out one arm in a useless attempt to steady herself. I let out a shout and moved forward to try to catch her just as Chuck yanked back on Luella's arm to keep her from tumbling down the steps.

After that, a couple things happened all at once.

The door to Suite #3 inched open and a sleepy-looking Chandra stepped out into the hallway, rubbing her eyes. She didn't stay sleepy-looking for long. Not once she realized what was happening.

The door to Suite #1 popped open, too, and her robe hanging open, Kate raced into the hallway.

And Chuck laughed.

"Now this is just perfect," he said, but not like he actually believed it. "I've got you all here." His gaze slid to me. "And here I was counting on you being home alone tonight." I didn't like the way he said that, or the look he gave me when he did. At the same time, I told myself not to panic, because that worst-case scenario hadn't materialized; I reminded myself that this scenario was bad enough.

Still hanging on tight to Luella, Chuck took another step in my direction, and I knew I had to do something to stall him. I didn't know what or how. I only knew that in spite of the fact that my knees knocked against each other and it felt as if there was a hand around my throat, I couldn't let him leave the house with Luella.

"You said it was her fault." I blurted out the words and pointed toward Luella. "You said you had to come back because of Luella. What were you talking about, Chuck?"

"Oh, come on!" His face twisted. "You haven't figured that out yet? You got the rest of it right. I mean, you knew who I was, so you must also have known about the loot I had hidden upstairs at that Chinese restaurant."

I nodded, then wondered if he could see me in the half dark. "Yeah. I know that. The night the storm started, you went to get the jewelry and ran into Peter. That's why you killed him, wasn't it?"

He rolled his eyes. "You make it sound like it matters."

"Everyone matters." I could have slapped myself the moment the words left my mouth. This was not the time for a can't-we-all-get-along speech. Chuck was in no mood to be conciliatory, and frankly, it wasn't sounding like all that good an idea to me, either. "You went back and got the jewelry. And last Saturday, you planted it in Levi's bedroll. Why?"

"It sure wasn't to make him look guilty, that was just dumb luck." Chuck was nearly to the top of the steps now. "The package ripped open. The one I had the bracelet in. Just when I stepped into the kitchen."

"Which is why you asked for that first cup of coffee. To distract me!" In hindsight, it seemed so obvious. "And rather than have the bracelet drop onto the floor where somebody might see it —"

"I kicked it into the sleeping bag. I thought I'd have time to go back and get it, but you four . . ." Chuck made a face. "You collected the bedroll for that stupid play of yours."

By this time, Luella and I were nearly toe to toe. I either had to stand my ground or give way to Chuck and let him lead her down the stairs and out the door.

That, or stall him a little while longer.

"That doesn't explain why you came back," I said. "Unless . . ." Honestly, I wasn't trying to impress the guy. I mean, really, who cares what a lying, murderous thief thinks of me? "You didn't just bring the bracelet with you from the restaurant. You had the rest of the jewelry, too. Those rings Hank said were never recovered."

"And my room was being cleaned," Chuck said. "Which means I couldn't stash the stuff in there. So I ducked into the only empty room." He tipped his head back toward Suite #6. "Then that little girl had to go and get sick."

"And someone was in the room with her for the rest of the weekend." It made sense. But it didn't help us out of the jam we were in. "You came back tonight, and you got what you came for," I told him. "And really, none of us cares if you leave with the jewelry."

"Right. Like you're not the four nosiest broads I've ever met." Chuck took a step forward.

And I saw my one and only chance.

I moved back just far enough to be out of his way, and as soon as his gaze dropped to the steps so he could see where he was going, I grabbed Luella's arm and pulled her to me for all I was worth. Chuck hadn't anticipated a move so bold, and he hesitated just long enough for me to whirl around and push Luella into Chandra's open arms.

"You can't do that!" Chuck swung his arm and I heard the swish of the knife cutting through the air right in front of my nose. Honest, that's the only reason I ducked and lurched forward. I had no intention — well, no conscious intention — of knocking him down the steps.

Anderson's feet went out from under him, but I suppose if prison teaches you nothing else, it hones your reflexes. Poised in mid-air and with no more than a nanosecond before he started to tumble, he snaked an arm around me and took me down the steps with him.

Somewhere between the top step where my left ankle twisted and the next one down where my arm landed under me, I heard Kate yell. "I've already called the police, Anderson." I got a quick look at her face as she peered over the side of the railing, and in one of those lucid moments that comes only at the most inconvenient times, wondered if Kate Wilder's face was the last thing I'd see while I was still alive.

Wouldn't that be a kick in the pants?

No worries. The next thing I saw was the carpeting on the stairway coming up to meet my nose.

And the knife that Anderson still clutched in one hand, dangerously close.

He hit, butt to step, grunted, and slid to the bottom of the stairway.

I wasn't quite so lucky. My shoulder smacked into a riser, and I oofed out a grunt of pain and bumped down the rest of the stairs.

I'm pretty sure I didn't black out. But the

next thing I knew, Anderson was standing over me, that knife of his dangling from one hand.

"You heard Kate." My right elbow hurt like hell but I managed to raise myself on it, anyway. Nothing says helpless like flat on your back, and there was no way I was going to send that message. Besides, from the sounds of the scrambling on the stairs, I knew Luella, Kate, and Chandra were on their way down. I couldn't afford to let them get too close. Not when there was venom in Anderson's grin and a bad intention inherent in every flick of the knife blade.

"You'd better leave while you can, Anderson." When I braced my feet against the floor and scooted toward the wall, pain shot through my ankle. "You heard Kate. She called the cops. It's not going to take them long to get here. If you're leaving with that jewelry . . ."

Right on cue, I heard the scream of a siren, and through the windows, saw the nighttime sky explode with pulsing red light.

Anderson was no dummy. Don't ask me where he was going or how he intended to get there, but like I said, no doubt prison teaches you all sorts of things. One of them was self-preservation.

With a curse, he scrambled for the door,

yanked it open, and took off down the front steps.

Good thing he was a big man, and after the tumble we'd both taken, not especially fast. He was just at the bottom of the steps when I reached that little table where I kept the basket of slipper socks. I grabbed the vase next to the basket, whispered a prayer for forgiveness to those gods who are in charge of things like Tiffany vases, and let fly.

When the cops screeched to a stop in front of the B and B, they found Chuck Anderson stunned at the bottom of the steps. And with one hell of a goose egg on the back of his head.

21

"I hear you had some excitement here last night."

I was sitting on the front porch sipping a cup of coffee, so really, I shouldn't have been startled when Levi showed up. I suppose my mind was a million miles away. That's why I didn't see him come up the front walk.

I set down my coffee mug on the table between the wicker rocker where I was sitting and the chair next to it. "No one got seriously hurt, though Luella was a little shaken up. I can't blame her."

"And you?" It was a sunny and pleasant morning (even if the world was still a little soggy from all that snow), and Levi's careful gaze skimmed from my pink bunny slippers to my ankle wrapped in an athletic bandage to where my bandaged knees showed right below where my denim capris ended. From there, he glanced to the sling on my right arm and the bruise on the side of my face. "You don't look so hot."

"Just what a girl wants to hear!" I managed a laugh and only winced a little when my ribs protested. "Nothing's broken. Everything's sore. I don't have any guests checking in for a couple weeks, so I've got plenty of time to rest and recover."

"You need anything?" he asked.

There was an opening if I ever heard one. Rather than give in to my baser instincts and list all the things I thought it might be interesting to get from him, I held out my empty mug. "Another cup of coffee would be perfect," I said, and when he disappeared into the house, I called after him, "and get one for yourself."

A minute later he brought me my coffee and a blueberry muffin, too. While I was out on the porch, Meg must have sneaked in the back door. Bless her!

Levi sat down on the chair next to mine, took a big bite of the muffin he'd brought for himself, and washed it down with a gulp of coffee. "This is way better than what they gave me for breakfast in jail," he said.

"Maybe I can use that when I advertise for the B and B. 'Breakfast better than what you get in jail.' It kind of has a nice ring to it. What do you think?"

"I think . . ." He'd been smiling and the expression faded. He took another drink before he set down his cup. "I think I'm grateful you believed in my innocence," he said.

"Except I never actually said I did."

He thought this over and conceded my point with a nod. "You didn't have to. I knew as soon as you brought me that cup of coffee. You wouldn't have done that. Not if you really thought I killed Peter or took that jewelry. Of course, I knew I was innocent. I just don't know how you did."

I'd been breaking off tiny bits of muffin and popping them in my mouth, and I set my plate on the table next to my cup and brushed crumbs from my hand. "Call it a hunch. It was the way you talked about your grandmother," I admitted. "You loved her a lot. Killing Peter isn't the way you'd honor her memory."

"I'm sorry I didn't listen to my own gut."

"About me?"

"About your safety. I should have known Anderson wouldn't be happy. Not when the cops had the bracelet. I should have figured that he wouldn't leave things at that."

"But none of us knew the rest of the jewelry was here. Or that it even still existed. He could have pawned those rings years ago. There was no way you could have known."

"I should have. I've been beating myself up about it since I heard what happened."

"Well, don't." The blueberry muffin was calling my name and I got back to it, dispensing with nibbling crumbs and taking a nice big bite. "In the great scheme of things, this is pretty much a happily ever after," I told him, just as Chandra's van roared up to the front of the house and she got out of it along with Luella and Kate. I made to wave and thought better of it when my arm twinged. "We got the bad guy. We solved the murder. All's right with the world, and all the secrets are out in the open."

"Not exactly." Levi got up and moved toward the stairs, taking the rest of his muffin with him. "I owe you," he said. "For believing in me."

"You don't owe me anything. Though I wouldn't mind a burger at your place one of these days when I actually feel like climbing up on a barstool."

"Done." He said it, he just didn't look happy about it, and before I could wonder why, he glanced over his shoulder at my friends, who were chatting as they came up the front walk. Apparently he made up his mind about something. He took a step toward me. "You should know," he said. "I did some checking. You know, about all that stuff Chandra told me about you. You should know that I know."

Good thing I'd put down my coffee mug, because the way my hands started to shake, I knew the coffee would have sloshed out on my lap. "And you know . . . ?"

Levi didn't smile. Not exactly. His honey-colored brows twitched. One corner of his mouth pulled up. "Don't worry, your secret is safe with me. But I know there was never a Martin Cartwright," he said. "Not one you were married to, anyway."

And with that, he turned around, offered a greeting to the three ladies just coming up the steps, and was gone.

Good thing Kate, Chandra, and Luella were deep in conversation about whatever Kate, Chandra, and Luella were talking about, because for a few minutes, all I could do is sit there with my mouth hanging open. And my brain whirling a mile a minute.

Levi knew.

At least part of the story.

And he wasn't going to spread the word.

By the time Chandra flopped down in the chair next to mine and Kate and Luella sat next to each other on the wicker settee across from me, I was smiling.

It looked like when it came to hunches, mine were pretty good.

"So . . ." Chandra leaned over and slapped my knee, and when I winced she made a horrified face and apologized. "We figured we'd check on you," she said.

"And thank you," Luella added.

"And get down to business." Kate pulled out her phone and scrolled through what must have been her calendar. "First things first. Since Chandra thought of it, she gets to announce the news."

Chandra sat up and pulled back her shoulders. "Our book discussion group," she said. "I figured we needed a name. So . . ." She drew out the moment and the drama. "We're now officially the League of Literary Ladies."

I liked it, and I told her so.

"And," Kate interrupted. "With that taken care of, we figure we might as well get started. I mean, with you being laid up, it's the perfect time."

"Not for another murder investigation, I hope."

Chandra barked out a laugh. "Of course not! To pick another book for our next discussion. We voted on the way over here, and we decided to let you make the choice."

I took a sip of coffee. The better to wash down the sudden knot of emotion in my throat. "Nothing scary," I said, and they all nodded their agreement. "And no Belgian detectives."

Chandra looked honestly disappointed.

"I'm thinking something old and wonderful and classic." I had any number of such books on the shelf in the parlor, and I hauled myself out of my chair to go have a look and make a choice.

Was it a good thing or a bad thing that I picked that particular moment to get up? I can't say. I only know I was just in time to discover that Jerry Garcia had wandered over from next door.

He was peeing in my pansies.

The employees of Thorndike Press hope you have enjoyed this Large Print book. All our Thorndike, Wheeler, and Kennebec Large Print titles are designed for easy reading, and all our books are made to last. Other Thorndike Press Large Print books are available at your library, through selected bookstores, or directly from us.

For information about titles, please call:
  (800) 223-1244

or visit our Web site at:
  http://gale.cengage.com/thorndike

To share your comments, please write:
  Publisher
  Thorndike Press
  10 Water St., Suite 310
  Waterville, ME 04901